AFTER THE WATER
LEVEL ROSE

AFTER THE WATER LEVEL ROSE

SEVEN SHORT STORIES

JOAN GIL

ISBN 978-0-578-36910-5 (Paperback)

Printed in the United States of America

Editorial assistance: Ms. Kathy Schleich
Cover & Interior Design: Creative Publishing Book Design
Cover image of Duck Boat with changes: Piotrus

TABLE OF CONTENTS

THANK YOU AND WELCOME

I SALUTE YOU, DEAR READER, in the hope of entertaining you with the following seven Short Novels (also known as Novellas). They include touching and very human episodes from the past, the present and the future. Most endings will surprise the reader.

1) You will explore life in a coastal city in the XXII Century after the rising of the water level caused by the climate change.

2) Back to present times, the reader will penetrate for a while the world of office intrigues, frustrations, and liaisons and see how it can end.

3) Most people in a small town would be troubled by an assassination next door, but not everybody.

4) A suffering heroine, immersed in self-pity, lives in social isolation, unable to find a companion or friend because of her ugliness and deformity. But she has an idea.

5) The next story will allow the reader to travel back in time and space to the Prussia of the XIX Century, when duels were still permitted and he will witness an absurd one.

6) One day in 1939 a horrible civil war ended in Spain, but the fascist victory did not bring peace to the defeated and the reader

will experience the conquest by the enemy and learn what a nice couple had to endure for years. It is inspired by a true story.

7) The final contribution may well surprise the most: it relates the discovery and exploration of the Earth and of Mankind in our days by an adventurous, undetectable alien spaceship that remains cloaked and cannot be observed. During their encounters with our people, the travelers manage to overcome many difficulties and even perils, buy they never reveal themselves. What opinion of humanity did they develop? The reader may wish to bid them farewell in their own language: FFRVQQGKZZZ!

The author frequently relies more on dialogues rather than descriptions. It maybe the result of an old interest in theater and movies, but in our days the public also seems happy watching streamed pieces, without missing analyses and descriptions which frequently are introspections. All we know about other people is only what we see and hear. If you have been entertained, please award the same courtesy to the figures in these stories. They deserve it.

Thank you again for coming and enjoy yourselves.

J.G.

AFTER THE WATER LEVEL ROSE

BEFORE THE TROUBLE AT the end of the XXI Century started, Beauville had been a medium-size town on the oceanic shore with an attractive and busy sports harbor, tourism, and some modest industry. First, the raining frequency and severity increased. Everybody had heard about global warming and assumed that the government would take care of the problem, but suddenly alarming warnings about the ongoing melting of the gigantic ice caps over Greenland and the Antarctic continent were discussed on TV and the Internet. Where would the freed water go after thawing? Somebody pointed out that the water volume on our planet is fixed and only its distribution can change. It was not thinkable to send the incoming water anywhere else. Slowly but majestically the water level of the ocean rose covering coastal, previously dry terrain. The Arctic pole was becoming an appealing summer vacationing paradise and many people had been happy about the warming. At the beginning, that is.

At the time that the water started to rise beyond its old confinement and visibly overran the coastal areas, Wilbur Ross was still a kid. The media and the government had been anticipating the development for a long time, without doing much to prevent it, but when it finally happened the citizens were as flabbergasted as impotent. Cries of

"What are we going to do" were followed with organized meetings to request federal help to build a containment wall around the city, but the government refused to do so because more important and better populated areas had priority needs. When the wharf became flush with the water, many astonished citizens sat into their hydrogen cars and drove to the harbor to inspect the novelty. Was it permanent? No, it would become much worse. At first the water appeared cleaner than in the past. Wilbur heard how his parents discussed the matter. Their big home on Walnut Street was close to the dry land's edge but it stood high over a mound, which soon was surrounded by salt water. The original name of the still dry land, "Uptown" had been surprisingly fitting but was nevertheless abandoned, replaced by "City." It had upset Wilbur during his childhood that the street was steep next to the front yard, which kept him from playing ball, because all balls rolled away. Now however the home stood dry above surrounding flooded intersections, sharing the good fortune with a small neighborhood of additional homes. It would become Wilbur's Island.

Surely, many people in the entire world had been displaced and forced to relocate, but not Wilbur. The city announced that they would build two navigable channels from the water to the dry areas, develop new beaches and plant water-absorbing vegetation in the new parks to replace demolished buildings. Some families and businesses managed to stay in the flooded area thanks to small artificial islands, some elevated areas like Wilbur's and artificial beaches that attracted visitors. When Wilbur learned that his home was destined to become an island and survive, he immediately inquired from his parents whether it would be feasible to fish from his bedroom window. Would he be able to watch whales or sharks swimming by?

The good Beauville residents, already nervous, still knew nothing about the worst problem that was coming their way: the immigration of hungry and needy fugitives from all continents both from the flooded and the hot areas, where survival had become too hard or impossible; would they increase Beauville's population and originate serious problems. Large columns of southerners of different races, creeds and native languages were invading the dry land. Because of their mild climate, many were attempting to reach Siberia or Canada, which was not easy. After the border was overrun, the federal army and many police forces were deployed to contain them, but there was no place where they could be sent back to be abandoned to a certain death. They were humans and wanted to survive. They were first labeled "economic refugees", but it was an insult because all they wanted was to survive. They had left nothing behind. Foreigners began arriving in increasingly organized groups. The police directed them to the high parts of town, the dry land, where cheap collective barracks and residential camps were readied. Their number increased but few resident cards were handed out. In view of the emergency, the government enacted laws that curtailed the citizen's civil rights and the police became authoritarian and reckless. Naturally, the new arrivals did not like the local arrangements and dreamed of resuming their journey to some better and more welcoming location. It was not easy to identify such destinations any more. As slums and overpopulated regions developed over the still habitable and more accessible parts of the globe and antagonisms between groups increased, then everybody understood that a new era had begun. Wilbur grew up in a changing, new world submerged in an insoluble and growing crisis. He missed the happy city life of his early infancy which he had briefly experienced, but the transformation and the worsening disaster were the realities that could not be ignored. The situation would not be stabilized during Wilbur's lifetime, and he had just discovered where he would spend his life.

* * *

Many years after the beginning, already in the XXII Century, Wilbur Ross man was heading home and trying to remember the original appearance of the mound on the old Chestnut Street where his home was located and he had played as a child. He could still see himself running downhill on the now nonexistent sidewalks trying to reach the ball. He had wished that the terrain were flat, but the mound turned out to save the integrity of his old home and of a few low-rise residential buildings. He remembered well the time when the salt water wetted for the first time the entrance to his home, first only during high tides, later continuously. Later, a crew of workers dug a navigable waterway of appropriate depth lined by a low containment wall outside of the house. One of the two planned navigable channels from the old harbor to the dry land had been designed across his former front yard and boats stopped on request at his door.

The channel that replaced the old Walnut Street was navigable only for duck boats, the flat boats without keel and relatively flat hull originally used in small lakes or ponds. Wilbur's island community owned one powered by a hydrogen engine that had been purchased with money from all residents and could be signed out for personal use. Wilbur was in charge. A larger passenger boat transported people and tourists every hour during the daytime and early evening toward the dry land and back. The water mostly emanated a foul odor. The boat-bus stopped on demand outside of Wilbur's home entrance, but the old man never liked it because it was noisy. Sometimes he reserved his community's small boat and sailed down the Chestnut Street canal toward the harbor. Flat boats without keel were not allowed into the former harbor, but he knew how to turn to the right toward a relatively remote island with a small artificial beach with shallow water where he spent hours patronizing a nice restaurant with ocean and beach views.

One day, returning home, he had encountered minimal boat traffic. He crossed only a large police boat transporting toward the detention center new illegal immigrants caught in the water.

Upon returning to his island, he could easily berth because the tide was low. Wilbur was already inside when his phone rang. He saw in the video screen his only son James.

"Hi, Jim. What is up?"

"Hi, Dad. Well, I had not talked to you for a while."

"That has never been a reason for you to call me."

"Is everything alright?"

Wilbur felt irritated.

"You know, Jim, I am reading in your face that you are upset. Just tell me what is not alright with you. Just get it out."

"Do you remember Miriam?"

"Your girlfriend? Sure, I do. You brought her here several times. I do not get many visitors."

"We do not live or go out together anymore."

"You mean that you broke up with her. Did you meet somebody else?"

A silence followed. Then James answered:

"Yes, but it has nothing to do with the breach. It had been coming for a long time."

Wilbur waited without answering. Additional details followed:

"I really liked Miriam, and we had good times together, but she was always upset and resented the condition of the city and of her employment. You may remember that she worked at the Financial Bank, which had kept a small branch open on one of the islands in the flooded area for the people who still worked in the territory and the tourists. It did not go very well and there was talk of closing. They had only two employees, she as girl-for-everything and a trained cashier from 9 to 4. She was even made to clean the floors and the two had been concerned that they faced a robbery risk. The only good side of her job was that she could live for free in a small attic over the public area, which may have been a dangerous place at night."

"You mean she was constantly nagging to you about the world and her life's circumstances?"

"Yes, Dad, something like this, and I had enough. She thought that I could resolve all her problems. I am sure that everything was better when you were a kid, but this was not in her memory. She had experienced that better past life as little as me. Things are now what they are, period. We should already be used to it, and there is no escape. She would not accept it. In the inland's countryside, where she was born, things are also bad. She had made inquiries in her home county about the possibility of getting a job and making a living there because she is a native citizen, but she got no offers, only discouragement. Everything was full. At least here we have scenery."

"And a water view."

"I could not take her perpetual nagging anymore."

"You said that before. You must know what you are doing. In my times we used to have a period of companionship with a woman followed by a marriage, but it seems that is not done anymore, not even by the couples who want children."

"Of course not. Just imagine that I needed a divorce now. What is the use?"

"You said you are in a new relationship. Tell me more. What is her name?"

"Aysha."

"Aysha? Is she Muslim?

"No. She is of African origin, but her parents came early, and she is a born citizen."

"Aha. So, maybe I will have finally a grandchild?"

"Who knows. That is the way things are going. In one more generation all the races and skin colors will be mixed all over the entire globe, and we will happily live together without racism, artificial ethnic fights, xenophobia or discrimination."

"You may be right, I hope. Give my regards to Aysha and bring her by sometime soon, but I must tell you that I liked Miriam."

* * *

Wilbur co-owned with his childhood friend Ron Miles a small bakery in the dry land. They had employed as caretakers an entire immigrant middle eastern family with two small children. The business yielded some modest revenue, but he and Ron had to supervise the operation on alternate dates and deposit the cash money and card receipts in the bank. The old man had given up his old car a long time ago. Parking was impossibly expensive, and he could reach the store by using the public boat from his home to the dry area. He could complete the trip in a bus, but he enjoyed walking.

He had returned home but felt tired. He overheard without paying attention the public boat from the harbor stopping outside. His doorbell rang.

Wilbur was surprised. He rarely received visitors, and never without announcement. Maybe another resident of his island? From the public boat? They frequently had problems with the reservation of the boat of common property, and Wilbur was accepted as the authority in charge. He opened the door and was flabbergasted.

"Miriam? What a surprise! James is not here."

Rather than answering, the young woman looked away, opened the mouth, and started crying loudly. She was poorly dressed and had brought with her a small suitcase.

"Come in, dear, come in. What is the matter?"

Miriam finally managed to express some coherent words.

"They threw me under the bus after so many years and James abandoned me."

Wilbur finally understood that the building where the bank branch was located was threatening ruin and somebody in the dry land had ordered it closed and abandoned. Miriam was paid a week's salary with a small bonus and was ordered to pack and leave. Everything she owned was in the suitcase. The woman had begged to be allowed to stay a little longer until she found a new roof where she could live, but the bank manager denied the request. She had attempted to reach to James for help but every time he saw her face on the phone, he refused to pick up. She had also sent him desperate emails which her former friend also ignored.

Wilbur thought that he would certainly not treat a faithful employee that way, but it was not his business and that woman was no longer Jim's companion. Why had she come?

Miriam dried with a paper towel her eyes and shyly looked around.

"You knew already that James and I have parted ways. I was born as a citizen in the dry countryside but my parents and all friends and relatives are dead and here, I only have casual acquaintances. In a few days, I will be penniless, and I have no place to go. It is almost impossible to find a job, so I thought."

She should have thought nothing, thought Wilbur irritated. She had sympathy for the woman and understood well her tough situation, but he could do nothing for her. Problems existed all over, half of mankind was in trouble, and he had nothing to share.

"I understand what you say, and I am very sorry, but I don't know what you expect from me."

"Anything you have, any crumbles from your table that you meant to discard. I will do anything you order me to do."

"I do not offer crumbles to a human being, Miriam, but I just cannot take care of you and your problem."

Miriam started crying again.

"Look, girl, there are resources for people in your situation. Since you are a citizen, you could go to the housing police in the dry land and ask for help, food, and a ceiling. They would have to give you something."

"You know what they would do to me? I have heard it many times. They would put me in a room like a cell in jail with other women. Maybe all their rooms are filled already, and I would have to sleep in a corridor and maybe somebody would rape me. Please, help me, Mr. Ross. I was always glad to see you when James brought me to this house. I thought that you are a charitable good man."

"I always liked you too, but I have nothing to offer. Only a small part of his house is habitable and has heated rooms. I am settled in my way of life and am in relatively good health. I have no need for a house helper. Sad as it is, I have nothing for you. My position is modestly safe, but I am by no means wealthy."

Miriam resumed her lamentations and fell on her knees. Wilbur felt embarrassed.

"Did you have dinner already? I have frozen food and some soup, and we can share it. I can also lend you some money, but you have to leave."

Wilbur went to the kitchen. Miriam followed him and tried to do all the work for him, which only troubled her host. In a way, the man was heartbroken, but he really could do nothing and there were too many people in trouble. In life, everybody must take the card that he is dealt.

At the table, Wilbur heard some additional disturbing details of the girl's dismissal. The man sighed. Justice had been different in past times. Now, nobody had rights. He shared some caffeine-free hot tea with the woman, but the conversation languished.

"We had an enjoyable time, Miriam. Thank you for coming. I will keep you in mind and let you know if I hear of something, but now it is time for you to leave. Shortly after 8 o'clock the last passenger boat toward the dry land will come by. If you signal, it will stop in front of you. You can take it, go there and you will easily find the housing and police place. I am sure that they will do something for you."

Miriam resumed her crying but was not ready to give up.

"Please, Mr. Ross, have pity. You know how much I loved your son" A long pause followed. "You know, if you want, I... Well, I mean you are a widower and must sleep alone. You know me and right now unfortunately... I am just saying that... When I say that I will do anything, I mean it, please. I will keep your home clean, even the bathrooms, but I have no other place to go."

Wilbur looked at her with sadness, and he shook his head.

"No, Miriam, no. You cannot offer any such thing in exchange for benefits. You had been my son's companion. I know you did not mean it" And after a while he stood up and added. "Sorry, but you must pick up your things and leave."

* * *

After closing the door behind Miriam, Wilbur called James. Now the young man understood why she had been trying to reach him, he answered. He was deeply sorry, but he had made it abundantly clear to Miriam that their relationship was for ever finished. Many adult people were having a tough time and were able to take care of themselves. He knew already about the situation and was sorry but could not do anything to change it. What would Aysha think? Maybe he could afford to give her some money but nothing else.

Wilbur could not sleep well. He rose early and walked into his kitchen, where he had succeeded in maintaining order and cleanliness and started preparing breakfast. He was surprised to hear some unusual noise coming from his door. He looked through the window but could see nothing. He opened the door and he found Miriam on the floor. She had slept outside the door covering herself with an old coat, but she was still shivering and pale. She raised to her feet looking at the ground.

"Pardon me, Mr. Ross. I told you yesterday that I had no place to go. I could not sleep and risk being raped on the floor of a police station."

Wilbur could not hide his astonishment and shock, close to true emotion. He was speechless.

"Please, Mr. Ross, I beg you on my knees. Have pity. I will obey you and do anything, anything but please help me" She started crying again.

"Come inside, Miriam and have some breakfast with me. It is cold outside" And he slowly added "Take your stuff inside too."

Wilbur was considering what it means to be a decent man and to what extent obligations toward those in need were implied. In the times of his childhood before the flooding and the mass migrations everything had been different, and certain things did not happen. He could never watch anyone's humiliations.

They had breakfast together. Wilbur thought that Miriam was dirty and poorly dressed. Did she have another set of clothes?

"Well, Miriam, I can only offer some emergency temporary help. I have a small room where Jim used to sleep, which is being used only for storage. I believe that I will be able to find a small bed and probably a mattress. For a while I can feed you. With the clothes you are wearing you would find work only as a janitor. Today is my day off at the store. We'll take the community's little boat if available and we'll go to a clothing store in the dry land, where we will find something more suitable for an educated woman searching for a job."

Miriam was almost overwhelmed and was unable to thank for Wilbur's generosity. She tried to speak but could not find the words. The man was also astonished. He had been moved by the girl's despair and spoken almost without considering what he was offering. His generous heart had surfaced without brain review and approval.

"If you can think of something else you need, let me know, but remember that this is only a temporary and brief arrangement. You will have to find a salaried job and move away to some housing of your own in the dry land. You will not owe to me any money. As soon as you are fitted with an acceptable dress, before we return, we shall stop at my bakery and get some sweets for the evening meal. Is that all clear?"

"Thank you, Sir, Mr. Ross, thank you with all my heart. You are marvelous and I am an unworthy freak. I do not deserve to have met such a compassionate and good man."

"Maybe you didn't but who are we to judge? I don't know what a freak is and never met one" answered Wilbur.

The small community-owned duck boat happened to be free and the old man and his new guest took it. Because of the low tide, Wilbur had difficulties reaching an accessible free mooring place in the dry land. They boarded a bus and walked into a large general store. Wilbur explained that he had owned an automobile, but it was not worth the expenditure of the upkeep. His own store was around the corner from the mooring. Well, almost so.

They entered a large department store and Miriam started checking everything in the women's section and selected a simple dress with a top suitable for the time of the year. She inquiringly looked at the price tag and showed it to Wilbur, who shrugged approvingly. He was almost regretting his generosity, but he had given his word and never took it back. Next, she needed a pair of shoes, because the ones she had, had been damaged by the salt water and the mud. The man shrugged again. Shyly she also inquired whether it would be possible for her to go to the hair salon, because her hairs... Wilbur inspected the mentioned scalp briefly and once again approved but for the last time, he said to himself. He would drink a coffee waiting in the refreshments area. He sat at the bar and a man next to him said:

"I saw you buying clothes for the brunette girl. She is not bad. There are lots of opportunities these days. No one needs to get married anymore."

Wilbur looked coldly at the man without answering.

After leaving the store with the purchases, the old man and Miriam walked a short distance toward Wilbur's co-owned bakery and pastry shop. Miriam felt overwhelmed when she saw and smelled it.

"All of this looks delicious."

"Listen, Miriam, come here and meet Ahmed and Fatima, who run the operations and have two beautiful boys. And here inside of the office, meet my good friend and business partner Ron Miles. Believe it or not, we have never had a fight."

The named man raised to his feet.

"And who would this beautiful young lady be?"

"You may have seen here before. She was friendly with my son Jim and now she is in trouble because the bank branch where she worked near the harbor closed and I am housing her for a few days."

"Oh, Wil, these times! Do you remember when we were young?"

"Don't even mention. Do you want to bring tears to my eyes? We may have lived too long. But say, you know better than me the dry land. Where could Miriam get a job? She could do many things in the bank, she has office training, is responsible with money and has secretarial skills."

"Oh, my friends! You really need good luck. There are huge lines of people applying for any opening, especially in banks."

"She is a born citizen. Does that not count for anything?"

"Not much, just a little. Only good friends and connections matter. I can direct her to the employment offices. They are easy to find. Anyplace where you see a lengthy line of people waiting on the street."

"Let us ask Ahmed or Fatima. She would be willing to consider anything that pays a salary."

But Ron just shook his head. It would be a waste of time and their employees would fear for their own jobs. They were probably already worried.

Wilbur remembered that he had not seen Ron for some time.

"How is business?"

"I will leave the new bank statements for you to see when you come tomorrow. We are making some money, but, quite frankly, it is great that we both have additional resources. It would be a suicide to raise prices because few people can pay. They come only for cheap bread and pitas. You tell me what we should do, we should really raise Ahmed's salary, but I don't see how."

Wilbur did not speak much during the ride back home in the boat.

"Miriam, you have seen how the situation and what your chances are. I helped you a little to make a good impression but now you are on your own. In the flooded area you will find nothing, even not cleaning the waterways. There is a regular boat service to the dry land every hour. Tomorrow I will be gone to the store early. If you also leave early, you may be able to avoid the waiting lines."

They had taken bread and some sweets from the business for dinner. Ron had critically watched the operation but said nothing. On the dinner table, they discussed the events of the day. Surprisingly, they laughed together.

The regular comings and goings of Miriam would become a routine that lasted two weeks. Evenings, she always returned tired and upset. No progress in the job search was being made. Wilbur believed in her sincerity and had started to like her. She was a transparent, friendly woman without double intentions. Maybe she could stay in his home a little longer, but she needed to find a job soon.

A few additional weeks passed by. Miriam was leaving in a morning passenger boat and returned home in the evening, frequently later than Wilbur. She enjoyed talking and describing her efforts and observations during the day to the old man, who appreciatively listened. Outside of his days in the store, he had direct contact with only few people and the video shows on TV bored him. He had already watched all that interested him. Talking to Miriam was different. She enjoyed life and found pleasure in all she did and discovered. But was she telling him all the truth?

At the beginning she had appeared desperate while looking for a job but now she was as relaxed as if she had one. She had purchased some modest new clothes and she had attended an early evening musical show. Where was she getting the money from? He asked once. The answer was simple "From my savings" she explained, laughing. Did Wilbur have musical instruments? She had found several friends in the dry land and all enjoyed to sing and play. It was for fun, no need to study music. Sometimes their new gang was even allowed to perform in evening clubs and they were rewarded with some cash. She had never been able to do that before.

"I suppose that James would not have liked this kind of occupation."

Miriam did not answer, but the old man, concerned, added some advice:

"I am pleased to hear that you are having an enjoyable time but be careful. There are dangerous people and desperate undocumented migrants in the dry land and the radio reports many crimes, especially in the evening."

"I am no little girl, Mr. Ross, and I have been around. I will not allow anyone to mess with me. I am glad and proud that you worry about me. You sound like the Daddy I never had." Having said this, she moved toward the surprised Wilbur and gave him a hug and a kiss. The man accepted both.

"You are a responsible grown up, but I am reminding you that there are dangers in the dry land. You may not know what other people want, but they desire everything you have. Do you really know who the friends in your gang are?"

"There are not all the same, Mr. Ross. Some have papers and work permits and jobs. I am friendly with one of them who has a permanent visa and can legally work and make money. Sometimes I help him in the place where he works in the afternoons, and we even play or sing together. Sometimes I even serve the clients to make some money" Miriam made a pause. "He believes we could make much more money during the evenings and late hours."

Wilbur sighed, inhaled and blew out the air. "You are a big girl, but you cannot have known this man long enough. The town is becoming dangerous and you have nobody to protect you. Think it over. I am sure that one way or the other you could find a regular job and get settled around stable and more reliable people. I am not pushing you out."

"But I always have you, Mr. Ross! I will be coming back every evening", she answered laughing.

She did not come back every evening. The first time she called advising that she had found a well-paid singing gig for a night only. But soon, her absences increased, and finally she came back to see Wilbur only on Mondays. The man started worrying about his young friend, whom he almost regarded as a daughter. He felt alone in his island and had become used to the conversations with the woman, who revealed the joy and enthusiasm for life which he had been missing. She had really changed a lot since the day when she appeared at his doorstep in despair. Sometimes he tried to reach her by phone during the week, but she apparently was too busy to answer. Miriam had been quite different from his son James. Maybe they had both missed or rejected something in the other. Still, he could not stop worrying. He finally called James asking him to investigate Miriam's activities.

"Why should I Dad? I was five years with Miriam and we decided to part ways. I am sorry that she lost her job immediately afterwards."

"But you separated in good terms, I believe. Don't you really care about her future? She is 35 years old already, but she is not settled with a stable job or a career. She came to me asking for help and I gave it to her. You never paid attention when I tried to explain to you that we must help each other."

"I will do something. She probably sings in cheap restaurants or entertainment businesses frequented by immigrants. She has never studied music. I agree that it sounds worrisome. Miriam always showed a touch of ingenuity which I view as dangerous in our current world. The way she came to you reveals it. Aysha, my companion, has a job at the police office with access to some of the computers. We'll see if she finds something out."

Wilbur was going to say that he missed Miriam's company and conversation, but he decided that James might understand it the wrong way. He viewed the woman just as a friend or daughter and some social companionship was the only thing he was after.

One Sunday Miriam came back late. From his window Wilbur noticed that she had hired a taxi boat and was dressed as a club hostess. Wilbur rushed to meet her. Her left eye was blueish, and she could not open it completely and she had some serious bruises and marks in her arm. The old man hugged her.

"What is wrong, Miriam? What happened to you?"

"Nothing, Mr. Ross. I had an accident. I slipped leaving the room where we live, and I fell hitting the banister with my face and you see what developed."

"Did the friend of yours assist you? Did you go to an emergency room?"

"No, no, it is not worth it; but it is bad enough that I could not join Brett at the stage tonight, so I decided to take the opportunity and visit you instead."

Wilbur reviewed again her condition and shook his head.

"What you describe is a strange story, Miriam. Has your friend hit you? If he did, he is not a friend."

"No, I told you what happened. Unfortunately, I will have to wait a few days before returning to work but I will learn how to apply make-up. Do you mind if I go to bed now? I feel very tired."

She went to bed. Outside, Wilbur could hear her cries of pain and rage.

The man had to go to work in the dry land next morning. From the bakery he called home and Miriam answered reporting that she felt alright and that her bruises looked better. When he returned home the woman had prepared some dinner for both and offered him a beer. She was smiling, but the blue eye was if anything even more noticeable. Wilbur engaged in some chitchat with Miriam before opening a serious discussion.

"How long have you known this guy, Brett? What is his full name?"

"I believe it is Brett Sayed. It is not important because we work at various places and meet new unknown people every day and it is not good to give away too much personal information. Brett has told me that he has used other names in the past as a protection. But he had nothing to do with my accident."

"I would like to point out that you are a citizen and that the law protects us against injuries, and nobody has the right to hurt another human being. Your brushes are intolerable. You should break up with this man."

"But... he is not perfect, but he is a good man. We kind of love each other, I think."

"The way you describe him, he sounds wayward. Maybe he could be running afoul of the law. No one uses more than one name, unless he is afraid of the police."

"The law, the police, what does it mean under the current conditions? Brett has had a hard life from the day he was born. Out there, all people must fight to survive. We earn money one evening from people who are worse off than us and need some entertainment and we don't know if we shall have a job tomorrow. What does the law mean for us? How does it protect us? The police neither helps nor protects."

"You are completely wrong. Things are what they are, but you can adapt your life to the circumstances and still obey the law and live safely" He still added:

"You worry me, Miriam. When I was a child, we all believed in law and order. Right now, maybe something is failing with the order, but we definitively still have law. You are a citizen and deserve better. I can accompany you to the police to file a complaint against Brett."

"No, Mr. Ross. It was all my fault. I did not pay attention to what he had told me, and I was not well prepared for the evening show, which is our main source of revenue."

Wilbur sighed.

Miriam still stayed two more days in the house and then navigated back to the dry land and to Brett. Wilbur was convinced that he needed to do something. He had developed some paternal feelings toward her.

He dialed James' phone number.

"Hi, Dad. How are things going?"

"I am alright, except that I worry a lot about Miriam."

"You worry about Miriam? She is nothing to us. You are good hearted but have no obligations. She should be grateful to you and period."

"She is, Jim. These are the recent events: she attempted to find a job, and nobody offered her anything. Then she met on the street some no good fellow named Brett Sayed and they started making money playing and singing in evening entertainment places for immigrants. She stopped coming here to sleep on a regular basis. Last Sunday Miriam suddenly appeared at my door covered with bruises because she had been beaten up by Brett."

This explanation was followed by a silence. Finally, James asked:

"This guy, Brett, is he a citizen?"

"No and I fear he is undocumented and living from obscure income sources."

"I am sorry to hear. I used to like Miriam, and I still wish her the best. What do you want me to do? I ask because I am sure that you want me to do something."

"This individual, Brett, seems to use different names. They perform in cheap places with immigrants, which must be a dangerous milieu. Do you know what can be done to find out something more specific? I remember the day you came here to introduce me to your Aysha, she confirmed that she worked at the police headquarters, as you had mentioned. You also told me in the phone that she has access to police records, but I haven't not heard from you again."

Jim sighed "Ah, and how is she going to find this appropriate? She knows that I am finished with Miriam and now you want me to do something for her."

"You really told me Aysha has access to many police files of immigrants. It would not be a big deal."

"So, you want her to find out who this Brett Sayed is? Aysha is going to be upset when I ask her. And if this man has a police file, what do you want to do? Are you going to report him? Do you have their precise address? And what will Miriam do after she loses her job and her income?"

"If she becomes again homeless, she will be welcome here. You know, I am getting old and sometimes I feel lonely. She has a pleasant conversation and is good company, a thing I sometimes was missing. You have abandoned me."

"My God, Dad. You want to jail or deport her boyfriend and you expect that this way she is going to come back to your home for conversation. Lots of luck."

James thought that his father no longer had the age to be interested in a much younger woman. Miriam was no good for anything because she was unable to care for herself and had always accepted without conditions the protection of men within her reach. She had been hired by the bank branch as an office help but two years earlier when his boss had demanded that she clean the office including the bathrooms as a condition to stay, she had submitted to doing it against James' advice. She obviously had difficulties dealing on her own with an increasingly tough world and needed to live in a subservient manner under somebody's shadow. Aysha was different and could take care of herself. The way how Miriam had chosen to spend the first night outside of his Dad's house to force his hand because he was the only man she knew, was revealing. James would talk to Aysha only when she had time and was in good mood, not right away. It would be a favor to his father because James did not feel responsible for anyone.

* * *

It had been raining during the following weeks and the city was under a heat wave. Wilbur did not receive an answer to his request from James. Miriam continued visiting Wilbur regularly on most Mondays.

Sometimes she brought little gifts or some food and the two had a pleasant dinner. The woman reported many things of which Wilbur was unaware of, but she went out of her way to avoid talking about Brett Sayed. She mentioned, however, that she found the people on the premises where she sang or served drinks to be good and pleasant company and that they made her laugh many times. She could not always understand their language. They mostly were suffering undocumented aliens, but it was better not to ask. It made her sad to realize in what dire and dangerous situation they found themselves and how much they had been forced to give up for an uncertain future.

Many things worried Wilbur, but now that it was summer the temperature was suffocating but Miriam always appeared warmly dressed in a buttoned and closed blouse with long sleeves. Was she trying to hide something from him, like additional bruises? He attempted to force a discussion on the issue, but she only related how much she enjoyed her job and the pay she was earning.

The man was not about to give up.

"Tell me where you live. What is your address? And the address of the place you sing? I worry about you."

"But Mr. Ross, you have my phone number. In certain neighborhoods of the dry land, it is difficult to recognize house numbers and street names because of disorganized overbuilding and small shacks. We had to move out once because the landlord wanted to raise the rent. Another time, a neighbor was making so much noise that he made Brett mad and he had to teach him a lesson. Then we moved again. Brett taught me how to look for new housing, which I did not know. That is the way things are. If you need me, just give me a call. If you feel sick, I will come and assist you."

"All of this lack of stability sounds, if you excuse me, a little pigheaded. There are better ways. When I go tomorrow to my store,

I will take some time out and visit the place where you work. I would not mind meeting your Brett."

"The establishment is named *Oasis of Hope* and is located on Liberty Street. I cannot describe it better. The clients will be surprised to see a man like you there. They are simple immigrants in need of some entertainment. As for Brett, I cannot promise that he will be there because there are other places where we can earn extra money. Currently we live a few blocks behind the *Oasis,* but I could never figure out the right number. We don't care because there is no mail service."

Wilbur waited until the following Friday before visiting the *Oasis.* He found it, but he thought that some people on the street were scary and that everything visible was unkept and dirty. He found the *Oasis* and entered. A sign at the entrance announced the availability of evening entertainment performed by Brett and his (unnamed) female singer. Inside, the room consisted of a little stage surrounded by numerous, mostly long tables with banks and chairs. Lining one of the walls an attached large bar offering alcoholic drinks was present. Wilbur approached an idle barmaid.

"Hi, lady. I am looking for a girl named Miriam, a good friend of mine, who sings and performs here in the evening."

"Do you say Miriam? No, I don't know her" And noticing a barman nearby she called him loudly "Ed, do you know a girl named Miriam?"

The barman shook his head. "No" But then he added "Is that the one that goes with Brett? She is Brett's sidekick"

Wilbur was immediately interested, and the man added:

"She sings here always as a part of Brett's show and she helps with the tables. It seems that she gets generous tips because she smiles so well. I haven't seen her for several days. But look, Brett is right there, next to the door. Why don't you ask him?"

Wilbur immediately approached the beefy and tall man identified as Brett and asked:

"Are you Brett? I am an old friend of Miriam. She has told me several times that she works with you. I am pleased to meet you, but I have come to talk to her. Where is she?"

"Do you say Miriam? I know many women, but I have no idea who this Miriam is. Excuse me, I have work to do" He rushed across the door disappearing in the next room.

Wilbur, very alarmed, decided to walk through the streets behind the *Oasis*, where Miriam had claimed she lived. It was a disheartening area filled with barracks. Most people he saw were probably undocumented aliens. He even tried to ask a few persons where Miriam and Brett Sayed lived, but nobody could say.

Wilbur, very worried, called James explaining the situation. Miriam had disappeared.

"Dad, I asked Aysha to look at the case in the computers with personal information. She found the individual named Brett Sayed, a man known to the police of different cities under several names suspected but never convicted of robbery and sale of illegal drugs. He was not known to have engaged in illegal activities during his brief stay in our city and the police is not looking for him. In summary, he is a very suspicious man, but he had not been arrested in Beauville, and his current address is unknown. As far as Miriam is concerned, her name does not appear in any records. The law would certainly be happy to receive and process a complaint from a credible witness and arrest Brett. That is all, go to the police."

"Miriam should have told me about Brett. She probably does not know the truth. I would have dragged her away from this man."

"You really believe that she did not know? Miriam was naive but not stupid."

"Was, you say? James, you must help me. Where do I go to report Miriam's disappearance?"

"Alright. I will ask Aysha again. Wait."

James finally told him that Aysha had advised to go in person to the Police Headquarters and ask for Detective Peter Nelson on the second floor, for whom she frequently worked. Wilbur rushed to the place.

Nelson worked in the section of disappeared people. Wilbur filled a form and gave it to an officer referring to Detective Nelson. Wilbur did not have to wait a long time.

Peter Nelson was an affable, smiling man who listened silently to the old man's explanations and concerns.

"So, you said that you talked to her for the last time six days ago. Normally we wait at least twice as long before we start searching for a missing citizen, but in this case, you explain that the young woman was involved out of sheer innocence, poverty, and absence of roots with a known subject with a police record currently identified in a problematic environment. Let us assume that it is true. Love of fun and of easy money is nearly universal, but it can become dangerous when driven by despair. Criminals cannot be recognized by the way they look or socialize. In this case, however, knowing that you are respected and well liked as an honest, mature, and charitable citizen and because your daughter-in-law Aysha helps me so much and is so dependable, I will show to you in the computer screen the faces of recently found and still unidentified female bodies. Do you feel prepared for that? It is tough."

Yes, Wilbur did feel prepared, but he felt how his heart had started racing.

The pictures were horrible. They consisted of a photograph of the whole body and a close-up of the mostly bloody face. The first one as the second and the third and the fourth pictures were of no interest, but the fifth one showed unquestionably Miriam. She had been savagely beaten with a heavy instrument, possibly a hammer; her arms showed defense injuries and her head had been crushed. Wilbur, profoundly shaken, recognized the dress she was wearing. The detective did not need anything else and closed the show.

"I understand that you have identified Miriam, Mr. Ross, and I am very sorry. Let me enter her name into the file. We did not know who she was nor what to do with her body."

"Are you going to arrest and punish this beast, this Brett?"

"I will try and would be pleased to do it, if I could, but now that you have asked him where Miriam was, he must be at least 100 miles away from here. We would never find proof that he was the one, nor there would be any witnesses willing to testify. They always run away when they see a uniform. This individual is a bad criminal who had used several names. Now you are going to ask me why he was not arrested earlier, and the answer is that we couldn't. We have been long wanting to do something about the *Oasis*, which is a nest of crime, drugs, and vice, but no judge will authorize it. I doubt that we can find this Brett, but I will enter in his file that he was a prime suspect in an assassination. Don't worry: this man will eventually meet his match. With us or with somebody else."

Wilbur was heavily breathing. The policeman watched him in silence. Finally, he asked:

"Would you wish to recover and take care of the body?"

Wilbur lifted his eyes, wet with tears, and did not know what to answer. Nelson explained:

"It is too expensive for most people to pay for a burial or even a cremation. Now that the indigent victim has already been identified, I can order her cremation at our expense. In consideration of Aysha, I would be willing to arrange for you to attend the cremation and accept the ashes. As for viewing the body, I do not advise it. I am deeply sorry, Mr. Ross. I see that the victim was young and meant a lot to you."

Crestfallen, Wilbur found the way to his home and sat in his chair first in the twilight, later in the darkness. Miriam was not going to come back. The telephone awakened him from his astonished and mourning sleepiness. It was James.

"How are you doing, Dad."

"Very badly, thank you. Do you know what that degenerate did to Miriam?"

"I do, Dad. The detective spoke to Aysha. He felt that you were shaken and afflicted."

"I certainly will miss her. She frequently came and talked to me, which you never do. She even made me laugh. You should not get ideas, she was like a daughter to me, nothing else. I had warned her that she was in danger, but she did not listen."

"Her problem is that she did not understand the reality and savagery of our current circumstances. She thought that she was surrounded only by unfortunate but good people. Things are what they are and to survive, you must first watch, suspect and then adapt."

Wilbur did not answer.

"Well, Dad, have you decided whether you want to go to the cremation? It will be done the day after tomorrow at 10AM."

"I do not know whether I can survive this or not. I feel sick."

"I have discussed this with Aysha. We will come along and keep you company. It will give you some closure."

So, they did. Wilbur decided to dress well for the occasion and chose an elegant but unfashionable old suit found in a walk-in closet he had not visited for months. His image in a mirror revealed how his appearance had changed. Noticing his dirty shoes, he tried to clean them. And a thought came to his mind: For whom was he doing it?

What had Miriam really meant to him? Why had he never considered the issue?

He had reserved the flat personal boat of the community for the entire day. He found James and Aysha already seated in front of the oven. Two workers wheeled in a box reminiscent of a coffin, placed it inside of the oven and studiously locked the door. The old man thought that the box may have contained a different cadaver, but it did not matter. Wilbur was asked whether he wanted to hear music. He agreed and some circumstantial music was piped in. Nobody had really seen the body. Was it important? Wilbur remembered the horrible picture shown by the detective. He would try to forget it and invoked the memory of a laughing Miriam.

They needed to wait a long time before receiving a container with the ashes. Wilbur took it and announced that they would go to some suitable place and drink to her memory like the Irish do prior to scattering the ashes. James and Aysha agreed.

The three sat in the boat. Wilburn was taciturn and did not speak. James and Aysha talked only to themselves. The boat headed toward the new artificial beach close to the former harbor which the old man enjoyed visiting. It occurred to him that he had never brought Miriam to the place. Now he was doing it. The three headed to the waterfront restaurant.

The box with the ashes was placed in the center of the table. A waitress brought them three large beer glasses. The three fell silent sitting around the urn, until Wilbur spoke:

"I question myself, why must a human being die at the age of 36 years? She was healthy and beautiful. I remember when you, Jim, were born. You were a little baby hoping for a long life, you went to good schools, you expected lots of things of life, you are healthy. Why did she not live to enjoy any of this? Are we not entitled, as human beings, to the fulfillment of minimal expectations? It is not right that an adult, honest and educated woman needs to go begging to get a bed because she had been mistreated. It is not right that a man can beat her repeatedly and brutally murder her, when all she was asking for was fun, food and companionship. Is that not worse than the flooding?"

James answered:

"Nothing of this was right. The only real problem was the climate change that brought the water to our doors and changed our society. It was not our fault and you tried to help her out of the goodness of your heart. Be proud of it. She was lucky to have found you."

The young man had evidently been angry, and Wilbur recognized some rage in his voice. All drank some beer again. James had something to add:

"Dad, you are blaming me because I broke with her. Well, I have discussed that openly with Aysha. She is my witness. I dropped her because she was not contributing to my life and I lost the love I had felt for her. She never had any initiative, she never made proposals. For her, being alive consisted of standing still, being told what to do and hoping that nobody would come and hurt her. We had been a couple where I was expected to order and she would merrily submit, thanking God for having found a master. That was not what I wanted. I needed a real companion with flesh, initiatives and understanding. I also had needs that she never recognized. *What do you want to do?* she used to tell me all the time. I heard it hundreds it if not thousands of times. Did she not have proposals or plans or her own? I could not take it anymore, so please do not blame me. Sleeping outside of your door until you felt pity and took her in was an example. She was in trouble and the solution was to find a new master to save her. She could have tried different things, but NO! She had to beg protection. And I am sure that every time the brute beat her, she answered crying that she recognized that all had been her fault and deserved the punishment promising that she would never do it again" James was really upset.

Aysha, after seizing James' hand, intervened:

"Wilbur, my parents came to this country early. They, like many others, noticed that their country was becoming a desert. It was extremely hot and it did not rain. They loved their homeland, their language, and had local family and friends, but they realized the need to take a tough decision. Soon it would be difficult to survive and it was mandatory to consider a radical step. To survive and be capable of living the existence they both wanted, they came legally here and obtained papers, well ahead of many other people who waited too long. They were able to immigrate before it was prohibited or made difficult. I understand that Miriam was a good, but weak woman. You know, no matter who- and whatever you are, if there is a fire you need to run away; if you fall into the water you need to swim, and if you will not or cannot do it, you will suffer grave consequences, because nothing was promised to us when we were born. Some will be assisted to survive because there are still good and compassionate people like you left, but eventually they will have to accept certain circumstances. Our world has turned ugly and dangerous for everybody. Think that our ancestors, all of them hunters and gatherers have been surviving tough environments for hundreds of thousands of years and here we are. Others did not survive and are gone. Don't you know that the first men had to continuously fight to stay alive? It is possible to survive and even succeed if you have the proper brain. James and I view this the same way. We are two equals who love and support each other. We have a future."

Wilbur had lowered his head.

"You are telling me that Miriam got what she had coming and that she was not equipped to survive in the current milieu. What happened to charity, to compassion, to solidarity? Has it been flooded and washed-out by the waters? For you she was a helpless girl unfit for independent life, who could not grow up and always needed a protective male. I do not remember anyone in my family like that, but I still wonder what we could have done to help her. Do you believe that she was not entitled to help? Would it really have been impossible for her to find among the millions of single men a suitable companion who liked her demeanor, her beauty, and her many qualities? Would she not have been a dependable and loyal wife? You are telling me, the world is crazy and dangerous, fight it or perish as you deserve, as in a boxing match and you don't see any alternatives. Well, I do not believe that I was born to fight anyone, and I never did it."

"Oh Dad" said James "you are right. She was a lovely and friendly woman who did not deserve to be brutally murdered, but she was not what I needed as a companion. Searching for a suitable partner and abandoning a dangerous one, however, should have been her self-preservation way out, not mine or yours. You should not be as troubled as you are."

For a moment, Wilbur gazed the ash container and then the window and he said: "There is sun, wind, and freedom outside, enough for everyone to enjoy in peace, and no one has the right to judge or disturb others, but if the others persist in their inhuman ways, one shining day all weak and feeble people will unite by locking their arms and will advance in peace creating a new world of smiles, peace, tolerance and justice, no matter what climate they have."

James and Aysha listened and were astonished with this harangue. They stood up. Wilbur grabbed the box wit the ashes pressing it against his chest and all three walked toward the shallow beach and the ocean. They removed their shoes and socks and entered the water, resuming their walk alongside the shore. It was not deep.

"Tell me, Jim. Do you remember something that she used to sing?"

"No, Dad. She had attempted to sing several times tunes from the radio, but she did poorly."

Wilbur started scattering the ashes over the water surface, as far inside as he could. Mentally, he was saying "Goodbye, my Miriam. Thank you for brightening my life in my old age. You were good and I will never forget you."

* * *

Two years had passed. Wilbur checked periodically the low containing wall built to keep his island dry and was worried, especially during high tides. The water level was still going up.

On his way to the dry land, he said to his companion: "If my house gets flooded, I do not want to live anymore."

A voice answered "You always find a way. Please, stay alive for years."

And Wilbur added: "Let us go to my store. Ron Miles is also getting too old to carry on. Maybe we could sell it."

"I am sure you will do the right thing" answered the voice.

But the man was still worried. "Maybe with my money I could rent a nice apartment, but I shall not know the neighbors and there are many dangerous people."

"You will handle it."

"I will get no money for my house if the island becomes flooded."

"Enjoy the weather today."

Wilbur took the bus to his bakery, which was already open. He took a croissant and went to his office. His partner Ron had been leaving the papers and drawers in an increasingly messy and untidy manner. He tried to order and file the bills. What was their financial condition? He said:

"This man is really getting to be too old. I really do not know whether we are still making money or not."

And the voice answered: "You will find out and make the right decisions."

"Right decisions? Do you mean that I should find and recommend him a nursing home? He has family, you know."

"You always do the right thing."

By noon he was finished. He saw three customers in the store. He thought that maybe everything was going well. He unexpectedly received a phone call from James. Wilbur was immediately worried:

"What is the matter, James? Is everything all right?"

"It could not be better, Dad. Look, here on my side is Aysha. She would like to tell you something."

The woman had been on James' side and was smiling.

"Hi, Wilbur. I have good news for you. We are expecting a baby. It is a boy."

"Hooray! I am going to be a grandfather. It is great. Do you think that he will be born knowing how to swim?"

James and Aysha laughed. "We'll teach him immediately."

The son had something else to add. "We have been thinking and weighing our options. We are both in our late thirties and have life experience. We have decided to get married."

"James, Aysha, you know how to make an old man happy."

Wilbur, who felt really happy, thought that life would continue after him and decided to have lunch in a small restaurant nearby to celebrate the great news. The establishment was full, but he found a last free seat at the counter. The voice told him: "You seem very pleased."

"I am. If I survive a few months, I shall become a grandfather and will get a great daughter-in-law."

"You will survive, congratulations."

The evening arrived. The man took, as always, the public passenger boat to his home. Inside, he removed his coat and went to the kitchen.

He decided that he never would leave it no matter what. He opened his freezer and selected a lobster box.

"The celebration will continue. It will be ready in 15 minutes and then I will eat it with a glass of white wine. It is an excellent wine. I have been saving it for a special occasion", he said to his imaginary friend.

"I am happy for you and your family, Mr. Ross" was the answer. "Do you want me to sing something for you?"

THE ACCOUNTANT'S
NEVER-ENDING TROUBLES

IT WAS A NICE spring day. Alex Weisman parked his modest car in the lot of his employer, a well-run toy company by the name PLAYFUL Inc. He rode the elevator as he did every day to the fourth floor and entered the *Accounting* department of the administrative suite. With closed eyes he walked toward his desk located in the last row of the section, near the window, in a slightly larger cubicle. He noticed that only one of the other accountants, Doug, had arrived and was standing in the corner of the coffee machine. He decided to join him.

"Good morning, boss" greeted Doug.

"I am not your boss. Are there any doughnuts left, or did you eat them all?"

"You are not? There are many times when it looks like it. I am finishing the cash-flow summary and the tax statement of the Aurora office, and I must bring it to you."

"It is only to help you because I am older and have more experience, but our only boss is Andrew Groves, the Controller. You know that. Do not call me boss. I don't like it."

Alex grabbed a doughnut and a cup of hot coffee and requested that Doug mail to his computer the Aurora spreadsheets as soon as possible and moved to his desk.

Doug had opened a wound. It was an injustice that he did not have an additional supervisor title and that he did not make more money. He had joined the firm 15 years ago and all accountants and secretaries relied on him for help and advice, which made him the de facto supervisor of the office. He was the one who always presented to the Controller the final cash flow book for distribution and felt qualified to take his job and the wounds ran deep. He had entered Andrew's office several times to find him laughing on the telephone or surfing the internet. Alex did not enjoy such leisure opportunities. The last time he had asked for a raise or a promotion, Andrew had offended him. He answered that it was a good career move to look for open jobs and advancement elsewhere after so many years and that he would give him good recommendations. Matter closed. Alex was so enraged that he really considered resigning. Jobs for plain accountants were available, but he wanted something better and had no answer when asked about leadership experience. Fifteen years in the same firm and he had never been promoted? How strange...

In his private life, Alex was a lonely man without a wife or a companion. Women viewed him first with interest, as a solid bet, but he turned out to be boring and unimaginative. He had never learned the proper way to come on to girls at parties or a bar. He had once considered joining one of the meeting webs on the Internet but on examination he recognized lies and deceptions, sometimes even dangers. He had concluded that nothing was wrong staying single. Maybe a girlfriend or a wife would decorate his apartment more tastefully or even find a better one but moving is always expensive and troublesome.

Alex had asked his superior for a personal secretary and she even interviewed candidates jointly with his boss. A young woman named Lisa was chosen and given a desk close to the Controller's office. On her first day, Alex approached the new employee to give instructions and to explain their work, but the new girl answered that she would be happy to help Alex and his bookkeepers if they were in trouble but that her main job was at the Controller's office. The man felt once again betrayed and scorned, as so many times before and once again considered leaving. "Let Lisa do my work, you imbecile", he thought meaning the Controller. This had happened almost three years earlier, but nothing had changed in the meantime. Maybe nothing was ever to change and maybe he had been born only to do his job.

* * *

The company was a small toy manufacturer that went public 10 years earlier, as the previous owner and founder, Mr. Holloway had decided. Alex had recognized that the move would give him extra work, but the firm hired additional accountants and Andrew, not Alex, became their first Controller. The boss had promised better salaries triggered by the move, but the salaries were only minimally raised. Alex had liked Mr. Holloway and was sad when he died. His only daughter Beth Holloway became the Chief Executive Officer, de facto the owner, and moved into her father's office. Somebody had proposed to her that sales figures could be enormously improved by reaching an agreement with a well-known Internet marketer. It worked out well and the company was able to open a second manufacturing plant. Alex noticed in his computer how the firm's income and benefits went up, but his personal earnings barely climbed above the inflation rate. As for Beth...nobody liked her too much. She organized and paid Christmas parties for the administrative staff but she was haughty and vainglorious. She rarely was insolent or rude, but she was perceived as high-flown and intemperate, well beyond what she was worthy of. Alex thought that after all she was keeping the company afloat, and everybody had a safe job. Most bosses behaved like her. Or worse.

Some time earlier, he had met Doug, a collaborator, mid-morning, as usual, next to the coffee maker. Mostly they talked about football or recent baseball broadcasts, but that day Doug displayed a mischievous, frisky look in his eyes. What's up, asked Alex, smiling, as Doug continued filling his mug. He finally talked:

"They have tried to keep it secret" said Doug happily inhaling, "but Mrs. Holloway, and our beloved boss, Andrew, are having an affair." The man smiled again and looked around. Undoubtedly the other employers had already heard or would soon learn, and he was the one who had found out.

Alex did not answer. His first reaction was "Who cares?" But he commented:

"Well, maybe that is why Andrew works so little. He is always playing computer games when I enter."

Doug laughed, but not loudly, checking at the same time if somebody else was listening. He answered:

"I have noticed it also."

Alex was not finished "I do most of his work and I am even not allowed to use his secretary. I noticed how she makes flight and hotel reservations and runs errands for Andrew. Sometimes he must call me when he needs to explain a bill to a client. He does not always understand what I am talking about."

"Let him enjoy it while it lasts. These things always end badly."

"The boss is older that any of us."

"Besides, the way she talks is funny. She says unexpected things and seems to have her own view of life and business. Besides, you know that Andrew is married. We have met his wife in the Christmas party. And so has Mrs. Holloway too."

Alex shrugged and drank some coffee.

"Yeah, the boss talks funny."

"She will have a fight with Andrew, and you will become the Controller."

"You think so? I doubt it. You know, when you have a good employee without leadership experience, you should keep him where he is and choose somebody else as boss. If you promote a competent employee, you risk losing the good employee you had and finding yourself with an incompetent boss."

"Come on, Alex. We know you and always follow your advice. You would deserve it and it would be great for the company."

Alex shrugged again and returned to his desk. This conversation had happened years ago and, as usual, nothing had changed.

Alex was close to the 16th anniversary of his arrival at Playful Inc. and once again he was cursing his weakness and inability to decide. He was already in his mid forties, and a change of job would become increasingly more difficult every day. If he stayed, maybe they would give him a golden watch for his 30th anniversary. What a joy would that be! He delivered a big sigh and turned to his computer entries, convinced that tomorrow would be the same. It was not.

His intercom sounded. It was Lisa, the Controller's secretary.

"Alex? Mr. Groves wants to see you immediately. He says that it is urgent."

"On my way."

Alex entered his boss' office. He found Andrew seated at his desk and somewhat disheveled. The accountant had never seen him this way.

"What is the matter, Andrew? You look worried."

"Well, the moment of reaching a crucial decision has arrived and I have no choice. Sometimes certain things need to be done. After my wife, you are the first to learn of it."

"Let me sit down before hearing it. Does your resolution concern me?"

"It may. I know that you have been here longer than myself and you are trusted and respected by everybody. Unfortunately for me, I see no personal way forward at Playful and in a recent meeting with other controllers I learned of better pay opportunities. Everybody needs experienced controllers, and I am quitting. Right now, it is the time to look for an upward job with better pay."

"I see. Where are you going?"

"Oh, the company is still not chosen. I have several offers."

"Would it not be more reasonable to wait for an offer before quitting here and losing your salary?"

"No, no. I got to leave right now. I can give no details at this time, but I am also considering out-of-town offers and I need to be available on short notice."

Alex slowly recovered from his surprise. It was evident that Andrew had been fired in a fulminant manner. What had he done? Had he stolen money? Certainly not from the company, it could not have been hidden from him. Did he have a fight with the CEO? Oh, well, this was Ms. Holloway, and he knew about the intimate relationship. It was more likely, but the relevant issue was whether Alex could be promoted to Controller, as he had wished for many years.

Alex stood up and offered his hand to Andrew. "I am deeply sorry to see you leave after such a long time. I will miss you because of our friendship and good collaboration, but you must know what is best for you. If I can do something for you, you know where to find me. Are you really leaving today?"

Alex felt some inner excitement while returning to his office. He had to think about means of taking advantage of the situation. Beyond his newly developed expectations, Andrew's situation did not interest him, because he had never liked the man. He returned to work, but he was unable to concentrate.

The coffee break was observed by all accountants. Alex was the last to reach the corner.

"Do you know what happened?" asked a voice. All turned their heads toward Alex.

"Do you mean that Andrew Groves has resigned? He had been here several years and now apparently he got a better offer."

All laughed shaking their heads.

"No, no. He had for years an affair with Ms. Holloway. Yesterday they had a fight and she fired Andrew on the spot."

"I had not been following this matter closely. None of our business."

"We all hope that you will be appointed Controller. You have been doing all the work for years."

"I know nothing about this. If so, I would insist on staying away from extraprofessional predicaments."

All laughed loudly. "You are not married like Andrew, watch out," and more voices were heard: "I would not mind at all" "Come on, she is old and ugly" "I find, she is not so old and not so ugly."

Feeling uneasy, Alex turned around to leave, but he still asked:

"How do you know about this development?"

Several men laughed for the third time. "Lisa, the secretary, is telling everybody. Go and ask her."

Back at this desk, Alex considered whether he should do something. Maybe he should request an appointment to see Ms. Holloway and apply for the job. But because his manner was as shy as serious, he took no initiatives, nor did he approve of other people's initiatives on his behalf. No, he did not enjoy starting anything. The people in charge of the company would easily identify him. This way of thinking and his abhorrence of self-promotion was one of the reasons he had never been promoted. Many in the company viewed him only as a diligent and helpful ant.

Alex' section was busy preparing the final earnings declaration, which might increase the value Playful Inc.'s shares at the stock market. Nobody noticed Andrew's absence. Occasionally Alex had to go to Lisa's desk in the empty Controller's office. One day, he asked whether they had chosen a new Controller, but Lisa knew nothing.

"The boss only says that there is no hurry because you cover the vacancy very well. She has asked me about you twice. She is convinced that there will be no problems with the earnings statement for Wall Street."

Of course not, thought Alex, extremely pleased. He had been doing the Controller's work alone for years. Maybe Ms. Holloway must be considering him. Of course! Why else would she be asking for evaluations? He joyfully returned to his desk. Everything was going the proper way.

The call from the Chief's office came one day late in the afternoon, when Alex was getting ready to leave. Ms. Holloway was expecting him in her office immediately. Alex felt heart palpitations in his chest. He went to the bathroom to check his appearance and fix his tie. The momentous day had arrived!

Over the years he had seen Ms. Holloway several times in the company's parties but they had never talked. She was a petite woman in her early or mid fifties, moderately obese and, to tell the truth, not particularly attractive. She had a scary, shrill, loud voice but spoke clearly. The company had been prospering and for Alex it was the only thing that mattered.

"Come on in, Alex, and sit down."

"Thank you, Madam. What can I do for you?"

"I was afraid that you might have left already."

"Oh, no, Madam. I am terribly busy finishing the earnings summary."

"Does it look good?"

"It is not quite finished but yes, Madam. It is going to be excellent. Your stock price will rise, I am sure. Your leadership is outstanding. I did not occur to me to bring some early data to show."

"Don't you miss Andrew Groves?"

Alex shrugged and denied with head movements.

"Lisa tells me that you had been doing most of his work for a long time. It is great to have people watching for the company's interests and ready to jump in to cover a hole whenever needed. Thank you, Alex."

The woman added a request. "You must help me with a problem. Our good client Kinder Inc. is disputing a big bill for toys we shipped. Can you fix that?"

"I really don't know but I can check with our fulfillment department and if there is no billing error, I will contact Kinder for clarifications and we'll take it from there. I have done it in the past."

The lady sighed loudly and looked up to the ceiling.

"Thank you, Alex. Now I am going to tell you why I have called you. We need to talk about Andrew's job."

The man inhaled and held his breath while his heart started racing again. Finally!

"I have discussed the situation with our board. You know that ours is a family operation and almost all members are relatives of mine. Genuinely nice people. It turns out that Auntie Evelyn's current husband has a nephew who has been doing bookkeeping work for a cooperative in Pittsburgh for years and had won many congratulations and awards for his work and he has always wanted to come here to stay with the family and have a better salary. I have been checking references and have spoken with our personnel director and I almost would like to appoint him as Controller, but I wanted to discuss it first with you. Please look at his CV and join me on the weekend interviewing him. I need to make sure that you both would work well together."

"I see. I feel honored that you trust and value my judgment so much. I am only a small accountant and..."

"Stop, don't thank me for anything. I just want to make sure that you stay with us and will help your new boss."

"Of course, Madam. If you do not have anything else for me, I do not want to bother you any longer."

Surprisingly, Ms. Holloway rose and picked up two small glasses and a bottle of bourbon from a drawer.

"Oh, don't go away so early, Alex, and humor me a little longer. Drink a glass with me."

Alex took the glass smiling. He did not know what to say.

"I understand that you are single despite your age. I like that because this has allowed you to go around, meet different people and stay free to do as you please. I have always done the same."

The poor, bitterly disappointed man, did not know how to explain to his mistress that she was sorely mistaken. He felt only frustrated and inadequate. Whatever the needs and expectations of this lady were, he was the wrong man to satisfy her. He would use the word "inadequate." Beth carried on:

"Andrew was such a disappointment to me! He took everything I gave him, he almost did not work, he requested and got raises, he was never available on weekends because he preferred to spend them with his family. With his family? What was I to him? I am over fifty. Shall I spend many more days of my life waiting for his divorce? He would never clarify this. Never! He had forgotten who I am and what power I wield!"

Alex looked sideways to the booze bottle. He felt that he needed a second glass. Ms. Holloway coincided and accepted.

"I feel free to reveal to you my intimate secrets because I know of your freedom, experience and your lack of attachments. You are the perfect man to understand what I am saying."

"Yes, Madam. I agree. I am sure that we shall find additional time to follow up on your stirring history."

"Is anyone waiting for you at home? I really need to open myself to a colleague I can trust. Charge me overtime if you wish."

"Madam, please..."

"Don't you Madam me anymore. My name is Beth. Call me Beth."

"Yes, Beth."

"Which persuasive means does a woman in my position need to find a companion?"

"It would be easy, Beth, if I may say so."

"You mean loathsome males who smell my money like Andrew?"

"Not necessarily, Beth, because a woman of your intelligence should be able to sort out and thrust out contemptible money diggers."

Alex was already considering a third liquor glass.

"I did not sort out Andrew. Outside of my fortune, what qualities do I have that would appeal to a real man?"

"Many, they would be hard to enumerate." He was going to add that he would need time to evaluate them but shut up on time.

Alex took a break to swallow his drink. He had always been a prudent and pondering man, aware that rushed and emotionally driven decisions were frequently wrong and who, despite his disappointments, valued having a stable job. He did not want to find a notice of dismissal on his desk next morning. Maybe if he drank slowly, Ms. Holloway might have forgotten her last question. He had identified no qualities in her boss and Alex' capability of lying for profit did not reach that far. He decided to stare instead silently into the eyes of the woman. He wished he were able to run away instead.

"Do you know, Alex, the kind of commitment that I expect from a life companion? To me, it is the same that binds a horsewoman to her stallion."

"You choose powerful metaphors. Yes, the thought of what you mean had crossed my mind, but I could never express it as perfectly. Carry on, please" answered Alex fearfully. He had not understood.

"Do you like to watch old Western movies? I do, I have a collection of them home. They reveal the true nature of the relation between human beings and their horses, a relation which I wish could be extended to human relationships. When riding, the owner and his horse form a unique single unit with two sets of brains and four strong legs that races at high speeds like a wind through empty prairies and forests. Decisions and orders from a single brain are accepted without resistance or arguments. No human could split the moving couple into separate units, no one could interfere with the objectives. After dismounting, the rider can tie the horse to a post, and it will stay there without complaining. When attached to a carriage, horses marvelously pull the vehicle uphill and downhill without growling; when mounted by a man or woman, the horse immediately responds to every wish, every direction it receives at any speed; same thing when led to a stable; when thirsty, it waits until water becomes available; it never makes advances or runs toward a female unless it is permitted or directed by the owner to do so. It is a perfect union, a real merger for the better between two living beings made possible by the will of God. The horse enjoys many advantages: it could run wildly in its youth before being schooled in its future life; it is fed for life; its horseshoes are replaced for free when needed; in the movies, unlike its much smaller rider, it is never wounded or killed. I thought of all this when I was a teenager and my Dad brought me to learn riding to a stable near my home. I started feeling that the horse was a part of myself complementing all I had without asking for no other recompense than a pat or a kiss. You cannot imagine my joy."

"Beth, you are so bright and open, your powerful images and symbols are transparent and diaphanous and reveal how much time you must have spent thinking about transcendent issues."

Alex considered for a moment that maybe he should neigh, but he was not sure that he knew how to do it correctly. He started feeling surrounded or captured and kept in defenseless condition. Maybe he was in front of the gallows and facing an alternative: either a warm stable with guaranteed food, air conditioning and occasional petting and walks, or the unemployment office. He felt a need to loudly whinny. He stood up and said:

"I feel gratified and enlightened by your insights and confidences. I will have to think for a long time about your lucid discourse to fully understand and assimilate it. Excuse me, but for now I must return to my office to finish the urgent work on your profits that I was doing in the sole interest of your firm."

"My firm you say? Haven't you spent half a life here? As a single man, what other home do you have?" Significantly smiling, she stretched her hand toward Alex, who took it. Was he supposed to kiss it? Should he consider prostrating? In doubt, he just respectfully bowed and left as fast as he could.

* * *

He said nothing in the office but three days later he was contacted by Ms. Holloway's secretary:

"Alex, Ms. Holloway says that you agreed to meet and evaluate the candidate to new Controller in her company. You are both invited for lunch tomorrow Saturday at 1PM at the *Prairie Restaurant*."

Evidently, the lady had not forgotten him, but the object of his ambition was going to somebody else. It would be a squabble and a humiliation, but he had missed the opportunity of presenting his credentials and asking for the job.

The *Prairie* was an exclusive and expensive local and he had never been inside. He felt very irritated. He should have refused and be already looking for another job. A waitress approached him asking whether he had a reservation. Probably, at the table of Ms. Holloway. The girl smiled, nodded, and guided him. Already seated at the table, Alex found a middle-aged man dressed like him in a cheap rack suit, who immediately smiled. Andrew used to be better clothed, he thought.

"You must be Alex. I am Matt Carter, the new Controller. Beth is all the time talking about you. She says that you are a fantastic accountant and that you are going to help me as much as you helped my predecessor. I am so happy to be able to join you."

Alex did not know what to answer and mentally cursed the intruder. His lips delineated a bitter smile.

"The moment that my aunt mentioned the opening, I jumped sky high. I have felt for a long time to be quite ready to become a Controller, maybe at some later time a Chief Financial Officer. In my present occupation and in my town, I found no suitable openings. Was I going to spend the rest of my life as a simple country accountant? I have a wife and two school children who will be going soon to College."

Alex understood the feelings, but he kept to himself that he silently shared them. Once again, he cursed himself for being there and lost his appetite.

Beth appeared. Alex was shocked when she smilingly kissed both men in the cheek.

"I am so glad that you both have met. You must become friends and work hard together. The previous Controller left all the work for

Alex, which was not right." Matt signaled that he harbored no such intention.

"Besides, the Controller must review items that accountants may not be able to discern" added Matt.

Insulted, Alex thought that stupid, lazy Controllers, are the ones with most problems.

"Well, my boys" concluded Beth, "you are really made for each other. Our sales are also rising, and I foresee great times ahead of us. You both understand our company's needs and know what to do. I could not be happier and so will you. Now that all is resolved, let us have a happy meal. I will have lobster with a side of Beluga caviar and some French champagne. Will anyone join me?" And she laughed.

Beth Holloway waited one week to execute her next move. This time she was the one who personally commanded Alex into her office. She called him while he was scanning a professional magazine for advertised openings.

"Oh, Ms. Hollo... I am mean Beth. What a pleasure to hear your voice. How can I be of service?"

"I was missing you, dear devil! We haven't met for one whole week."

"A long time, indeed. Did you hire Matt Carter?"

"Yes, yes, as you recommended, because I did not want to upset you. He will be starting next month."

"I am looking forward. Is everything all right with you?"

"Do you have something to do this evening? I wanted to invite you to dinner at the *Basque Cuisine*."

"Oh, well, it is too expensive for me."

"Don't worry, my dear. I have an account and they know me very well. We will meet at the restaurant at 8PM."

One second after hanging up the telephone, Alex regretted having accepted. Everything was a humiliation from an abusive boss. She was a nepotist who had given away the job he deserved and wanted; she had offered no salary hike, but now she was gratuitously displaying money in front of his nose. She took the initiative in everything, she was ugly, intrusive, irritating, but how could he cancel now? Did he own proper clothing for such an evening outing among wealthy people? Maybe he should leave at once and visit a famous man's store. Did he have enough credit left in his card? He decided not to do anything of the kind. By appearing in rags, maybe he could get rid of the woman. Finally, he dressed as he had last time.

He arrived 10 minutes ahead of time and was shown to an empty table. He looked around and concluded that he did not belong there.

Beth arrived half an hour late. The maître rushed to meet and guide the lady toward the table and announced that he would immediately serve her favorite drink. "And the gentleman?"

As the evening and the expensive meal progressed, Alex could not help but feel impressed. Wearing a beautiful attire, Beth did not look so horrible as he had felt in their original meeting. A very well-dressed gentleman approached her addressing her by the first name. She introduced the unknown to the somewhat-embarrassed Alex. "This is Charlie, and this is my very good friend Alex" she said. After the unknown, always smiling, left, Beth explained:

"You did not know Charlie, really? He is the Chief Executive of ALMIRA. You know, the computer people."

She made a pause critically examining Alex. "I don't mean to criticize you, but you can easily see that evenings gentlemen are dressed differently. Somebody might be surprised about the way you dress and mistake you for a low-level employee of my company. I am thinking about coming visits. It is one of the things I did not like about Andrew. There was no way of suggesting anything. Nor of telling him the truth. Listen: I will send to you tomorrow the secretary with a card I have from the Century Men's Store. You can show it and they will fit you appropriately. Many men sitting here go to the same clothes company. You do not have to worry about the bill. They give me a discount."

Alex thought NO, NO and NO, but said nothing at first. Then he decided that it was now or never. He tentatively chose NOW, aware that he might regret it for the rest of his life.

"I am grateful, Beth and will do as you say. I must tell you something about my position in the firm. I never mentioned it, but I had hopes of being considered myself for the position of Controller. I had been performing most of Andrew's work for years and many colleagues wondered why I did not have the job. I am qualified."

"Oh, do not be angry, my poor little fellow. The way things are, there is no alternative to considering certain friends or relatives. To prosper in life, you must know and accept the world. They say that the United States are a democracy, but this has never meant that you can do as you please, nor that we are all equal. You can read about equal rights if it gives you comfort, but there are outside of the situation we are discussing. There are family rules that you must accept or else you will find yourself by the wayside. I can offer you other rewards."

Alex lowered his head. He knew the world, but he continued: "Except for small costs of living adjustments, my salary has been almost unchanged for fifteen years and I have never been promoted. I noticed that you approved a number of unscheduled bonuses for Andrew, occasionally for things I had done myself."

"So, I did. What do you want? The Controller job is out but tell me clearly what else you want."

"Promote me to section supervisor with a raise."

"How much."

"10%."

Beth laughed. "I will give you 20%. I want you to be happy and keep helping my Controller. Matt is a good boy, beloved by my family, but I know that he has a lot to learn and will need your help. We three shall meet regularly and discuss how things are going. The firm is prospering, and I want that everybody loves each other and lives in peace."

After this, they were able to conduct a friendly conversation until 10:30. As they were leaving, Beth stopped and, looking at Alex, she proposed: "I want to take a cab. Will you come with me to have a coffee in my home?"

Alex was not surprised but he was tense. He thought that he had been chased like a rabbit. Both stood at the door while the doorman was trying to fetch a taxi. And then...

Alex noticed it late. His colleague Doug from the office and a woman companion had stopped on the other side of the street and were looking at the couple with visible surprise and curiosity.

Alex stiffened his body in a rage. He did not deserve that. Now everybody was going to know. He hesitated. Should he wave to Doug or ignore him? Could he talk to him offering explanations next day? He decided to talk only to Beth as before, ignore the couple and do nothing else. What had he become? A gigolo? A kept single man? How many stories of this kind had he heard before? Would his colleagues regard him with suspicion and fear? No, he would go to the police and report a case of reverse sexual harassment. He had read of similar cases in the papers.

His fury kept him going but then calm triumphed over despair and he thought that he needed time to reflect and consider the consequences before doing or saying anything. The evening had not displeased him entirely and he had won a raise and a promotion. His life had so far been miserable. Being aware that the tram comes rarely, one must climb into the first one that appears, because it may be the last. A cab arrived. Alex accepted his destiny and climbed into the tram named Beth.

Against his custom, the next day he arrived at his office late. He noted an unusual silence as he walked in. Lisa, the secretary, came in and respectfully smiling, she deposited papers on Alex's desk. He had the feeling that everybody was looking mockingly at him. He shrugged. He owed them nothing. He knew that everybody in the room was going to see his new salary and comment. They should simply congratulate him. When they learned that he had not made it to Controller, there would even be more cheap talk. What was he getting for his services? He knew, the accountants were going to see it.

* * *

Matt Carter was anointed new Controller and took possession. Alex had known from the beginning that the new employee lacked experience and necessary knowledge, and this became evident to everybody. Doug once dared to ask:

"And how come, Alex, that you were not the one promoted? This guy does not know anything."

"None of your business. I am now your supervisor, and I am quite pleased. Matt is simply not familiar with the way things are here and we must help him to get started. I do it all the time."

But nobody mentioned Beth Holloway in his presence. Alex occasionally received her phone calls:

"Hello, my dear. I want just to thank you for all you are doing for my cousin. You know, the owner's family is like a royal house. We all need help, and we have the right to expect necessary services. We always remember."

"Except when you forget. Yes, you explained. Equal rights do not reach remote corners" answered the accountant.

Beth laughed loudly. "You know and understand the world and are a realist. That's why I love you so much."

"More than your horse?"

Beth laughed again, this time louder. "You are my thoroughbred, my stallion! I want to have dinner with you this evening.

"Are you inviting Matt too?"

"You are a bad boy. No, it will be a hot meeting."

Time passed by. Sometimes Alex stared his wristwatch. "Why does it not move slower? I am wasting my life like a gigolo. I should bill her by the minute. I get fed everyday and nobody cares. I am no longer young, and I still have not achieved anything worth remembering. My parents must have been happy when I was born, maybe they thought that I would become somebody. Thousands of people can do the same things I do. Matt knows less than I do but it does not matter, and he makes more money than I do. I am getting old. I wish, I could slow down time until something good happens to me." And what about Beth? He had no warm feelings for her, but she was sufficiently grotesque to make him laugh. If he dropped her, he would lose the job, and where would he go? To suffer that woman was better than being alone in a cold street. Yes, time passed by. Actually, it raced.

Alex met Beth mostly in her home and he frequently stayed the night. She had an outstanding cook. Little by little, the woman started reporting things about the company and its personnel that he had not been aware of. Slowly something akin to friendship developed between them. She really had an atrocious way of reporting her thoughts in an explosive, almost reckless manner, but Alex thought that it was preferable to the constant lies of many others. Sometimes Beth even solicited and followed the man's advice, especially if it was formulated in a concise manner. Better than other bosses, he thought. He no longer considered himself a prisoner or a toy, although that was exactly what he was. Given a proper amount of time, most people can get used to everything.

The shocking surprise was approaching. Beth was increasingly upset about the behavior of her relatives in the Board meetings. She felt that they would be eating soup in a poor's house without the help of her father and could not tolerate being contradicted. A nephew had dared say to her: "Why do you seem so unsettled and discomforted when we express other opinions? We are here to help and support you, Auntie. You are already in your mid fifties and you might take a deserved retirement after so many great years." The auntie was so upset that she started yelling, pounding the desk with her fists and closed the meeting. They were lusting in advance her money! Maybe she should serve them for lunch a soup of hundreds. The boy came to apologize, but it was in vain. Beth had learned the truth about her relatives. They were just waiting. "Maybe they are already looking for a hit man to kill me," she added at the end of her confession to Alex.

Alex answered that greed was one of the most powerful human motivations. Impertinent avidity for money would confront her with her best friends and closer relatives. She should continue enjoying a long and prosperous life and forget them. To show that she was the boss, she could pick up someone and fire him from the Board, maybe the shameless nephew. And he shrugged.

Beth looked strangely at him and fell silent.

"I see, Alex, that you are the most prudent and clever man I know, and I couldn't work or live away from you. As you know, in few years I will be 60-year-old and I had no expectation of ever becoming a wife. When I was a young girl, I dreamed of walking into a church dressed in white and joining a good-looking man in matrimony forever. Destiny, my father and my own character failures deprived me of that joy."

Alex swallowed hard. Beth was an interesting but not glamorous woman in her mid-to-late fifties, overweight, with few friends but with lots of money. He was in his mid forties and his life had never found a destination. Should he accept the implied offer o decline?

Beth was not going to give him time to decline. She had approached him months earlier originally thinking that he was a stupid mule and now she had discovered that he was the clever mustang of her dreams, an obedient, muscular creature with some brain. The decision had been taken. They would be joined in holy matrimony.

What did Alex think? He kept thinking about his obscure, disappointing and unfulfilling previous life. Beth had some modest qualities, if one knew how to handle her, but above all she had money. He looked into the eyes of the woman. For one moment he saw only a ridiculous, fat, and not-alluring sex addict. He felt a nausea. He raised his arms forward embracing Beth, pushing her to him and pressing his face against hers. He lied:

"Yes, my beloved. I had never expected that you would fulfill my dreams and desires." He felt tears coming out of Beth's eyes. He trembled in a rage because he was doing for money the wrong thing.

Before we humans speak, the content of our real thinking must be formed in an unreachable part of the brain, but to learn about its meaning, we must wait until the message arrives in another part of the brain and requests permission to move to our mouth. Alex knew that the words "Get out of me, dirty whore" were coming into his consciousness but he managed to stop them in time. Instead, he desperately tried to remember what virtues or qualities were present in the ugly, domineering woman. But he could not forget or ignore his humiliation as a bedraggled and impotent mendicant. He had failed to obtain what he wanted the right way and now it was too late. Matt was younger and Alex would never become Controller. Beth had chosen her groom the way he would have chosen a bride. So, he was the bride.

* * *

Discussions and arguments about the incoming wedding spread over Beth's entire family and even the company. She finally announced that she preferred to organize the wedding not in a church but in the large garden of her suburban property. A pastor who was her friend had agreed to officiate. And she was going to finally realize her old dream of getting married in a white dress. Her aunts were shocked. A white dress at almost 60 years of age? Nobody dared mention her increasingly growing belly, but she spontaneously made it known that she was on a diet. Besides, Alex liked her the way she was. And, she added laughing, it was not a pregnancy. A somewhat perplexed fashion specialist had a bridal white dress sewn for her and offered an old-fashioned corset to push back the protruding belly and obviate the need for a diet. After all, she paid well.

Alex was unable to learn much about the way the news were received in the company. Doug and other bookkeepers came to congratulate and shake hands with him, but Alex noticed how they all turned their eyes from him. Only Matt Carter and Lisa, the secretary, seemed to be happy. Matt added that he was grateful for all the help Alex had offered in friendship. "Friendship to whom?" asked Alex himself. "Besides, I am making extra money, she is paying me to do your work" he added in his mind, but externally he only smiled. In the following days Alex overheard some discussion on what present they should offer and how much everybody was expected to contribute. He did not enjoy that customary ritual. Sometimes the thought of Beth dressed in a bridal gown sickened him. All the time he was unable to put aside and desist of all his scruples and misgivings. He knew that he was doing the wrong thing, but the other side of the same coin was unemployment and return to a lower living standard. He felt like a coward, a kept man, and he could not discuss his situation with anyone. Should he go to a therapist?

He would never give him advice relevant to his dilemma. Maybe Beth would soon die and leave him some money. That is what despicable people like him expected. In the days preceding the ceremony, Alex could barely sleep.

The accountant started to manifest disdain whenever Beth made affectionate intimate moves "Beth, we have our entire lives ahead of us" he countered. And the woman inquired "Are you nervous about the step we are going to take?"

After a while Alex sighing answered, "It is for the rest of our lives, my dear."

"Yes, it is", and she hugged him. "I am so happy..."

Alex smiled but he internally thought the following: "You should have met and known me years ago, when I still thought that I was a free but decent man and you had been entertaining yourself with a married man. Now you should despise me. Why don't you tell me what you would do if I refused to marry you? You know, I could still run away, find a simple job or sell hamburgers and recover my decency and my honor." And he caressed her tenderly, while the woman hid her face on his breast. "I should have reported you to the authorities for sexual harassment," was Alex final conceited lucubration.

Two days before the wedding's date, Alex was seated by the window watching the birds in the park-like backyard of Beth's residence, when his uncle Larry appeared outside. The newcomer noticed his nephew across the window and winked. Alex immediately recognized him and rushed to meet him outside.

"Uncle Larry! I am so pleased to see you and I am happy that you were able to come to my wedding. I am sorry I could not meet you at the airport."

"You must have been terribly busy, but the Hotel room that you reserved for me and my wife is great. It is a short walk from here."

"Come in and I will introduce you to Beth. You are almost my only family."

"Would you not like to undertake a little stroll with me? I can meet your bride later."

"Alright, uncle. What has become of you? Are you still a College professor?"

"I am. When I was young, I missed my opportunity to learn some useful trade and that is why I had to spend the rest of my sad life teaching repeatedly every year the same to moderately clever students at a nearly unknown and small provincial College. You were clever choosing accounting. Jobs for accountants are ubiquitous."

Alex considered not answering, but he finally replied:

"It is true, there are many existing jobs but few good ones. With the passage of time, everybody would like to be promoted and earn better. That is where the abundance ends."

"Mm. Do you believe that this situation is better in Colleges? I would not be where I am. Sometimes I look forward to retirement. Becoming chairman or dean does not depend on your brain or accomplishments but on your social skills and connections. You, of course, are going to be well settled now."

"What do you mean? Do you believe that this is the reason I am getting married?" asked Alex alarmed.

Uncle Larry scratched his nose, as he habitually did when he was thinking.

"By chance, one of my College friends has had for some time close contacts with your firm. One day recently, I happened to mention your name and your marriage plans. My neighbor told me that he had already heard of both you and your plans and that he was happy for both of you. He had met Beth at least two times. She was a fantastic CEO, much better than her father and she was a good person who treated her employees well. She had a funny way of talking but everybody thought it was a consequence of her superior intelligence. Sometimes it was difficult to understand what she meant, but at the end, she was always right. She neglected her private life because of her devotion to the business. Time passed her by, and she was lonely and single, in her fifties. Everybody felt sorry for her. Then an outstanding man of great reputation, an experienced and beloved accountant in the office of the Controller, took a personal interest in her and both became close friends, and now finally they are going to get married. Everybody in the firm is happy and wishes you both the best."

This time, Alex was speechless, irritated, dumbstruck. Why was he relating this sweetened version? He had never seen things quite that way. The uncle carried on:

"I understand you, Alex. Maybe you have felt before that I spoke with disdain of my position and teaching career. If so, you were wrong. In the long evenings of my recent life, I see myself in a beautiful garden like yours in company of my ever-young wife and we both enjoy the breeze, watch the birds, and smell the flowers, thanking the heavens for having granted us such a rewarding life and a chance to do useful work for our fellow humans. As I teach to my students, our forefathers of very ancient generations lived side by side half or full naked in caves. When hungry or attacked, their survival depended on their capability of successfully fighting off animals or other beings, killing when necessary. But in the following centuries and millenniums mankind grew in social cohesion and capability and our predecessors were blessed with the knowledge of natural law and learned that doing harm or killing others was wrong and acquired religions that taught them how to forgive and love each other. But unfortunately, that was not all, because after the day the night arrives and although nicely decorated with brilliant stars, sometimes wind, clouds, or rain arrive. This is the time when humans must seek cover and protection at all costs and forget their solidary obligations and for a moment the reign of God may be replaced by that of Satan and hope is lost. It is a grievous mistake because the night will end, and the sun will shine again and see the truth from the heights. Hope returnes and the old rules can be restored. Some may cry remembering what they had done, but finally most individually understand that they had done only what they needed to do to survive."

Perplexed, Alex tried to understand what Larry really knew and meant. What had this relative learned so far away?

"I salute you, my dear Alexander! I do not know why you did not find a nice female companion in your youth like I did, but years later, you understood how to fulfill the purpose of your life in helping a desperate, aging woman to regain her footing and fulfill her expectations. I am also pleased that it came with nice side benefits. Why not? I have also tried to help others. I and your aunt came here to cheer for you."

Alex, enraged, thought that he had been targeted for a prepared sermon. Who or what had Larry become? Maybe an Angel of God in human form? Or more likely a listening troublemaker who enjoyed discerning other people's problems. Who could have told him of his real situation? How did he dare speak to him like that? He knew nothing and understood nothing. The reign of Satan?

A while later both men returned to the beautiful mansion and saluted its owner. Larry asked her whether he could get a discount for the popular game *Earth's Electronic Wars* which his grandson vehemently desired. Beth, laughing, replied that it would be delivered to his address free of charge and that she would appreciate free advertisements. All three laughed with variable degrees of enthusiasm. Alex once again felt that Beth was old and ugly but strangely, he felt taken in by sympathy and pity. She should do something about her prominent belly after the ceremony. The old man shook hands and then after rejecting an invitation to lunch because his wife was not there, he kissed Beth, and both appeared happy.

The day of the ceremony arrived. The park was filled with company employees and people unknown to Alex, who had contributed to the crowd just four family members. He had insisted that the accountants including the secretary Lisa were also to be invited, but they had to stand in the back because all chairs were taken by more important people. They were not invited to the reception prepared inside of the mansion by a famous catering company.

How did Beth look like? She loomed up, as she had announced, dressed in the magnificent wedding gown for which she had longed all her life. Did she appear ridiculous because of her age? Difficult to say. Her enlarged belly was totally contained and mastered by an invisible corset and she revealed a passable figure with attractive shoulders for a 56-year-old woman. Her head was crowned by beautiful flowers and she approached on the arm of an uncle while a small orchestra played a wedding march. The notable feature was the happy, defeating smile that she dedicated to all guests. She really was a happy woman who was getting her deepest dream fulfilled after 20 or 30 years. For the first time Alex discovered something magnificent, proud, and dignified in her aspect, like a color picture taken from a coffee table book. He thought "What am I getting?" and his face became perplexed, revealing awe for the woman in front of him.

After the marriage vows, the Pastor gave permission to kiss the bride and Alex did so with more enthusiasm and sincerity that he had ever previously felt, and Beth whispered in his ear: "It is the happiest day of my life, my love, my man. I had waited so many years for this culmination, a moment of fulfillment. We will never forget it!" And Alex responded: "Yes, my beloved Beth! We will never forget."

Despite his concerns, Alex had recognized that Beth had done a perfect job and survived gloriously the challenge.

The wedding trip took them to Paris, Pisa, Florence, and Rome. In Paris, Alex was surprised to see that his wife spoke French and was able to communicate with all natives. He had assumed that all French fluently speak English and was upset to discover that it was not the case. Beth insisted on in visiting Museums, but Alex felt bored. They hired a cab with driver to visit Versailles and entered the Mirror's Room where an armistice had been signed. Alex viewed himself in a mirror wall next to Beth who again looked aged. Her unsightly belly had returned. What did other people think of them? Did somebody realize that he was a paid gigolo? Or was he being mistaken for a young man with his mom? They took a long walk through the magnificent palace garden, like kings may have done. Alex no longer wanted to look at Beth. He had become the assistant of a better educated woman who had again turned old and ugly.

They landed in Florence and rented a chauffeured limousine from the airport to the city of Pisa. Alex had seen pictures of a leaning tower, but he did not find it logical that the tower had never been straightened. "The tower is like humans: it shows peculiarities that beautify it. The same is true of you" answered Beth. At least he was not being compared to a horse, thought Alex. For him, the tower was like an original but messed up spreadsheet that needed to be fixed before being released. They attempted to climb to the top. Alex could not take the contradiction of having to descend steps to continue climbing. It made Beth feel dizzy too. Given the circumstances, Alex preferred the adjoining cathedral, a marvelous beautifully finished white building that inspired peace and content.

In Florence, Beth led him to the entrance of the old Signoria, seat of the historic old government and made a casual reference to the tyranny of Savonarola. "Who was that? A communist leader?" asked Alex. Not exactly. He immediately had noticed the nude David's statue in the little plaza outside of the Museum building. "I know that, I have seen pictures of this statue many times" He was wrong, explained Beth. He was seeing only a copy, the original was inside, well protected, because it is one of the world's masterworks. Alex did not like the way the old woman talked to him. She sounded like an old teacher. The man replied that he had enjoyed and knew about these things at school, which was not true.

They jointly visited Florence's Cathedral. Alex was told that the dome's cupola had been a true wonderous work of technology, thought to be impossible to build in that century. An architect had designed it beautifully, but nobody knew how to possibly build a cupola of that size and it took a long time and a review of old roman ruins before they found a capable engineer. Remarkedly, it has stood like that for centuries! The man found it interesting, but he really did not care much for the architectural feats of the Renaissance. They should instead explore more intensely the good restaurants and maybe find a local place with genuine dancing in old dresses. He was not behaving like a good student in the company of an old teacher. The woman was spoiling with lectures Alex' first visit to Europe. He wanted to see the old Italy and Paris of the World War II movies.

It was enough of a sacrifice to have to be with the learned character the entire day. They briefly stopped in Rome, where the accountant surprisingly opined that in America, the government would have rebuilt the Forum and the Coliseum. Beth silently laughed. Somewhat flabbergasted, the newlywed woman, amused, did not find words to formulate an answer and she looked with concern and pity at her husband. How many things had he missed because of the years he had been forced to sit in front of tables and numbers? He had done it, she was sure, to help her and her company. Now she was going to repay by educating him. She enjoyed the thought. Beth wanted to visit the Vatican Museum, but Alex resolutely declined. They had visited enough museums. Maybe they could go to the Sant'Angelo castle. He determined that it was not possible to swim in the Tiber. Was this the one that Julius Cesar crossed to start a war? asked Alex. No, answered a horrified Beth! That was the Rubicon, far to the north and flowing to the Adriatic Sea. The time to fly back home at least arrived. It had only been a moderate success, more from Beth's point of view than Alex'.

The new husband, however, had made an important observation: now that they were married, he had some authority, he would be able to challenge and talk back. He no longer had to shut up and obey. Punishing him would no longer be easy, dismissing him from work, as she had done with Andrew, was nearly impossible. He decided that it was time to raise his voice at home and teach the woman some lesson at the first opportunity. With the charm of the trip behind, he felt his old antipathy against Beth rising again. He went out at night without inviting Beth and refused to give explanations next day. Everything would be different. The prisoner was breaking out of jail.

They had been home already 5 days, and Beth was back at work, where she had every opportunity of describing the joy and enthusiasm that her beloved husband had felt viewing the marvelous European works of art, and they were currently studying the leading national art houses with an eye on making purchases. She had attempted to discuss this project with Alex, who was completely indifferent and pointed out that the walls were already covered with "stuff."

Alex was not sure that he wanted to return to her former job. He felt it humiliating to work as a simple accountant in a business owned by his wife. How would Matt Carter, the Controller view it? He knew

that Doug could easily replace him and there was no rush. He decided
to raise the issue with Beth.

"What would you want to do, then?" asked Beth. "I know that you
ogled Matt's job, who is very fond of you, but Matt was an obligation
I had. Besides, he has done nothing to be fired."

"Now I have personally met the directors of all departments of
JOYFUL Inc. I knew only their names and salaries. I do not know
how they are doing but I would have the qualifications to replace
several of them."

"Maybe you would have their knowledge, but neither their connections nor experience. Do not forget how well we are doing in business
and in Wall Street. The people you mention are critical."

"What about a job with responsibilities at your office?"

"I've had a skilled staff for years. What would you want to do?
Work as a secretary or bring me coffee?"

Alex felt insulted.

"Will you allow that your husband works as a nobody in a corner of
your own company? Then I will prefer to rather stay here and become
a house husband. I will cook for you and clean the bathrooms."

Beth was visibly irritated. "There is nothing I can do. Go back to
your office, continue helping Matt and I will double your salary. And
you are welcome to take as many free days as you wish as long as you
do not create a problem for Matt. That is all I have to offer. Sorry if
you are not pleased. You really cannot complain about anything."

Alex felt a mixture of envy, hatred, disappointment, humiliation
and above all rage. The situation had changed, but nothing else had
changed. She continued to be his mistress, old, unpleasant, and ugly as
always. He would teach her a lesson. What had she turned him into?
He knew the answer: into an overpaid accountant probably despised
by all his former friends.

* * *

Beth used to go to her family doctor at three months intervals. Her secretary advised her that she had an appointment next day at 2PM. She appreciated it because she was not feeling well. Her abdomen and gird were increasing in size and she had lost appetite. She reported these complaints to the doctor who, as always, examined her carefully, more so than in previous occasions. After he was done, he returned to his desk and Beth found him writing.

"Well, doctor, how am I doing? Will you prescribe something to shrink my belly? My husband does not like it" she said, laughing.

"We'll fix the problem with your bloated abdomen, but first we must run some tests to figure out what it is."

"But I already know, Doctor. When preparing for my wedding I had too much to eat and drink."

The physician raised his eyebrows. "I am not sure of that, Beth. This enlargement of your gird is more suspicious for fluid than fat."

"Fluid? You mean water? I drink too much, but it had never happened before. What do you think it is?"

"It is pointless and confusing to discuss problems before the tests come back. I am ordering some blood studies and MRI images of your body. As soon as the results are back, we shall know more and then it will be the time to discuss what it is and what to do."

"You are scaring me, doctor. Is there nothing we can do about my belly right away?"

"We'll be able to help with that, I assure you. We have your phone, and I will stay in touch with you."

Beth submitted to the blood extraction and left the office. She meant to walk back to the company, but her gait had become unsteady, and she called a cab.

In the evening, she sat at the table with Alex. She was uncommonly silent, which surprised the man.

"Well," said Alex to start some conversation. "I started going back to my office. Matt was happy to see me and asked a couple of things. And Doug, my first assistant, asked about our honeymoon trip. Everything is fine."

Beth was not eating. "Good. Do you remember how unhappy I was about my belly?"

"Sure, you needed a corset to fit into your white gown."

"I went to my doctor and he ordered tests. I am afraid. So many people have died of cancer..."

Alex answered that her concerns were exaggerated. It looked like a minor problem. If she insisted, he would be happy to accompany her to the doctor. He failed to reassure her. The man noticed that Beth's hands were trembling. What was that now? No alternative way of soothing her came to his mind. He resumed eating and drinking some wine. Beth left and went alone to the bedroom. Alex wanted to watch some television. Beth would have her MRI pictures taken the following day.

Finally, Beth's personal assistant entered her office to report that the doctor's office was on the phone. Trembling, the woman picked up her office phone. A friendly voice reported that the doctor would like to see her again. Would she be available next morning at 10 AM?

"Can I talk to the doctor right now?" asked Beth anxiously.

"No, sorry, the doctor went to the Hospital. He will see you tomorrow at 10AM."

The following night, Beth was awake most of the time. She asked Alex to come along and grabbed his hand anxiously. Yes, he would come along, and he was sure that there was no reason to be alarmed.

The demeanor of the doctor was unusually serious. He greeted the husband and invited the couple to sit in two chairs.

"The news I have, Beth, are not good. What you have in the abdomen is indeed water, as I had suspected. Your belly seemed to be growing, but actually you were losing weight."

"Why do I have water in my belly?"

"A mass coming out of one of your ovaries has been growing for a while and has seeded malignant cells into the abdominal cavity. These cells have managed to get implanted in the peritoneal membrane that lines all organs and they have grown in several places creating metastases."

Beth opened the mouth and was speechless. Alex did not quite understand what the doctor was saying, but his wife had understood.

"A cancer! You are telling me that I have an ovarian cancer."

"Yes, but please calm down. I can refer you to an outstanding oncologist, the best in town, who has treated many of my patients, but since you obviously have the means, you might wish to consult the Mayo Clinic or the Sloan Kettering Memorial Hospital in Manhattan."

"Am I going to die? I am only in my fifties and I just got married."

Alex feigned all the concern and pain that actors in the movies show in such cases. He even tried to embrace Beth. The doctor continued:

"Whether or not you wish to go for a consultation, additional tests and small procedures will be needed to confirm that it is an ovarian cancer and then you will be treated. It is easy to evacuate the fluid, but it may repeat itself. Medical science has been advancing a lot in recent times. There is no need to be so worried as in the past. It is a genuine problem, but major studies have introduced remedies, even large survivals, and even some cures. You will be guided by specialists to do the right thing and there is no reason to give up hope."

Alex, however, was almost as worried as Beth, but about different issues. Would he be able to keep his exorbitant salary and an acceptable position after Beth's death? Because of his recent history, it would not be easy to go out asking for a comparable job.

One-week later Beth heard for the first time the ugly word "Chemotherapy." She came back home in company of Alex. The man was trying to comfort her, but Beth was an intelligent woman struggling to reject the terrible truth which she already knew.

"Is it going to hurt me? I have heard horrible things."

"No, Beth. I know nothing, but the Medicine has made extraordinary progress and patients no longer must suffer. They will give you whatever is needed to prevent pain, and if not, you go to another doctor. Besides, you soon will be healthy again. We could go back to Italy and you will be able to explain to me everything about the ruins and the history of Rome."

The woman smiled sadly.

"If you wish, I will even learn Latin!" announced Alex.

Beth was not able to contain a laughter and hugged Alex. She felt that despite the many employees of the company and the people who benefited from her largesse, she had only Alex. She could not talk with anyone else who really cared about her. She remembered the words of the oncologist and, although he had not said so, he had not expressed any hope of survival. How much time did she have left? She felt blessed to have found Alex and leaned her face against his. She cried.

The husband took it upon himself to make sure that Beth observed all orders of the medical team and went along for almost all the chemotherapy infusions. Most of the time he sat next to the patient reading a book. When the session was finished, he would pick up the car and drive her home. She generally felt sick after each session. After an abdominal puncture in the doctor's office, her waistline had returned to normal, and she playfully invited Alex to dance with her. Her face, however, looked gaunt, which displeased her man. She, however, did not notice and continued playing and smiling.

Alex allowed himself a few sorties from the residence to visit a luxurious evening salon that he had recently discovered. When he returned home, he always thought "Now, back to work." Visits from Beth's family were infrequent and short. They invariably ended asking Alex about Beth's health...and prognosis. Alex knew nothing about her health, but she was being treated by excellent doctors.

One night, he came back late and was surprised to see lights on in the mansion. He entered and the live-in house maid approached him running. "Sir, thanks God you are here. The lady has felt extremely sick and vomited. She was crying for you, but I did not know how to reach you."

Alex ran upstairs. Beth was seated in bed, clearly disheveled and pale, maybe uglier than usually.

"Where have you been? I was terribly ill, and you weren't here with me."

"I am sorry. You had looked good and even had some dinner with me, and you kept it down, how could I know?"

Beth started to cry "Do not abandon me, I have nobody else and feel very sick." Alex was worried by her demeanor and appearance.

"I would never abandon you, my love. I just wanted to have a few drinks with some friends. What can I do when you feel sick? My heart is broken, but all we can do is call the emergency number of the doctors."

"Listen, Alex. I have been thinking about your position in my firm and I know that you are not pleased but you are especially important to me and I want you to be happy. I have called a Board Meeting for tomorrow in the early afternoon. You know that all the members, but one, are family. Since you are now family, too, I have decided to appoint you also a member. To make it possible I told my lawyer this morning to transfer to you a packet of 100 regular shares."

"This is generous, Beth. How can I thank you?"

"You can correspond by taking care of me. I feel old and sick, and you are all I have. Don't leave me alone."

Next morning, Beth had recovered from her condition the previous evening and was able to hold some breakfast. She was losing weight and her girth was growing again. She no longer was trying to conceal it.

The board meeting was brief. Beth made her announcement and all members clapped unenthusiastically with long faces. The only additional major issue was the approval of a new electronic toy strongly supported by Beth. The responsible developer would come to the next meeting and make a presentation. Alex was surprised but did not speak. The Board appointment did guarantee his future but it did not suffice. He was unable to pay much attention because he was thinking about his future after Beth's death. Was he going to lose everything to which he had become used? What happens to gigolo boys and proteges once their job is concluded? Back to the office? He had not been there for weeks. He felt spoiled and lazy. His former colleagues would be ashamed or at least embarrassed to speak to him again. The Board would fire him at once, and then what? He had given up his former apartment.

Alex did not feel like visiting his favorite night local and retired to the bedroom next to Beth's after wishing good night to the woman and expressing again gratitude. Next day, he reappeared in his office. He greeted Matt and told him that now he was a Board member and therefore a Director. The Controller was flabbergasted but he reacted well and congratulated. Doug approached him asking "Is it true?" Alex answered "Yes" and thought that now everybody knew what kind of shameless, despicable adventurer he was. The health condition of Beth was being suspected, but he always falsely answered that since she was in the hands of great doctors, full recovery was expected. Something inside told him that it was not true and uncontrollable sorrow grew inside of his chest. He had become a repulsive paid man without sense of honor or dignity and soon he would stumble in public, and people would spit at him. He had been quite different before that obnoxious freak drew him into her bed. He needed to take revenge.

He was half intoxicated by bourbon when Beth appeared in the living room. She was smiling and returned to the apocalyptic language of her earlier times. Kissing him in the cheek she said:

"Here rests the great knight who has just defeated his perverse enemies and comes to the rescue of a feeble damsel."

"Who would the perverse enemies be? Your uncles and the cousin?"

"They are all salivating about my inheritance. They do not wish me good health. I can change my will anytime, but they know nothing else. I have every intention to favor some good charities." She smiled again expecting interest, but Alex was partially intoxicated.

"Why do you talk about wills and charities? You are never going to die. From what do you need to be rescued? You live with fantasies, but you insist on imposing your will to everybody."

Beth was surprised. "What are you complaining about? To whom do I impose my will? As a chief executive I do my job and seek the best for my company and therefore I must give orders. Nothing works without a vigilant boss. It is the same in all places."

"You don't seek the best for your workers. Some married men in the factory cannot sustain their family with your salaries and need second jobs."

"We pay as much as anyone else for each category."

"How come that they do not have cars or servants as you do?"

"Business is like a chess game, where each figure has its place and attributes."

"And you are the Queen, of course, the only one who can do as she pleases."

"Of course, I am. You cannot complain about my generosity. You get enough."

"That is too much. Leave me in peace!"

Alex stood up and left. He slept in a guest room. Beth stayed behind whimpering.

Next day, she stayed in bed until late. Alex came back from the office mid-afternoon and cautiously entered the room, after being reassured by the maid that his wife was awake and watching TV.

"Hi, Beth! How are you feeling?"

The woman did not answer.

"Listen, Beth, we both had a dreadful day yesterday. I am sorry if I offended you."

"Oh, please. Take care of me. Do not upset me and never leave me. I really need you badly. I am terribly ill."

"You are being treated by the best doctors. You will soon be all right. I will never leave you, my dear Beth, never. People who love each other, sometimes fight. If they never do, it means they do not love each other and they do not live in the same world."

"What a way of proving love. There ought to be some better way for senior people."

"Who is a senior? Don't be absurd. We are no seniors. Some people never learn anything, but we have the life experience to do it. Give me a hug and a kiss, my beauty, and let us forget yesterday."

Power and money, however, are sources of conflict that never seem to go away. The next Board meeting, the first for Alex as a director, was finally scheduled to take place in two weeks. Beth had officially concluded her medical treatment and the doctors had reported that the tumor had receded. It had been a nightmare that kept her from eating, drinking, sleeping, and exercising, but now it was over. Her physical appearance improved, her face rejuvenated, she gained weight, life was joyful and filled with enthusiasm. Alex noticed all of this in the strong hugs that the woman regularly administered to him. He thought, nevertheless, that the choice of words of the main doctor had not quite supported such unbridled enthusiasm. He had avoided saying that she was cured. Alex found Beth's jubilant attitude exaggerated and misleading. Mentally he did not feel up to the challenge, but he tried to keep smiling.

Yes dear, yes dear, you are right, dear. Rest well, dear. Then, he tried to rest himself. He was going back regularly again to his office, where the Controller Matt never failed to inquire about Beth's condition. Alex assumed that he was sincere. Everybody had the right to act sincerely except Alex. Sometimes he wanted to cry out in rage in the presence of other people and walk away, but he never could.

The Board meeting started on time, as Beth always demanded. All participants took their places. An employee from Development and his section director were also present. Having taken care of a few minor administrative problems, Beth addressed the main reason why this unexpected Board meeting had been called. He introduced Joe Bassett, the well-known genius who had already successfully developed many of JOYFUL Inc's most successful money-bringing electronic games. He had come to describe his plans for a new entertainment product to be targeted to pre-teenager clients, tentatively named *Marvel's Coffer*. The presentation included a financial request to purchase additional equipment. The production line would be installed in areas currently occupied by less rewarding old product lines of little interest, which would be discontinued. "I have reviewed his analysis and fully agree with his conclusions. We wish to clean out old junk and open the firm to the future with a state-of-the-art computer-based video toy", and she sat after signaling Joe Bassett to speak.

Joe was ebullient and described his proposal with great enthusiasm. Maybe he did not notice that only Beth and Joe's section chief seemed to be approving. After he finished, his boss added that he would personally answer any financial issue. The *Coffer* would be an expensive project that would require a major investment, but the effort would prove rewarding in one or maybe two years, as it was in tune with the sector's market directions. The man sat, at which time he noticed that only Ms. Beth Holloway was happily smiling. He raised his eyes through the window to the sky which had changed color presaging an imminent threatening storm with lightening and donner. The board members looked at each other. Assessing the situation, Beth invited them to raise additional questions. They did that.

"Is the budget not too high? It could get us in trouble if the toy fails."

"Is that not too similar to the new product of the competition?"

"I saw a few days ago something similar and cheap in the Supermarket."

"It sounds all great, Joe, but don't you feel that there are already too many games of that kind in the market?"

"Do you remember what happened to our competition last Christmas? They were forced to slash the price of toys they were advertising. We will have to do the same."

"Many parents complain that they cannot understand and explain to a child how these expensive items work. The boy starts to cry, and the father wants his money back."

"We should have further information on the successful old toys being built in the production lines that you want to shut down. Many customers have been buying these items for generations."

"Oh, really? Did your grandparents play video games?"

Finally, one of the members managed to really upset Beth:

"A project of this magnitude assumes that the company leadership will be stable for the near future. What if it is not?"

Beth was enraged.

"What are you suggesting, son of a bitch? For your knowledge, the doctors have informed me that I am free of disease and I will live longer than any of you. How do you dare? Who is paying you money to sit here? Pay more attention to how your wife wastes money and try to shrink her luxury vacations. You are all odious children of Satan, you envious and lying devils."

It became impossible to continue the session. Joe and his supervisor discreetly disappeared but all family members had loudly risen against Beth. Alex attempted to pull her out of the room with the help of her secretary. Her face was red and her breathing labored. She was yelling: "You will never replace me, never! You are all empty-headed, feeble-minded, inane morons, and dimwits!"

Alex offered to drive her home. He was thinking that the remark that had started the fight was ill-timed but had some merit. It is quite natural that a Board worries about the future when the CEO had an incurable cancer in temporary remission.

Beth was crying in the car.

"I am going to throw him out. He is an imbecile. They all believe that they are going to inherit my company after I die. They want me all to die. They hate me. They insult me in public. The *Coffer* was going to be my legacy. Children all over the entire world would play with it. The supreme figure on the screen was going to be called Beth. That is why they hate me and want to lay obstacles in my way so that I am forgotten. I will do it anyway and you will help me. I am the boss."

Alex thought "Yes, Madam" but said "Of course, anything I can do. We should be celebrating that you are healthy again. Instead, you are crying because of the greed and disrespect of your family."

The woman leaned against her husband "Only you understand me, Alex. Only you."

"I see that you are tired and need rest. If it is alright with you, I would like to go out. I meet friends and colleagues for conversation in a bar. I hope it is alright with you. I also need some fresh air."

"Of course, my love. Maybe you could bring me there too sometime, but today I am tired and keep thinking of my foolish and stupid family."

Nothing much happened in the following two months. Beth naturally restarted the *Coffer* project. Alex did not like it, but he recognized that he was not an expert. It had to be exceedingly difficult to guess what the public will like or not and bet money on it, but Beth really had guessed right a couple of times and the company was doing well despite the illness and the board's concerns.

Beth appeared to have developed a deep feeling approaching love for Alex, who felt bothered and tried to respond in a friendly manner. He understood that she had nobody else to turn to, and he thought that he had no alternative job if he lost the current one. He would wait and see, but he really found the old, ugly woman irritating. It helped him to go back to work every day. He even retrieved his old enthusiasm for the job and developed a companionship with Matt Carter. The Controller was not dumb, he was only untrained and inexperienced when he arrived, but he was catching up. They frequently sat and laughed together. Alex had figured out that his safest alternative was to start saving salary money for an uncertain future while attempting some safe investments. His stock in the Company might tank as soon as it becomes known that Beth is passing away. How long was she going to live? As usual, he came back home late weighing that it was time to start bringing her back to a movie or stage theater. Al least she did not speak during the show.

* * *

And the sad news once again arrived two months later. Beth had felt some pain and went back with Alex to her main doctor, who ordered a scan. The tumor had returned. "So, what do we do now?" she wanted to know. The doctor made an inscrutable face. "Now, we start again chemotherapy with different medications."

"Shall I live?" asked the woman anxiously. The doctor did not answer immediately. He crossed his hands and responded, "There are things that only God knows, and it is better that way."

She pressed the doctor nervously "How long, Doctor? How long?"

"I really don't know, Beth. If the chemo works, maybe a long time. On the other hand... Just resume normal life and do your best to enjoy it."

Alex seized her hands and kissed them "We are going to go trough all of this together, my dear Beth" He had to physically support her as both left the medical building. Beth was crying all the way home.

She rejected dinner and Alex accompanied her to the bedroom. "I wish, I knew what to tell you, but you are going to make it. You will survive. I will always be on your side and we'll fight together whatever, comes our way."

He thought that he had heard the final warning. It was time to plan his future. He had to hide his irritation every time he saw his wife's face, but he had learned how to control himself. Except that one day he could not control himself anymore.

The weather was splendid, and Alex proposed to drive to a park near the lake, but Beth did not want to join him.

"Why not? It is sunny, one can feel the breeze, the temperature is great. It will do you good."

"I can not. I am feeling sick today."

"That's what you always say when I propose to go somewhere. Yesterday you did not want to come to the movies, although I really wanted to see the movie. On TV, you only watch stupid investigative reports and documentaries, but never funny sitcoms. It is always the same. You spend your life sitting in a corner or on the bed. Cheer up. I keep trying to entertain you. I do my best."

"To entertain me? I must take care of my company, which you are incapable of doing. I would like to see what you would do in my place feeling as sick as I do, thinking about the future and my impossible family."

"Am I one of your stupid family members that understand nothing? I was terribly ill when I was a teenager. My parents brought me to the doctor many times and was also afraid that I was to die. My mother felt that I was making theatre and slapped me in the face. She told me to try to overcome my pain and go outside, which I did. But you seem to enjoy being sick, going to the doctor and needing medicines. It makes you feel interesting, but even your horse can one day be tired of you and kick you in the rear."

"Why do you insult and tell me such cruel things? Don't I pay you enough?"

At this point Alex could not take it anymore. He stood up and ran to his car without answering. Was that the reason why he was being paid a salary? He needed fresh air.

He noticed in his phone several calls from his home but chose to ignore them. He sat in a business having lunch and drinking coffee. He kept thinking that Beth would have felt great in that place, had she not been so domineering and moody. They could do together only what she proposed.

It was mid-afternoon when Alex returned home. As he entered the house maid ran scared to meet him.

"Sir, Madam was very sick. She made me call the doctor and an ambulance brought her to the Hospital. She has not called, and I know nothing of her condition. *Ay, Señor, qué susto tan grande!* I am afraid. Should I have driven with her to the Hospital?"

Alex ran upstairs and entered a very disorderly bedroom. The door to the toilet was open. He looked inside, and something called his attention. Beth had written on the mirror something in red with her lip stick. It said: "Alex, I will leave nothing to you."

Alex considered taking a picture but dismissed the idea as absurd. Instead, he attempted to clean it hoping against reason that the maid had not seen it. Then he called Beth's main doctor and explained that he had been out of town. The doctor simply reported that Beth had a nervous episode related to her disease and additionally explained "You know what she has, and it is not getting any better. In such cases I refer the family to a special counselor. My secretary will give you the number." A while letter Alex drove to the Hospital intent on apologizing. Next day, he met the counselor.

Time passed by and Beth's condition worsened. Alex did his duty: he frequently visited, talked to her, offered his services for anything. He was pleased that at least the matrimonial relations had ended. Soon 24-hour caretakers were hired. Alex was reluctant to go to his job because of the many questions for which he had not answer. An earth-shaking power change was imminent. Members of the family were making daily inquiries from Beth's secretary and they had informally met several times. Alex viewed them with bitterness and stayed out of their way. Curiously, they rarely called to her home.

But he had enough of the situation. He had to overcome his dissatisfaction, his nausea and found it increasingly difficult to fulfill his duties. He had started making phone calls regarding possible openings for accountants, but he found it difficult to conduct specific discussions because everybody knew him. He would have liked to know what they thought professionally of him. Should he deal with a low-level personnel chief or call straight the boss, whom he knew? What was it worse? Slowly he started getting the message that he should move to another city, as far away as possible. It was great that he had started saving money. He would also sell the 100 stock shares Beth had given him. Maybe he should try relocating abroad.

He visited the dying woman twice in the morning and twice in the afternoon. Whenever she did not answer, he quietly caressed her head murmuring something in her ear. When she moaned loudly, the nurse came and administered something, but Alex could not stand the scene and had to leave.

One afternoon the nurse came to Alex and told him that she had to leave because of a family emergency. She had called the office and a replacement was already on her way, but she had to leave right away. No, Beth was not doing alright, and she was sorry, but it would be a fleeting time. Alex answered that he would go immediately upstairs.

He was alone with the patient as she died. The man walked two steps backward and breathed deeply. He did his best to repress an internal voice that cried "Thanks God! It was time" He turned his back toward the bed, walked out of the room and slammed the door violently, as if to close a sad episode of his life that had cost him his reputation, career and future. His past reappeared in front of his eyes. When had he fallen into the dirt and why? How could a puppet have become a puppeteer in charge of his master? And above all stuck with his financial and professional worries, what should he do?

The nurse arrived and found him in pain and profoundly distraught, but she did not understand the real reason. The woman went through the usual list, as she had done with others. Beth was pronounced dead. He had to accept it and concentrate on the funeral. Who should be notified? How much would it cost? Who and how would pay for it? And then, he had to prepare for the storm that always follows a demise.

Alex looked at the house door and thought "They will kick me in the rear und throw me out that way."

* * *

A few hours later, Beth's body was taken to the funeral home and Alex stayed for the first time alone in the house. He had charged Beth's secretary with taking all the calls. He did not want to speak with anyone. The woman, however, approached Alex with a sealed envelope addressed to him. The secretary informed him that two weeks earlier Beth had dictated to her a private and confidential letter addressed to him. She had requested that the text be handwritten rather than printed. She followed her instructions. Beth had read the missive from the grave at least twice and signed it. She instructed the secretary to seal the letter without telling anyone and deliver it to Alex immediately after her demise. Both women had been crying.

Alex, astonished, took the letter, withdrew to his personal room, and sat next to the window. Clearly worried, he opened the letter. It was indeed handwritten by the secretary, but the signature was Beth's.

Dear Alex, my life's only love:

I wish you luck and happiness for the rest of your life. I die realizing how fortunate I was to have found at the end of my life the realization of my dream of finally meeting and living with a man like you. I am aware that the manner I first approached you may have displeased you and if you still remember I wish to apologize. But think of poor me: I was single, ugly, not nice- looking, almost old, desperate for companionship, dismayed by the passage of time. After I broke with Andrew, how could I have found anyone else if not by offering what I had, and most people want? I had never found or knew any other way to attract a man and I failed to understand that you were not a shameless lazy profiteer like Andrew. I felt that I needed a companion at any price, and I am blessed that I found a great one.

For the first time in my life, I loved you and learned what love means. I felt that you corresponded. Yes, you became my only companion, the only one who came to my sick bed, who brought me to the doctor, who comforted and spoke nicely to me. I saw how you had to leave my room and go away from my side because you could not stand seeing my pain and suffering and anticipating the end of our companionship. When still possible, you brought me to places I had never seen, you tolerated my cries and constant complaints but continued offering me love and solace. You made me happy.

In the hour of my declivity, I die cherishing and blessing our time together, your fidelity, your concern and sweetness. It was my last chance but I will not die without having enjoyed true love and companionship.

Yours, until my last breath,

Beth

Perplex, astonished, flabbergasted... Alex could not find the word. He was a dull, simple professional man who had never understood human relationships. Sluggish as he was, he would have to reread and try to interpret and understand the meaning of the letter. She had misunderstood everything, ignored his disgust, raised him absurdly to a false altar where he did not belong. But what had he done? Had he unjustly cursed and despised a lonely, abandoned woman who was looking to anyone's friendship for relief of her solitude before meeting death? Had he behaved like a decent human being? Had he tortured a defenseless old Beth without reason?

He could not continue analyzing the letter. He needed to relax, remember, and redirect his thinking before being able to understand. Enough now. No more, no more. It would take two days at least.

To do something else, he ran toward his car and drove to his dead wife's lawyer. The receptionist admitted him immediately to the boss' office.

"Hi, Peter."

"Hi, Alex. I am glad to see you to express my deepest condolence."

"Thanks. I wanted to discuss with you how to pay for the burial. I do not know how to cover all the things they are organizing. The whole family has grandiose and lunatic ideas, as if a queen had died. I have little money and I could never pay for it. Where do we find the funds?"

The lawyer looked at him with amazement. Then, he loudly laughed:

"I find it hilarious that you come here asking for money. Don't you know that Beth changed her last will leaving everything to you? Everything: the company, money, stock, the house. Everything. Congratulations. You are a very wealthy man. I hope you keep me as your lawyer."

MURDER NEXT DOOR

IT ALL HAPPENED IN a small, always quiet, and peaceful rural town named Emmett, located in the Roosevelt County, embedded in of one of the free and sovereign fifty States that constitute the Great American Union. When bored or tired of cable TV, especially in winter, the residents had the option of driving 20 miles to the much larger municipality of Great Falls, seat of the County executive and host to many more interesting stores and entertainment locations. The four Emmett bakeries made a point of selling only bread made of local grains, as all residents preferred.

Charles Glenn was a 65-year-old retired automobile mechanic. He had owned a gas station with a small repair shop, where he had worked during much of his adult life with a single employee. Some 5 or 6 years before retirement he had noticed that the new cars were becoming increasingly complicated with lots of computer stuff, maybe too perplexing for him. His employee, trained in Great Falls, appeared to know more than him about newer models, which Charlie found unacceptable and worrisome. With the time, the older models disappeared and were replaced by new ones, true computers on wheels, increasingly difficult to fix. To put an end to his growing unease and sense of humiliation, he decided to sell or liquidate his business. Over the years he had saved some money and had inherited from his parents several acres of fertile land. It was leased to the regional big agricultural company, an arrangement which yielded some income and caused few problems. He was additionally entitled to Social Security and Medicare. His guaranteed income was small but secure.

In considering the new life into which he was ready to engage, Charlie could never forget how his wife had died of cancer at an early age ten years ago leaving him with two grown sons. They lived in remote parts of the state with their own families and sometimes came back to visit with or without their children. The old man continued to reside in the inherited house where he had been born. The neighborhood was modest. His residence's size was unexpected in the small town and contrasted with his street's other homes. This awarded Charlie a near aristocratic status. The home had been originally built in the XIX Century and at the time of its construction, it probably was surrounded by empty fields. The sizes of the front- and backyard were, even for Emmett, unusually big. Charlie had been carefully watching the house's condition over many years. He had personally carried through repairs, regularly painted the walls, repaired the roof, upgraded the kitchen and toilets, and had hidden all electrical cables inside of the walls. He was aware that the property represented his main asset and financial security. As a jack-of-all-trades he knew how to take care of everything and extend the building's life. He kept a little area with a work bench in the basement.

An unusual fact strengthened his opinion that the land had been home to wealthy people. The lateral yard surrounding the home was on its left side irregular, as if somebody had taken a bite out of it. A neighboring house built in this diminutive piece of land was old, cheap-looking, and ugly. The windows were unequal, mostly of the wrong size, as if the builder had had some surplus windows and made holes on the wall of the size required to accommodate the available frames. It consisted of a first and a second floor which gave it the appearance of a narrow tower. How ugly! Nobody in the City Hall could explain the origin of the strange property but Charlie had developed on his own the theory that the small building had been developed by a wealthy owners family and was meant to house temporal workers or servants. At some later time, an ancestor may have needed money and sold it to strangers including the minute piece of land on which it stood. Currently it was owned by a local part-time real estate firm which leased it. Charlie concluded that he did not have enough cash to buy the homely house, but it bothered him.

As it was to be expected, the residents of the mini home had frequently been anxious to move somewhere else and Charlie had noticed many young residents coming and going after short stays without bothering to contact him. There was no fence to mark the boundaries of both properties and many times Charlie had caught unknown neighbors inside of his property peering through a window into his living room. Was it dangerous? The place was a revolving door that hurt the neighborhood.

The lateral outside wall of Charlie's home facing the hideous tower had a short, but wide bench covered with ceramic tiles. Despite the view, Charlie liked the pew and many evenings or nights when the temperature was right, he would sit there, remembering the deceased wife who had also been sitting on the bench next to him and the intimate talks between them. If he ever should need money and was forced to list his property for sale, the presence of that ugly thing next door would undercut the price.

The retired man knew the names of almost everybody in the street and since he lived alone, he was always trying to develop and keep personal relationships with all his neighbors. He spent Sundays playing games with some of them, but the residents of the oddball tower had never been receptive. Another social rejecting problem originated in the house immediately next to the tower, on the other side. The man in that house was beefy, bearded, had a loud imperious voice and his physiognomy and demeanor were perceived as threatening. He was an independent trucker who had occasionally parked his trailer in the street. He was married to an equally unpleasant overweight woman who never showed up on the street outside of her car. Charlie had met her in the grocery store twice, but she pretended not to see him. She really bought plenty of food, he thought. She was an unseemly fat broad.

The current residents of the objectionable tower were a black couple with a beautiful 4-year-old daughter. Charlie liked children and would have enormously enjoyed a chance of playing ball with the little girl and inviting the whole family in, but her mother, Deirdre, did not seem interested. Too bad, he rarely saw his own grandchildren. Charlie, who enjoyed trying to be mischievous and witty, thought that if the little girl grew fast, the couple would have to leave for lack of space, and laughed. Deirdre was thin, and poorly, but cleanly dressed. Whatever few words she uttered, it was always done in a friendly, respectful manner. Her fiancé, Audell, mostly came through as an unfriendly person, always dressed in unwashed clothes; he did not have a beard, but he was rarely clean-shaven and sometimes smelled badly. He came and left at irregular times, which left questions about his occupation open. Charlie thought that maybe the couple lacked a shower in the minute house. He would have been willing to let them use his own bathroom if their attitude had been different. With the time, during incidental encounters, Deirdre occasionally smiled at him and sustained brief conversations about her toddler. Charlie learned that Audell was the girl's father but not Deirdre's husband. What job did he have? Oh, she was not sure but apparently, he found work helping farming companies in the area, as a simple farmhand. He was looking for a permanent position. Like many others, thought Charlie.

Charlie offered her his services if their old car broke down. He had kept tools and was happy to see and service outmoded models, like the jalopy they owned. Deirdre smiled. "The car is old, but it shows only 50,000 miles."

"It may be actually 150 or 250,000 miles" answered Charlie. Both laughed, but Charlie had been serious.

A few days later Caitlin, a neighbor woman, reported to him confidentially that Audell was rumored to be a drug dealer.

"Really?" asked Charlie. "That cannot be, Emmett is too small for that. Maybe he works in Great Falls?"

"No, no. I have it from a reliable source. A friend confided in me that her husband and son occasionally inhale cocaine. This town is not that small. There are thousands of residents with young people at home. Do not forget the many who have left for the city to find a job and return to visit bringing their unhealthy habits with them. I hope, Charlie, that you are not in danger."

"If I were, everybody would be. Bullets fly across streets." Charlie thought that real drug dealers have money, and they would choose better accommodations. Now, he would no longer think of offering this family access to his shower.

The Fourth of July, the National Holiday, was approaching. Most types of fireworks were prohibited although they were offered for sale by most local shops. The city would organize a large fireworks display in a town park, known as the place where most teenagers went to make up. People had to bring their chairs or blankets and the loudspeakers played suitable music. In early years, Charlie had attended the municipal event, but he discontinued doing so after his wife's death. Many town people came with children. It was a kind of annual show repeat.

The evening before, Charlie had been eating sandwiches and drinking beer at the home of his good neighbors across the street Pete and Rose Schmidt.

"Did you see the raucous fight outside this morning?" asked Rose.

"No, I wasn't home. How interesting! Tell me, what happened?"

"There was a fist fight between the black guy next to your home and Jim Powell, who lives next door."

"You mean Audell and his neighbor the trucker? How did it start? I am sure that the big man won."

"It was already going on when I saw it in the window. Jim had come with his truck, which he wanted to park outside. Apparently, the trouble had something to do with the black man's jalopy, which was keeping him from parking his rig where he wanted. Jim went to your neighbor's home and shouted that Audell had to move the car immediately."

Charlie laughed. "Maybe the car was broken and could not be moved. It must be about to fall apart and disintegrate."

"Both guys started yelling and threatening each other with vulgarities. Jim, who is an appreciably bigger fellow started the fight and hit Audell in the face. It got worse. I called Pete to go outside and stop it."

Here Pete, Rose's husband, joined the conversation. "Jesus, I was afraid to get involved. Jim was using racial slurs, which is not right, but the negro was defending himself well. He hit the bigger man in the middle of the nose, and it started bleeding. Two or three of us ran to them and stopped the fight. Jim's wife, the fat woman who talks to nobody, was also outside insulting the black neighbor with racial slurs. Jim was the one in trouble. Finally, everybody calmed down, Audell moved the car and the trucker and his wife went home. Jim is a nasty man and he was really bleeding and probably had a broken nose. He was upset and threatened revenge. His wife could not calm him down, but she finally dragged him inside."

"Well," commented Charlie, "if he burns down the tiny house it will be an improvement to the neighborhood."

All three laughed, mischievously. They were happy that something resonant had happened, a story to be followed up. Life in in a small town was boring, especially for seniors.

The city of Emmett employed a sheriff and two deputies, but nobody had called them to settle the squabble. Charlie occasionally walked by the precinct mostly to check out the two cars they had. The retired mechanic always viewed the patrol cars as too old, too prone to repairs and too slow. He had mentioned it to the sheriff, who answered that he should report it to the town manager. The old man remembered how Caitlin had confidentially claimed that Audell was a drug dealer. He could not have chosen a safer place. The town's three police officers were even not up to identify a low-level dealer.

Charlie was visited by one of his two children in the company of wife and kids for a late lunch on the Fourth of July. After the meal the son announced that they were going to go visit an old friend in Great Falls. The son had only talked about sports and the daughter-in-law about food prices and recipes. The grandkids had almost ignored him. Left alone at home, Charlie decided to watch the fireworks of New York City on TV. He could also overhear the remote noise coming from the park.

Approximately at 10PM the two police cars of the town appeared preceded by sirens and parked outside of Charlie's and Audell's homes without stopping the blue lights. Charlie looked out the window and noticed the two uniformed officers entering Audell and Deirdre's home. He walked down the stairs and opened his door. He could not see anything happening, but nonetheless he waited until one of the two cops came out of the little house and ran toward his car parked in front of Charlie's door to call the Sheriff. Charlie, still in his pajamas and barefooted, tried to listen in but did not quite understand what it was all about. He finally asked.

"We cannot talk about anything before the Sheriff arrives, sorry" was the answer.

"Come on, Mike, we have known each other for years. I used to fix your car and I know all the people who live in the area. I will find out one way or the other."

The officer looked around him and finally said: "You haven't heard it from me, but the black man, Audell, has been murdered by gun shots."

Before he retired, Charlie noticed lights in several neighbor's houses. Agitated, people were outside asking the same. Finally, Charlie loudly shouted across the street: "The police says that Audell has been shot and killed. More information tomorrow." And he went back to bed. The neighbors heard the announcement in silence and perplexity. Charlie had good reputation and was credible. Calm returned.

Paralleling the situation, the weather next day was murky. Charlie noticed small groups of people on the street, all of them respectfully distanced from the small tower. Charlie was sure: everybody was saying that this had never happened in Emmett, but our man could remember a similar case when he was an adolescent. One of the police cars was still parked outside of the crime scene, but no police activity could be noticed. After a while, the sheriff arrived in the second car and entered the house. Deirdre, the young widow, and her little daughter could not be seen anywhere. At last, a funerary vehicle and two cars with detectives from Great Falls arrived to complete the scene. Following an examination by the detectives, pictures were recorded and Audell's body was removed. The medical examiner's vehicle left, whereas all police cars stayed for a long time. His neighbors evidently believed that Charlie was the best-informed source and the most intelligent among all street residents. Many of them were discretely removing from the entrances their US flags and other patriotic ornaments.

Little by little, the emergent, high-priority question, was heard everywhere: who had been the murderer? Were Deirdre and the girl safe? Why were they not appearing in public? All remembered the recent fist fight between Audell and the brutal trucker Jim Powell, who had threatened to kill the black man one day earlier and was nowhere to be seen. This was suspicious and had implications. Had Audell been killed over a parking dispute? Several neighbors remembered having read on a paper or seen on TV similar cases. That is why they were always careful and advised their families to repress road rage. Jim Powell should be taken to jail. Tired of these speculations, Charlie returned home and closed the door.

What about the criminal drug leaders who worked with the dead man? Everybody was repeating that Audell was a dealer, which meant that it was proved. One of the neighbors talked. His son had confessed to have acquired illegal substances from a black man stationed at the Lion's Den, Emmett's most popular watering hole, and he had observed how the provider covertly talked to Audell, who as a black man was easy to notice. Ah! said the people in spontaneous conversation groups upon receiving that shocking information. Emmett had become a new Medellin, as some neighbors had been wisely predicting for a long time. Now nobody else would be safe. The gangsters are heavily armed. Poor Deirdre! To be alone with a little girl of such small age! She probably had suffered a lot. A woman commented that she could not imagine living with a drug dealer under the same roof. There were government charities to shelter women and children in jeopardy. It was a bad example for her little girl and the county should have taken the girl away from her and that house. But how come that they never came to church on Sunday? She probably was in cahoots with her man.

Now it was for the police to do something about this situation. Hear, hear, said most participants.

Around 1 PM, Charlie's doorbell rang. He opened and two police detectives in street clothes from the county asked for permission to enter and talk to him. Charlie invited them into his living room.

"I know what happened next door. Did you figure out who did it?"

"We are not free to discuss that. It is too early. The victim was killed by two shots in the chest in his living room. The murderer had neither left a trace of him nor stolen anything known. There is little in the house worthy of a robbery. We have noticed that there is no physical separation or fence between your property and the house where the event took place. We have not yet been able to find the gun, but the lack of separation between your and your neighbors yard concerns us. Do you authorize us to search in your backyard? We have no warrant."

"Of course, here you do not need a warrant. I am always ready to be of help. But please, tell me what you would be looking for in my yard?"

"We are searching for the gun used in the crime."

"And you think that it could be found in my yard? That is exciting. Am I a suspect?"

Both detectives simultaneously shook their heads laughing.

"No, Mr. Glenn, nothing of the kind. Whenever a partner in a couple is murdered, the surviving partner or spouse always becomes the first person of interest. We understand that Deirdre did not leave the house during the evening and stayed home during the event, therefore we speculate that any weapon might be hidden here. The victim's immediate south side neighbors have a fence and were in bad terms with the deceased but we have already searched their yard and house without results. Besides, the neighbor has been given an alibi by his wife."

Charlie opened his mouth in disbelief. "So, you are now considering that such a meek and kind woman as Deirdre, mother of a small girl, could have murdered Audell?" He shook his head.

"We haven't said any such thing. We follow routines. Did you notice any unusual activity in the area yesterday between 9 and 10 PM?"

"Not at all. I watched the fireworks in New York which started at 9PM and then I fell asleep."

"Did you hear any shotguns being fired?"

"Well, how would I distinguish that noise from the one of the New York fireworks on TV? Or from the local Emmet pyrotechnics? Besides, I told you that I fell asleep soon. I woke up around 10 o'clock, when I heard police cars outside my door. I ran downstairs and a local policeman told me about the crime. I went back to bed, but I could hardly sleep."

"One last question, Mr. Glenn. Have you noticed luxurious automobiles or large SUVs in this street?"

"You mean the kind of car drug dealers use?"

"What do you know about this? Was the deceased a drug dealer?"

"This is just loose talk of the neighbors. I do not go to night locals, nor do I spy on neighbors. Answering your question, on rare occasions I have seen big cars in the neighborhood. Think that I earned money as a car mechanic, and I am still interested in cars. But you would see many more such cars in Great Falls. No, I have never seen a fancy car parked outside of my house. Audell owned only an old and downtrodden vehicle that must still be around. I do not know how he could pass the inspections if he did."

The two policemen left thanking him again and spent more than one hour in his backyard pointing at items, collecting them in a bag and taking pictures. Charlie concluded that they knew nothing.

The following day Charlie kept watching the small house but could not see anything of interest, except that one of the local police cars was driving by very slowly. He was surprised that Deirdre did not receive visits of friends or relatives. He decided to go in.

Charlie had to knock three times at the door. Knowing that Deirdre was inside, he insisted. Finally, the door was opened, and Deirdre and her girl appeared. Charlie immediately recognized in the woman's face marks of a severe beating; the woman could hardly open the left eye. "Nobody has mentioned that" Charlie thought trying to smile.

"Hi, Deirdre. We have known each other for months. I know that you are a kind and honest woman, I know what has happened and I am concerned. I came to ask if you need something. I could buy food or even cook something simple for you and the child or drive you somewhere. I want to tell you that you are not alone."

Deirdre moved aside and Charlie entered. He had not been inside the house for years.

"Thank you for coming. Nobody else cares about me. Nobody phones me."

The little girl, laughing, had started pulling on Charlie's leg.

"Oh, little one, what do you want? Let me go back to my home and get some cookies for you" He asked Deirdre "Do you have milk? Tell me what you need."

"They believe that I killed Audell."

"What?" asked Charlie.

"That is only because he beat me brutally, as you can see, in the face and other parts before the assassination and that is why they think that I murdered him in retaliation. As if it were the first time that he abused me. Me! I never held a gun in my hands and would not know how to use it."

Charlie opened his mouth.

"I can't believe that! This is impossible. Did Audell own a gun?"

"Yes. I know that Audell did because one day when he was intoxicated, he showed it to me. I cannot describe it. I know nothing about guns. The police claims that it must have been unregistered but they cannot find it."

Charlie understood why the detectives had checked out his backyard. "What did Audell need a gun for?"

"He just mentioned his second amendment rights. He owned only one, because they are expensive. His dream was to own an assault rifle."

"What did he do for a living?"

"I do not know. He went out in the evening and sometimes he said that he had found temporary work as a farmhand. Mostly he went to Great Falls. He never gave me much money but on the other side, we had everything we needed. My family did not like him, and we decided to leave Nashville and come to a rural area in another state to make a fresh start, but we were not going anywhere. He had little schooling and few skills. And maybe an unfriendly nature, too."

Charlie kept asking himself why she did not volunteer any explanation for the brutal injuries she had suffered.

He left to take his usual walk in the neighborhood. When he returned, he noticed that Pete & Rose Schmidt, his neighbors across the street, had been watching him from a window. Both ran to open their door and pulled Charlie in.

"We saw you talking to Deirdre. What did she say?"

"It seems that Audell had been a world class wife abuser and beater. Poor Deirdre had recent injuries all over her face and body. The police has decided nothing, but they suspect Deirdre and she is worried."

"Oh" cried, Rose. "He really looked like a wife beater. This must be the reason why she shot him."

"What?" complained Pete. "We do not know that she has killed anyone."

Rose insisted "It is what I would do if my husband were abusing me."

Charlie intervened: "With what gun would she have shot Audell? She called the police immediately after the shooting and there was no gun in the house. She could not possibly have disposed of it. The detectives looked all over. Besides, she did not know how to use a gun."

"Well," added Pete. "We all saw how Audell was able to beat up the trucker and how the man swore to take revenge. It was only one day before the crime and this guy has always scared me."

"Me too" said approvingly Rose, "and the police also searched his house and yard. But according to Elvira who has talked to his wife, she can alibi him and swear that Jim had spent the whole night with her without leaving for a second."

A silence followed, but Charlie was skeptical. "We are talking about rumors, that Elvira said to Rose that according to a conversation Jim had done or not done something. Then you tell your husband and me and if a second independent person repeats it in your presence, the case is already proven. It seems to me that an alibi from a wife for a husband has limited credibility. Let us wait and see what the police says."

"We'll see if they arrest somebody."

"In general," clarified Charlie, "they need the permission of the county attorney in Great Falls to charge anybody and it is going to take weeks."

"You know so many things, Charlie. These are the requirements. But did you hear something about the drug dealing angle? These people are extremely dangerous gangsters and murder people. And I have seen that many drug dealers on TV are black. One of them must have come and left at once, taking the gun with him. I have heard that the police was searching for his accomplices in Great Falls."

"Ah! Stop listening to rumors. We all stay home, meet once every week to eat and play a game and eventually we shall learn from reliable sources what happened and who is going to jail."

"You are right, Charlie, but we are not used to these excitements. We all thought that Emmett is a peaceful and God-loving community."

"Sorry for Deirdre but excitements are rare."

Charlie had noticed an increasing number of police visits to both Deirdre's and the trucker's home. It was easy to recognize their unmarked vehicles because they parked on the street. All the visitors seemed to be detectives from Great Falls. They spent time inside Deirdre's and the trucker's homes, but their interviewed targets did not explain anything. Only once they approached Charlie to ask if he was sure that he had not seen any unknown luxury or black SUV on the street the day of the crime. But Charlie answered again that he had been watching the fireworks on TV or had fallen asleep. And had he not heard any gunshots? No, just fireworks. Had he ever found an unknown gun? Of course not! He would have immediately reported it. Like most residents, he owned an old, properly registered gun which he had not used for years. Did they want to see it? Not necessary, Sir, thank you. Had he noticed any suspicious black individuals entering the crime house? No, neither suspicious nor unsuspicious of any color, but he did not spend the day watching the street. The detectives appeared satisfied.

During one of his walks, Charlie bumped into the younger officer Bill Cummings.

"Good to see you, Bill. Tell me something. What is going on with the crime on Elm Street? You are aware that I live next door and know everybody. We are all worried. We never had an assassin in this town. What have you found out?"

"Oh, Charlie, we cannot discuss this. It is being investigated exclusively by the county detectives and they have warned us."

"Come on, Bill, I attended the party that your dad gave when you were born, and I fixed your first High School car for you."

Bill breathed deeply and looked around. "Look, Charlie, don't mention this to anyone but it seems that we are going to have to arrest Deirdre and charge her with murder two."

"I don't believe that!" protested the old man.

"What are you talking about? I have said nothing."

Two days later Charlie watched from his home the arrival of three police cars. Half an hour later, the sheriff and his two policemen came out leading Deirdre in handcuffs toward one of the automobiles. They were followed by a woman bringing the crying little girl to a temporary foster home.

"Where are you bringing her?" cried Charlie to the policemen.

"To the jail in Great Falls," answered the Sheriff.

Across the street Rose Schmidt almost cried "So she did it! A criminal in our street! I need to call Pete."

But Charlie warned her: "Don't rush to conclusions. There is much to be seen and said about this." Soon the entire town would have a single topic of conversation.

Three days later our old man received an unexpected phone call from Great Falls:

"Hi, Mr. Glenn. We have never met, but I have been appointed defense lawyer for Deirdre. My name is Peter Ayles I am a junior partner of our firm. The County Attorney informed my boss that the judge had chosen us to defend this unfortunate and extremely poor woman. Our managing partner called me to his office and informed me that being the youngest associate I was being given a once-in-a-lifetime chance of being promoted. I asked Deirdre what friends or family members she had, to try to form a support group and testify about past events and her character. She told me that she had nobody but after thinking a while she mentioned your name. Would you be willing to assist her? Before you answer, let me assure you that in my opinion she is innocent. Election time is approaching, the County Attorney and the Judge want some blood to show how tough on crime they are, and a black woman living with an alleged drug dealer is their perfect target."

It took Charlie a moment to recover from the surprise and after a second he answered: "Yes, of course, Mr. Ayles, I am completely at your service and being retired I have plenty of time. You can call me Charlie."

"And you call me Peter. The prosecutor claims that in the absence of other possible suspects, the surviving partner is always the prime suspect. They wonder about the amount of Deirdre's blood found on the face of the victim. They think that Deirdre was violently beaten, but that she overcame Audell and shot him while they were on the ground, since otherwise the finding of facial blood of Deirdre cannot be explained. They have even ordered DNA tests. Deirdre herself cannot explain it and simply says that she was so savagely beaten that she cannot remember what she did, except that she had no gun, knows nothing about guns and has never had one in her hands. She claims that Audell had indeed a gun, but I cannot find a registration. It must have been illegal. The main issue, however, is that no gun has been found! I will repeat this in the trial as frequently as needed. A woman is alone in the house, so badly hurt that she can hardly speak or move, she hears shots downstairs and immediately calls the police. What chance did she have to get rid of the gun? How? Audell was murdered by somebody who entered the house and left while Deirdre was upstairs recovering from her injuries, and the police is no longer looking for this person. It would be outrageous to convict her to help reelect the County executives, but with a good defense, she cannot and will not be convicted. They have no evidence."

"I fully agree with everything you say. Deirdre is safe in your hands, Peter."

"Would you be willing to visit Deirdre in the County jail? She feels lonely and abandoned. She meets me and nobody else."

"Of course, I will. Can I bring her food or something?"

The following day Charlie drove to Peter Ayles' firm in Great Falls. He found that Peter was a pleasant young man.

"Charlie, I am giving you a pass to be able to see Deirdre without being a relative. I had to explain to them that she has no other friends or relatives."

"She does not. I am bringing her some food, a great sandwich and two apples."

"It will be all right. I must warn you about something. They are not allowed to listen to or record my conversations with Deirdre because I am her defense lawyer, but they have the right to hear and record everything you say. None of your conversations will be private. Please do not mention under any circumstances anything pertaining to the case, because this would reveal our strategy to the prosecutor and could be used against her. Besides, they do not know if you could be a witness. Something else more pressing: she was arraigned yesterday and naturally we pleaded not guilty. The prosecutor, who is a lawyer in the other firm in town, requested a bail of $100,000, but Deirdre does not have a penny. The bail is an injustice that hurts only poor people. I complained and the judge reduced the bail to only $50,000. We will have a trial very early, probably in 4 months only, but if we do not find the money, $5,000 in cash and the rest in a bond, the poor woman will spend four months in jail without visitors. Can you think of something?"

Charlie blew air out of his mouth "No, I don't have 5,000 bucks and my home is already mortgaged."

Peter was ready to push his point. "She told me that she never went to church but most people in your town do. Do you think that you could mobilize church people to support her? She is an attractive case for that group: a young innocent woman with a little girl, badly battered by her companion, who is a drug dealer, without friends because she is black in a nearly completely white village, to be tried only with minimal, unconvincing proves and a gun that was never found. How can she be guilty? This prosecution is an electoral racist outrage."

"And you cannot produce the money?"

"No! It is prohibited. I could be disbarred. I cannot lend money to a client."

"I hear you. I will beat the drum and see whether I can get some social or religious support. Besides, there are a few black people in Emmett and I will find them. I have your phone number."

The County detention center was close to the Courthouse. Charlie had never been inside. He was frisked and led to a room with a glass wall perforated by windows and lined by a narrow table on both sides. He was warned that physical contact with the detainee (which was impossible) was strictly prohibited and they had only 15 minutes. The man sat in front of one of the windows and after a moment Deirdre appeared on the other side.

"Oh, Charlie! How great that you could come! I feel so lonely and almost the other detainees are whores, drug offenders or thieves. But they will be released after a few days and I am locked for at least four months, maybe for life."

The woman started crying.

"Listen, my dear, one should worry only about today's problems. Nobody knows what the future will bring. Look, I brought you a sandwich, two apples and cookies and I will keep coming with goodies." He added "Many people remember you in Emmett", which was probably true but not in a good sense.

"I would enjoy having friends but what I mostly miss is my dear daughter. They only tell me that she is well cared for, but I would give anything to see her. No child is well cared with foster parents."

"Have you been informed of your trial date?"

"Peter tells me that it is going to happen in four months or more and that I will stay locked here for at least so long."

"I am not sure that I can fix anything, but I will try to get the bail money. Are you a religious person?"

Charlie spent the night weighing a tentative to raise the bail money. The obvious first step was to contact his neighbor Pete Schmidt, a devout Christian who never missed a church service on Sunday and was a Council member of his congregation. Charlie was displeased when Rose joined them in the conversation. The old neighbor liked her but thought that she talked too much to too many people.

"Our neighbor Deirdre is feeling as well as one could imagine under the circumstances."

Rose interrupted him. "She should not have murdered her husband or friend, or whatever."

"Rose, that is exactly what I wanted to discuss with you and your husband. Having met her for almost one year, did you ever feel that she was a dangerous person capable of a heinous crime? To me, she was a likable young woman with a beautiful little daughter, quite different from Audell. The law has found no proof that she had or knew how to fire a gun, nor has anyone found one. Getting rid of a gun is not so easy and she could not possibly have disposed of it in the few minutes between the shots and the arrival of the police. The fact that Audell was a drug dealer does not leave my mind. These people kill each other and always carry firearms. And what about the alibi of the trucker? Can he be ruled out simply because his wife claims that she was with her husband all the time? How come nobody talks about the horrible beating that poor Deirdre took from Audell before the assassination? Days later, I could still see the scars left and the blue eye. Many men seem to think that they have the right of hurting their wives simply because they can. It is a national tragedy and it is not what the Bible says. What can you do if are hopelessly locked in a small house which is all you can afford and must share small living quarters with a dangerous person who insults or beats you?"

Charlie had been following Rose's expression and now she and Pete had lowered their eyes and seemed to be thinking.

"The judge, the county attorney and the other office holders are close to election time and have found a perfect victim to show how tough on crime they are. A single black woman living in sin with a drug dealer! Could that not be dangerous for our children and community? Nobody will accuse the town people of being racists although they would be engaging in a cruel case of racist abuse. Look at Deirdre, an isolated and completely innocent victim chosen because she was upstairs recovering from a beating while a visitor murdered her man. He must have been a professional killer because he left no traces behind and took the gun with him. Is the police looking for him? I will tell you: it is all racism to blame a defenseless woman of color. Are we Christians going to tolerate it?"

Finally, Pete revealed his thinking. "Yes, Charlie, you are putting us to shame. We rushed to judgment because we do not understand the law. I did not see the injuries in Deirdre but..." He grabbed and pressed Rose's hand. "I would never watch in silence how a woman is hurt because of her race. Everything you say is right and I am sure that subconscious low-level racism exists among us although the Bible teaches that we are all equal and must love each other. I always thought that Deirdre was only a weak woman scared of her companion, always afraid of speaking her mind without risking punishment."

Now it was Rose's turn to speak. "Deirdre was always isolated. I said so many times, but nobody paid attention. We could have protected her, invited her to our meetings, but we were indifferent. Now she is been used for a dirty political game." Charlie appeared satisfied:

"You are right Rose. People should have listened to you. I wanted to propose a penance to compensate for and remedy the neglect that has led to the present situation. The bail is fixed at 50,000, ten percent in cash, the rest in a bond that guarantees it, like some property. It is a safe investment that could be lost only if Deirdre were to run away, a ridiculous idea. I, like most of our neighbors, do not have the means to cover that temporary loan. Deirdre will be tried in less than four months. If she could make bail, she would return and be here with her daughter. If she cannot, she will have to spend the four months in unjust imprisonment, for which she will never receive a cent in compensation. If enough people share our opinion about the injustice and abuse of power which includes violence in our midst, we could ask your Grace of God community to provide the funds."

"What", almost shouted Pete. "I am a member of the Council, and we are completely out of money. Probably most of us would sympathize with Deirdre but we got no money."

"Think about it: the temporary investment would be a Christian act designed to strengthen our community. It would be required only for four months and immediately returned. I am sure that you have as much as $5,000 in cash and the additional $45,000 could come for instance from listing the house of the Pastor as collateral."

"What, what? We'll need to talk about this."

"Do so, please. Deirdre's lawyer, Peter Ayles, has assured me that he would be willing to attend one of our services any Sunday, explain the situation and answer any questions. If your Council wishes, his presentation could be followed by a general discussion and a vote of all congregants. If you require specific answers, for instance what outcome of the trial can be reasonably expected or how safe would the Pastor's home be, I will give you his phone number and e-mail address. I am no lawyer."

The Schmidt's were left thoughtful and in doubts, but Charlie felt increasingly optimistic and started sharing his expectations with others. Deirdre advised him that she knew several black people, maybe three or four, but there might be more in Emmett, and, if approached, they might attend the meeting and maybe join the congregation. Attorney Ayles was ready to attend a service anytime and deliver a presentation.

The Sunday arrived. Everybody was talking about the cases of injustice in their County that they had observed or suffered. At least four months in jail for nothing! One more victim of male abuse ignored by the system, like many others, as some women say. Charlie, a clever man of good reputation, had hit a nerve and the Church felt that they had an obligation to help. Some found that the Pastor's residence should not be put in jeopardy. But it would not be and it was time to fight and end racism. The Lord would help, and the Reverend would keep his home.

On Sunday, the Church was full. Four black men and two women had appeared und were sitting in the last pew. Charlie, Ayles and the Community president were in the front row. The Preacher had ended his sermon remembering Martin Luther King's *I have a dream* speech about racial fraternity and his call to the solidarity between all believers and all human races and any faith. "The community is shaken by the case of a young, isolated black woman, now falsely accused of a crime she could not have committed, now deprived of freedom and in need of a help that nobody else can provide. I salute several Afro-Americans who are our brothers, knew her and are welcome among us. Now, Deirdre's attorney will speak to you."

Peter Ayles raised and moved to the front:

"Good morning, brothers and sisters. I am Peter Ayles, the attorney chosen by the judge to be Deirdre's defender, because being poor she could not afford one of her own. You know that Deirdre sits in jail because she cannot afford a horrendous $50,000 bail. How many in this room would be able to deposit that much money to recover an unjustly lost freedom and be able to live with your daughter? Only wealthy people have so much money. Listen to their charge against Deirdre: her partner and father of her daughter, suspected of being a drug dealer, always pugnacious and quarrelsome even with neighbors, came back home intoxicated in the early evening of the 4th of July. He was in the habit of beating and insulting her, and on that day, he hit Deirdre brutally to the point that she briefly passed away, all this ignoring the patriotic and fraternizing spirit of our National Holiday. Hurt as she was, she managed to climb to the first floor of her minute home, where he found her toddler desperately crying. She laid down next to her beloved daughter to try to sleep. A while later, she heard two gunshots downstairs. She cried for Audell, who did not respond. Hurt as she was, she dragged herself downstairs to investigate and found her man dead on the floor. She could see nobody else around and she immediately called 911. Now you will ask, how could this unlucky woman be arrested? The County officials say that in cases of assassination of a person in a stable union, the surviving partner is the leading suspect. A wonderful way of resolving a crime when they cannot find the criminal! Just blame the victim's wife. They say that Audell hit her, she grabbed a gun and killed him. Oh, yeah? Where did she get the gun? And where is it now? Deirdre is a little, weak woman who had never held one in her hands and no gun has been found anywhere. It has not been found because the unidentified murderer took it with him. How could the gravely wounded Deirdre make it instantaneously disappear? She was no magician."

"They claim that no neighbor saw an unknown person or a car in the street. Where were you? Maybe watching on television the fireworks from New York or Washington? Or the shows that followed? Were you watching your windows? To commit an abuse, the County Attorney always looks to blame somebody weak and defenseless. Just imagine what a lucky coincidence that Deirdre happens to be black too. Several black citizens have joined us today. Ask them if they feel embedded and protected by the society where they live and by the police. Or do they fear to undergo the same destiny as Deirdre? In a few months, we shall reelect or replace all our County executives. Have you made up your minds? Will you prefer one who claims to be tough and can find a guilty person for every crime? Or one who believes in and worships Justice, respects weak women and believes in racial equality?"

"In despair, we come here asking for $50,000 which we have not found anywhere else. If you refuse to help, the innocent woman I defend will be imprisoned and separated from her young child for months. We recognize that it is your right to deny us the funds and that you have no obligation of any kind whatsoever, but I am a Christian too and know that our Lord Jesus Christ teaches and expects from us solidarity and love for our neighbors. You can resolve the issue by posting 5,000 in cash and a bond guaranteed by a building you own. After the sentence, whether she is found guilty or innocent, every single penny will be returned to you, and you will be proud of what you have done. Thank you to the Council President and to your Pastor, and God and our Lord Jesus Christ will bless you."

Many in the audience had tears in the eyes, including the Preacher, who invited to black attendees to come forward and identify themselves. Two of them, named Jadyn and Efrem claimed to know Deirdre well and testified to her kindness, good character, and love for her daughter. Audell, the victim, had been quite different and nobody liked him. They had all been members of the Ethiopian Church in Great Falls, but they had no community of their own in Emmett. If accepted, they would like to join the present Congregation. Most attendees enthusiastically agreed and stood up applauding and crying. Some even came to hug the Afro-Americans. It was a moment of true fraternity.

Two days later the Pastor, Jadyn and Charlie took all the bail papers to Peter Ayles in Charlie's car. The lawyer found them in order, and they ran together to the Courthouse. On the way, the lawyer mentioned to Charlie that he was trying to get the extraordinary case of the Church's Christian and exemplary decision and sacrifice published in the local paper and, if he was lucky, in a national media organization. His intent was to inform, not to taint the juror pool, of course. He laughed. Two hours later, a joyous Deirdre was seated in the car with the three friends and supporters on her way back to Emmett. The Pastor insisted on buying her some food. On the same day, Peter presented to the judge a motion to dismiss the case for lack of evidence and foundation, but he was turned down, as expected. Nothing had been resolved. The child protection authority had refused to return the little girl until after the trial, but Deidre was allowed to visit weekly, only once and in Great Falls.

In the following days, Charlie stopped at Deirdre's several times offering to shop for her, knowing that the woman probably had little money, if any, but she smilingly always declined the offer. After the third rejection, Charlie added that in case she needed some assistance, he was next door. He had noticed outside her door the old and dirty pick-up truck of Jadyn, one of the young black men who claimed to have known Deirdre before and had insisted on coming along for the bail formalities. The prehistoric vehicle, not much younger than the one owned by Audell and now Deirdre, stayed there for hours, sometimes during the evening. Charlie shrugged his shoulders. Good for them, they were young and Deirdre was an attractive unwed mother. He considered offering to look at the engine for free. One day he was walking back home when Deirdre opened her door announcing good news. Her friend Jadyn had found for her a paid cleaning job in the business where he worked and was trying to find additional family jobs. Peter Ayles had told her that she would need some proof of income to get her daughter back and now she had it. Charlie congratulated. Being a janitor or a cleaning woman was little, but like Jadyn, she had never graduated from High School.

The four-months interlude passed by without any additional incidents. Charlie would have wanted to invite Deirdre and Jadyn, but he was unable to cook anything that could be offered. A sandwich, maybe? He tried to convince Rose Schmidt. Her husband Pete agreed. Jadyn declined the invitation, but Deirdre accepted, and all four had a nice evening at the Schmidt's. After the meal, Charlie offered to escort the young woman across the street. Somehow, they talked about the deceased Audell, and Deirdre unexpectedly offered some information:

"All say that he was a drug dealer, which is ridiculous. One day when he was intoxicated, he explained to me that he drove to Great Falls to get some little packs of cocaine from unknown people in a dark corner. He never knew their names. In Emmett he had fond two drug-addicted men and he offered them some insignificant amounts of free cocaine in exchange for selling the rest at a higher price. He pocketed the price difference and went back to Great Falls for more. He did not use himself, but once he made me snore a little amount. It hurt my stomach, gave me heart palpitations and belly ache and I could not sleep. I never knew where he made the little money he had, but it was not from the cocaine activities. I cannot imagine that anybody in the drug business would care to murder him. I feared that he may have been a thief."

"You should not be talking about this before the trial."

"Mr. Ayles warned me already."

"And you disobeyed him. Never do it again."

Charlie turned around and waved to the Schmidt's while Deirdre entered her home. It had been a pleasant evening. Would the trial mess up everything?

Time rapidly passed by. The weather was still pleasant outside. An evening Charlie, seated outside his door, saw Deirdre and Jadyn coming out of the neighboring house holding each other's hands. Deirdre hugged and kissed her friend. After the young man had left, Charlie approached Deirdre.

"How are things going, neighbor? I rarely see you here anymore."

"It is because Jadyn has found me lots of decent work. They allow me to visit my daughter only once every week for two hours and I regularly talk to Peter Ayles. I must tell you something, Charlie, because I know that you understand me. I am afraid of the trial and cannot sleep at night. Do you think that they could sentence me to death?"

"No!" answered Charlie laughingly. "You will be found not guilty but even otherwise you would get only a few years."

"You always say the same things as Peter."

"When I was young, before owning my repair shop, I worked with a union and was well acquainted and talked a lot with our best lawyers. I never mention it here. People do not like unions."

"You both say that it is unlikely that they give me the needle, but they may do it and I am scared."

"The death penalty is nothing. Dying is like falling asleep and everything is resolved and finished. What is hard is to be sent to a jail for years, without medical care, sharing a tiny cell with an unknown, losing all your civil rights, being abused, or raped and eating disgusting food. Animals are better treated."

"Will you come to the trial, Charlie?"

"Of course, if that is what you want. Peter may want me to testify."

"I do. Jadyn and the Preacher will also be there."

The trial took place in late October, only weeks ahead of the local elections. Peter had predicted that it was going to be truly short. The Pastor and some members of the Congregation also said that they wanted to attend. Deirdre and her new boyfriend arrived in Charlie's car. The first day started with a short Voit Dire.

"Bua what?" asked Jadyn.

"They will be choosing the jurors and asking them questions in front of the judge and the public, to rule out accepting prejudiced people" explained Charlie. "Once they have found 12 jurors and two extra ones as reserve, the real trial will start, probably tomorrow."

The following day, the Prosecutor started his charge against Deirdre without ever mentioning what everybody saw, that is, that she was a black woman. He repeated the story that everybody knew but characterizing the young woman as a scheming and resourceful person of whom little was know. As frequent in these cases, she had never completed High School and was living with a partner active in the drug business. He recognized that the murder weapon had never been found despite the efforts of the police, but Deirdre was a clever woman capable of self-defense and above all (and this had never been mentioned before) that her blood had been identified on the left side of the face and the shirt of the victim, as well as on Deirdre's blouse, clearly proving close contact between the two people at the time of Audell's death. This was inconsistent with the claim that after the beating Deirdre had run upstairs and stayed there until after hearing the two shots. How could her blood have been found on the victim? He victoriously smiled after claiming this.

Peter delivered a brief opening. "Deirdre is a minority woman victim of repeated abuses and cruelty from her partner. She lacked the resources for leaving him and was forced to stay as a common-law wife for the benefit of their daughter. She is currently forced to work hard as a janitor, lacking any kind of training, health insurance or social support on the very day of our National Holiday, when the country was celebrating the might, justice, and constitutional rule of our great nation. Simultaneously, on that very day, an indifferent, intoxicated or drugged evil lawbreaker had chosen the feast to beat my defendant to the point of unconsciousness. She escaped going upstairs, bleeding, half-unconscious, unable to leave their small, precarious home, unaware of the legal resources that might have protected her. She threw herself onto her bed, trying to forget, reflexing on the cruelty of her circumstances and the hopelessness of her condition. Fireworks illuminated the skies, and everybody was filled with patriotic feelings, but Deirdre was alone attempting to recover from a horrendous physical attack and humiliation and was covered with her own blood. She did not know that was happening next, but she had clearly heard two shots and came down despite her pitiful condition to find her partner dead on the floor. She did not see the assailant but immediately called the police. If she had been the shooter, how could she possibly have gotten rid of the gun? She was in need of urgent medical care, which was denied! How?" he repeated for effect. "Audell had clearly been the victim of a distressed, unidentified business partner and the police had not diligently sought him, merrily blaming a poor, unfortunate and isolated woman, aggravating her misfortune. The criminal had intentionally chosen our National Holiday to better be able to hide himself despite the noise that a gunshot always causes. He had been successful at Deidre's expense. The Prosecutor has no credible evidence to sustain his charge."

The rest of the day was uneventful. The State called a detective and the forensic medical examiner. How could the doctor explain the presence of the accused's blood on the victim's face under her narration of the facts? The doctor found it impossible to explain unless the murder had taken place with the shooter in contact or close proximity to the victim. Another police officer testified on the existence of drug rings in the County and that women had occasionally been identified in the gang's operations, but never Deirdre. The prosecutor subpoenaed to testify an alleged drug dealer who invoked his fifth amendment rights and refused to answer. The judge ignored all the defender's objections.

Peter Ayles started calling witnesses in the afternoon. He did not have many people to vouch for Deirdre's character. He called Charlie, who simply related their friendly encounters and pleasant neighboring relations. Deirdre was the loving mother of a beautiful little girl. He had never noticed any luxury cars or big SUVs in the street, but it did not mean anything. He did not want to spend the rest of his life identifying cars in his street. On the Fourth he had been watching TV and had never recognized any shots for what they were if he had heard them. He recognized that seating in front of a TV monitor, he might have missed a car on his street, but he pointed out that he would have recognized the engine's noise and probably been motivated to rise and look through the window.

Attorney Ayles had already challenged the police officers and the forensic discovery of Deirdre's blood in the face of the victim. Had the doctor even seen or heard anything comparable? When a woman shoots a man, does her blood appear on the victim's face? Is this really a convincing argument of Deirdre's guilt or just the opposite?

The judge ended the session and he announced that both lawyers would make the closing statements the following day. Deirdre, Charlie, Jadyn, and the Pastor returned to Emmett in the Pastor's automobile. All hoped that the following day would be the last. They were all optimistic.

The closing statements were boring. The audience already knew what the lawyers would say. Peter Ayles made it brief and sweet:

"As a defender I must prove nothing to you. I must only point out that the prosecutor has not presented a single piece of credible evidence and I must remind you of your obligation under these circumstances to find the accused not guilty. Think for a moment about the story that the prosecutor has presented to you: a socially isolated young woman, a janitor who had never handled a gun, exposed to the brutal violence of her partner. On the night when she has suffered the most cruel assault, she passes out and is half-inconscient in her bedroom upstairs when she hears two shots. She runs downstairs as fast as she can, finding the partner dead and calls the police. If she were the one, who did it, where is the gun? How could an uneducated woman in her condition make it disappear instantaneously? The city and county police searched for it everywhere. If they cannot present a gun, you must acquit. Look at the other argument, that blood of my client was found on the deceased's face and clothes. Just imagine: a major beating against a defenseless woman with the fists. According to the prosecutor, the only way her blood could have landed on Audell was if the man were shot by Deirdre. Do you believe that? The police did not check for gun powder in Deirdre's hands, and they neither sought nor found any other suspicious people. They were content closing the case by dragging Deirdre to this place, adding pain and separation of her daughter to her long suffering. Members of the jury, do your obligation: Acquit!"

The judge gave some brief instructions to the jurors, who retired to deliberate briefly after 11 o'clock AM. Deirdre's supporters decided to have lunch without the woman in a small restaurant across the street which mostly catered to lawyers. Peter joined them. The men were smiling. Peter was happy to receive his friends' praise. The job of the defender was to force the state to prove its case and he had shown very easily that the prosecutor had no case. One way or the other, the Pastor would immediately recover the bail his community had so generously posted.

The meal lasted longer than usually. They even had some beer and laughed. Then Peter received an iPhone message: The jury was back; the verdict would be read in one hour. The lawyer was astonished but also worried because he knew that in most cases a fast jury decision means little discussion and a guilty verdict. They all returned to the Court House and hugged Deirdre individually. Charlie observed how moved Jadyn, Deirdre's new boyfriend appeared. All sat down waiting.

The Pastor noted "Justice will be done" to which Charlie pensively answered "Only God in Heaven knows what Justice means. Here we have only human laws. Laws threateningly demanding punishments are different in each state and country. How can they represent the will of the silent God?"

The judge finally asked to the jurors the decisive question: "In the case of Deirdre...what say you?" and listened to the answer "We the jurors unanimously find the defendant not guilty."

Deirdre's friends raised their arms and felt a strong need to hug each other and the woman again. Peter Ayles was in a cloud, congratulating himself on a job well done. Jadyn was openly crying. A while later, Charlie, Deirdre, Jadyn, and the Pastor were in the car headed to Emmett bringing back as a trophy the rescued woman. The two young people were openly kissing each other. At one time, they all started singing. They arrived in triumph to Deirdre's home. Even the hourly news bulletin of the National Broadcasting Service mentioned the outcome and the support of the church. Neighbors, mostly women, came out to the street and upon hearing the news, cried, and applauded in celebration. It had been a great, memorable day of victory. The

Pastor received back the money and the bond. A Christian job very well done! Savings are needed for emergencies.

The children protective service immediately returned to Deirdre her little girl. A while later Charlie noticed both playing in his yard and approached them ready to join. Jadyn was working in the grass but he also eventually joined with the biggest and most sincere smile of which he was capable.

Weeks and a month passed by. A jolly Charlie was always looking for opportunities to buddy up to the almost 5-year-old girl. They plaid ball with each other and he looked like a happy grandpa with his granddaughter. Deirdre was frequently away, earning money and Jadyn's old pick-up truck was parked outside both houses until late in the evening almost everyday. It was a good life, thought the old man. Things were as they should be.

* * *

One afternoon, Charlie had been charged with watching the girl in his yard while her mother went shopping. Upon her return, Deirdre went inside her home for a moment and came back. After kissing the girl, she addressed Charlie:

"Charlie, I am sorry that I must tell you that Jadyn and myself are leaving on Sunday and will not return. I will miss you. You have helped me so much and were almost like a father to me and a grandfather to my daughter. Consider our situation. Jadyn and I are still in our early thirties. If we choose to stay here, we know what our future will hold. We would like to change it and improve our life. I cannot go back to my birthplace because they threw me out, but Jadyn's family in Atlanta is ready to welcome us and the girl. We never finished High School, but Jadyn has been making inquiries and over there in Atlanta we might be able to finish, get a diploma and qualify for better jobs and earnings.

We have decided that to make it easier, Jadyn and myself can study together. We have tried and it works perfectly." She paused for several seconds and added "I feel much better with Jadyn than with Audell. We have even talked about getting married. I feared that I would die without a wedding."

"I have been suspecting that. I care a lot about the three of you. To wish to improve and educate yourselves and fight for a better future, is great and intelligent. You are both still young enough. What you say about what your future in this town would be, is only too true. There is never equal opportunity, except for those who were born already in possession of the equal opportunity."

"Charlie, I cannot tell you how much I and Jadyn thank you. We deeply regret having to bid farewell. You are a great and lovely man, and we will miss you." She hugged the man, while the toddler was pulling on her skirt. "I really wish to offer you something. I have no money for a proper farewell party, but I bought some coffee and sweets. Come inside my home, please. I need to express my gratitude."

"Gratitude? Humans have an obligation to do what is right and that does not entitle anyone to any rewards. Come here with me for a moment, Deirdre. I want to reveal something." Charlie guided the surprised woman and her child to the little stone ceramic-covered bench in his yard.

"Have you tried sitting here? Do so. It offers an excellent view inside of your little living room. Your window is unusually large for such a small home. I spend time here many evenings."

Deirdre sat on the bench and for a moment stopped breathing. A dark shadow of worry and fear was crossing in front of her eyes. What was Charlie going to say?

"I must confess something else. I am a naughty child! It is not only the view. In summertime when the window is open, one can even hear what is spoken inside. My hearing is getting worse every day. I tried to get one of these horrible ear devices advertised on TV, but they cost $4,000. I rather went to a discounter and got a simple ear amplifier for a few dollars. It works perfectly and I can hear lots of things. I don't do it to spy. It is an expression of love and deep interest in mankind's ways and nature. Before I die, I want to learn what humans are, and it helps listening to their conversations. Most people unfortunately are intellectual desert areas. Empty coconut heads." He laughed.

Deirdre's face had changed. She was no longer smiling. Her eyes were fixed, directed first to the sky and later to her window. She was ignoring her daughter's antiques. Charlie changed the topic:

"I accept your kind invitation. Let us go to your place, drink some celebratory coffee, and have our final conversation."

Deirdre took the girl in her arms and walked ahead of Charlie toward her door. He went to the kitchen and returned to the sitting room in front of the big window with a pot of hot coffee and a plate with cheap grocery store sweets. Charlie had started throwing back and fort a ball with the girl and both were laughing but Deirdre was heavily breathing and sat in a chair without saying anything. She was not smiling. The old man could not look happier and split a cookie to share it with the little playmate.

He finally talked to Deirdre.

"I find that stone bench so comfortable that I occasionally fall asleep in it and dream. Let me explain to you what I dreamed of in the night of the last 4th of July. I did not want to watch fireworks on TV, they always look the same. Maybe the rockets should be recyclable. I imagined that I was seeing in your window a drunken black man alone. A while later, a visibly distressed woman entered and started to imprecate him. She was using a terrible language. I was glad that as a man I had street experience. It took me a while, but I finally understood that the woman was charging the man with sexually molesting her little girl, being also the man's daughter, apparently in the same house. The man denied it first, but the woman claimed that she had proof, that she would not tolerate it and that she might go to the police. The man rose and loudly cried *"You know, stupid bitch, you are talking about MY daughter, and I can do anything I want to her, and I owe no explanations and need no permission of you. If you keep bothering me, I will throw you to the street and you will see how much charity food you find, but the girl stays here as long as I need her. Period."* Still in my dream, this was followed by a silence and the woman started to silently cry. She turned toward the man and yelled to his face *"You have no decency, you are evil, God will punish you"* She was rewarded with a violent slap across her face and almost fell to the ground, but she recovered and went back to her torturer *"Hit me as much as you want, as you have already done many times, but please, for the love of your mother, for everything that is sacred, do not touch our daughter again. She cannot protect herself."* If I correctly remember, here the man loudly and sarcastically laughed, closed his fists, and started brutally hitting the woman, who was unable to defend herself. I cannot repeat it without wet eyes. To the chest, to the head, again to the head, to the eyes. The woman could not cry for help and she got no help. Unconscious, she fell to the ground in a corner and the man did not assist. My instinct was to raise, go to my shop, pick up my sledgehammer, enter the house and kill the bastard. But I waited and I saw that the woman was moving again. She succeeded in standing up and once again, with a face covered in blood told the man *"I beg you. I am used to everything but do not touch my daughter or I will kill you, I swear"* *"Oh, really, you stupid whore, worthless bitch! If you want to kill me, I can help you. Here is my loaded gun. Kill me"* I did not see well, but he seemed to take a small gun out of his pocket, and placed it on a coffee table, exactly like the one you have here. The man resumed laughing. *"You are really uselessly imbecilic. You do not know how to use a gun. I will continue doing what I want with your daughter. Who knows whether she is mine or not and I could not care less. Go ahead, kill me."* And the woman, still bleeding and crying, suddenly grabbed the gun, pointed it at her partner and shot twice. The man fell backwards outside of my view while I cried *Well done, girl!"* After a break, Charlie considered the fiction of his dream finished, and spoke on:

"You cried a while and bent over the body. I think that your nose was bleeding, and this must be why your blood fell on Audell's face and on the gun. Your daughter, awakened by the noise, started crying loudly and you ran upstairs."

Deirdre had stood up and was silently facing Charlie. She obviously had difficulty breathing. While she was standing there, Charlie had resumed taking sips of coffee and trying to resume playing with the little girl. Finally, Deirdre asked:

"What do you want?"

"Nothing, my dear. It was all well done. You are a very brave woman and have unjustly suffered so much. I need nothing from you" He again took another half a pastry and gave it smilingly to the toddler, who immediately took and bit it laughing louder. Then the old neighbor grabbed the coffee mug and raised it toward Deirdre:

"I drink this to you, Deirdre, I drink to liberty, I drink to the right to do what is right, I drink to be entitled to follow my conscience. I drink to celebrate how well this affair ended and I drink to you and your future with Jadyn and with your beautiful daughter. She will grow surrounded by the peace and love that Audell denied to you both. The ordeal was tremendous, but you did well and now everything is resolved and you will have a better life."

Deirdre's lip was trembling. She wanted to speak but could not. Charlie asked:

"Have you told what you did to Jadyn or anyone else?"

"No, I was in doubt."

"Doubt no more. *Do not do it under any circumstances.* Betraying a secret confidentially is like placing an ad in your local newspaper. It would destroy your life, your family would mistrust or fear you, you would lose most friends except for some curious weirdos and reporters would crave your story. No, no and no. Never, to anyone, not now or in years. The main reason why I decided to talk to you today was to make this clear to you. You have no reason to worry. There is no double jeopardy in this country. Forget it yourself and organize your new life."

"May I ask you something? You have mentioned the gun stained with my blood. What happened to the gun? I threw it away in the trash can, but I cannot understand why the police never found it. I was afraid all the time."

Charlie could not contain a loud laughter while sitting the little one on his lap. He was having an enjoyable time relating his adventures and displaying his wisdom. "That was the funniest part of all, dear Deirdre. I was not sure that I should do or say anything. I went back into my house and turned all the lights off to keep the police from bothering me when they arrived. Standing next to the window of my dining room, I saw you coming down again and leaving your home through the rear door toward the trash can. Clever as you must evidently recognize that I am, I immediately thought that you were trying to make the gun disappear, wrapped in a supermarket bag. But into the garbage can? What an absurdity, how could you! Even our dumb local police officers would have found it in 5 minutes, and you would be now in jail and would have forever lost your daughter. A really dumb move. I noticed how you made a useless effort to hide the pack at the bottom of the can and went back inside. I could not wait long. I ran out of the house in the darkness toward the can. It was very dirty and filled with repulsive soft stuff and unbearable stench. I do not understand what you put inside but it was disgusting. I had to roll up my sleeve to retrieve the weapon but I had no gloves. I was in and out with the gun in less than five minutes. I brought it to my workbench in the basement. And you know what the best was?" She fed another cookie to the child, who rewarded him with a smile and a kiss. "When the two Great Falls detectives came to my home the following day asking for permission to search for the gun in my yard, I had it on my worktable in the basement. When they knocked at the door, I had to stop cleaning the fingerprints and the blood. Oh boy! It was one of the most thrilling moments of my adult life. We would have gone to jail together!"

"Peter was wrong to claim that I did not know how to handle a gun. We had been shooting in the woods at least twice. Where is the gun now?"

"You did not set the gun safety and it could have hurt somebody else. I just secured and took it apart, removed the bullets and discarded the parts separately in two of the deepest river crossings we have in the neighboring county. Even if they ever find it, there will be no fingerprints. We are both safe." He fed another cookie to her little friend, who acknowledged. Both were laughing.

Deirdre was paralyzed and speechless, standing in the center of the room. She slowly turned toward Charlie: "My mother was unmarried, and my father hated and hit me for nothing until he finally left. Nobody paid attention to me or loved me. All found me dumb and useless. I never got any presents. I had to wear my sister's old clothes. My mother beat me and made me leave when she had a visitor. I never had in the pocket a penny to buy sweets and could not celebrate my birthdays. Everybody told me that I was ugly and stupid. I did not finish school because the other kids harassed me for being black, and the teachers ignored me. I could never afford fashion clothing or any kind of new dresses. All men I could meet as an adult abused and exploited me. Audell beat me and told me that I had to obey him. What a dark and hopeless life I had ahead of me! Only my girl brought me joy in my life. And then, one day..." She could not continue talking. For a moment, Charlie was listening. "...when everything was lost... and there was no hope and I was going to lose my daughter, who is what I most love in this world, and be beaten to death... It was hell on Earth forever, without hope. Then, an unknown old man who owed nothing to me, for the first time in my life helps me, comes forward, arranges for a bail, saves me from jail exposing himself to danger, he even facilitates how I get acquainted to Jadyn and plan a better future. Everything changes and is resolved. You have fixed everything, I am a reborn new woman ready to restart. You brought me from Hell to Heaven. And you want nothing from me? How, how can this have happened? You made me a free woman for the first time and I see you playing with my daughter like the grandfather she never will have! Is everything a dream?"

Charlie took the question seriously but needed a while to formulate his reflection:

"Your problem is that you don't know that there are many good people around capable of helping whether you push their buttons or not. In school you only learned how to think and obey in silence, to accept from others what they explain what is good and what is bad, to consult and ask for permission before using your own judgement, to abuse power if you get any, to be indifferent to human suffering, to repress the internal sunlight that reveals to humans traces of real Justice. You don't have to thank any man who gives you what you need, because it is your birthright."

Charlie hugged and kissed for the last time the little girl he had come to love and started walking toward the door ignoring her babbling. If she was losing her grandpa, maybe her mom and Jadyn would find another one. On the way out, Charlie announced to Deirdre that they would never meet again. It was the last farewell. The woman still grabbed his arm to stop him:

"I am perplexed and again helpless, Charlie. I thought that I understood the world, but I did not. I had met only people who hated, abused, or despised me. I learned that I needed to avoid them whenever possible, lower my head and hide my troubles. Now you tell me that there are also good people and sunshine around. It sounds great, but how shall I identify them? Am I going to make mistakes? How do I know who is good and who is bad?"

"Your plan to move to a city with Jadyn and complete your education is solid and promising. At the end, you will make something out of yourself. Give my best regards to your future husband."

Charlie had reached the door and started to open it, but he stopped before leaving and turned for the last time toward Deirdre:

"It was clever to keep the facts to yourself. You will always know what to do and you will be all right." And very slowly, stopping after each word, he added his farewell message: "Because... because I know that you and I, we both are exactly the same."

THE HUNCHBACK'S TALE

STANDING IN A CORNER of an ugly, dark, and scarcely furnished walk-up studio, the non-denominational goddess of Self-Pity grinningly ogled her victim. She had known, celebrated and motivated the young woman for years. Her unsuspecting devotee, speaking to an image of herself in the small mirror on the wall over the apartment's washbasin, moaned theatrically:

"Am I to be blamed and punished for having been born unsightly and deformed? Is it right that at my age I must live alone and look forward to the liberating arrival of the grim reaper? Don't they say that all humans are born equal? Did I not get good scores in High School? Mirror, mirror on the wall, am I really the ugliest of them all?"

The mirror, possibly astounded but unworried and always committed to the truth, seemed to quiver sharing its owner's indignation but continued to cruelly reflect the same misshapen image. The problem with self-pity is that it never changes anything and offers only a brief period of undiscerning consolation.

"Is it my fault to be as ugly as I am? Tell me, mirror on the wall. How did I deserve it? Is there a reason why I must endure causing revulsion and loathing? I try to connect only with people who by reason of their clothing belong to the low socio-economic class, like myself.

Don't they teach in school that it is only the soul that counts? Young as I am, must I already resign myself to this? Couples of the street talk to each other, even kiss, and laugh, but nothing of this is available to me. For me it is all the forbidden fruit. How could I possibly find a companion? I wish I could forget. As a kid in school, some children touched and rubbed my little hump claiming that it would bring them good luck. And in the recreation court, they mockingly pointed their fingers at me. When I tried to play, they never passed me the ball. A teacher once called me Quasimoda and everybody laughed. The parents of these atrocious children had money and could keep their children healthy, but mine had no insurance and could not afford a doctor to treat my vertebral column deviation when it was still time to fix it. The priest in the church instructed us to love and respect each other, as if it were easy when dealing with hyenas. Sure, it may be possible but only when it is mutual. I never had the strength of Quasimodo. I almost begged others to treat me with love and respect and was ready to pay in kind, but no one cared about me. Even now when I approach some one, I get a short answer and the person turns his back on me. I am well educated, I think and read about the problems of life and religion, I am compassionate, but I am treated as if I were not qualified to sustain a conversation or befriend anyone. What I am, I am not by choice. I wish I had the courage to counter and cry to their face that I am a human being, not objectionable, not malcontent, not dangerous. My appearance may be drab, but what resides inside my brain is lovely, believe me, and would match any demands or expectations. I am only 29 years old and I have been denied comfort, warmth, and companionship all my life. I see in the movies and TV how people conduct clever conversations about significant issues, politics, or economy, but nobody wants to talk to me about anything of importance, even not about feelings. Yet, I have opinions! Was I born to expect anything of this world? How many years may I be able to survive this torture?"

After a pause, Missy Bru looked away from the sincere mirror that had become her moaning wall. She dressed her evening gown, went to bed, and tried to sleep. "I never have dreams because I scare the spirits and angelical apparitions that come attempting to end my solitude and bring me solace and peace. It is not the winter of my discontent, but the cold summer without blossoms of hope."

* * *

The subway station was full as usually. Missy had always seen it crowded whether she was going or returning from work. Like most passengers she had to accept overcrowding and she did not know how an empty subway train may look. Shyly and without calling any attention she inspected the face features and expressions of the people waiting on the platform. She liked some. May be these strangers were enjoying fitful memories of the sort of engagements with mankind unavailable to her. It would be great to have a conversation with certain people in the crowd, for instance a middle-aged woman dressed in blue. She noticed a tall man who was as handsome as unreachable, like a museum display. "He must have several girlfriends, but I never had a single boyfriend" she thought. She liked to sit on a bench, but she found them taken by fat women who invariably deposited their bags on their sides. A middle-aged man noticed her while she was looking for a place to sit down and stood up offering it. "He must have pity with me because I am a cripple" thought Missy and rejected the offer. Sometimes, she acted in a self-defeating manner. Did she want or did she not want to be capable of conversation with others? She should try at least! Being like everybody else was not in the cards.

She felt tired, bitter, and enraged. She was unable to stand her situation any longer. Nothing was going to change. She was impotent. Everybody would want to stay away from her for the rest of her accursed life. Her birth had been a mistake. Her father should have drowned her when she was a baby as he once did with newborn kittens. No more!

The train was approaching and could already be heard. Blinded by inner pain, Missy started walking between waiting people toward the edge of the platform. Her gaze was lost, her feet were moving by themselves.

"Hey!" What are you doing?" cried a strong man grabbing Missy's arm and drawing her backwards. "What were you going to do?" He looked into her eyes. The train came to a screeching halt and many standing passengers inside lost their balance and almost fell. The conductor jumped out of his cabin yelling "Ep, you! Are you crazy or stupid? What were you going to do? You know, I never killed anyone and have a family to feed. I must now write an incident report and some passenger may be hurt and I will be blamed. And these people need to go to work. Get lost and find another place!"

Missy noticed that everybody in the platform was looking at her. The unknown man who had pulled her back to life, lowered his voice "What you wanted to do was wrong. We are humans. We care about each other. You surely have somebody who cares about you and will be happy to see you again. Tomorrow everything will look different." People in the grocery store were possibly waiting for her to start her shift, she thought, but nobody really cared for her. What was the man talking about? She overheard hostile comments. A young man shouted, "Let her do it. She lacks the guts. It's all theater." Confused, angry, ashamed, desperate she turned her back to both men and felt observed by everybody. She started running toward the stairs. An elderly woman cried something about God loving her. And why had God made her a cripple?

She decided to walk to her job. *Food Delight* was one of the biggest supermarkets in town. Therein Annie had found her first permanent position two years earlier. She had been lucky to get one of the daytime regular jobs. She had been first assigned to the lowest entry level position replenishing empty shelves and printing and placing price tags. Her big boss, the store manager, was named Rudy Barnes and frequently could be seen walking in the aisles. He had a few times stopped checking on Missy, but he only smiled and continued his rounds. The woman had only been able to exchange a few words with him but knew that he enjoyed the reputation of being a fair person. Her main problem was that she was unable to reach the upper shelves and required help. Finally, she was moved to the bakery section, where among other activities she attended to special wishes of the clients. There were never complaints against her. But some employees reported privately to the manager that Missy was not attracting people to her counter and that the section did not meet the expected sales volume.

She did not want to go back to the subway station where people might have recognized her. She needed a while to calm down. While walking to work, she felt riddled and was incapable of concentrating. What did she want? What expectations had she? Had she really wanted to die or just tripped at the end of the platform?

At the end, she clocked her card at the store 20 minutes late. It had never happened before in two years. After changing, she rushed toward her workplace and was surprised finding an unknow woman carrying out her usual duties.

"Hallo. I am Missy. I know that I am late today. Have you taken my job?"

The new employee was clearly embarrassed and flabbergasted.

"Hi, Missy. I am Betty. It is my first day and I was told that you are moving to a different job. Maybe they would allow you to teach me a few things that I do not understand before you relocate. I am pleased to meet you."

The hunchback concluded that she had been fired. Maybe killing herself would have been the right thing to do. She had to go to the office and pick up her last check. She noticed, however, that Jerry, the bakery chief, was waving to her to approach.

"You are half an hour late," said the man. Only 20 minutes or less, thought Missy but she saw no point in arguing with him. He had never liked her. Who knows, maybe he was right. She was ugly like sin and had arrived 20 minutes late. No reason to keep her in the store. But Jerry was not finished:

"Missy, yesterday evening before going home Mr. Barnes called me and mentioned that he is going to reassign you. You must go to his office and talk to him."

"Reassign me? And he started a new woman in my old job?" thought Missy. "How am I going to find a new employer? Maybe I will have to go to a different subway station and try again."

Thinking that life is a bitch, she slowly walked toward the manager's office. She would take the opportunity to collect her last check. The secretary told her that in fact Mr. Barnes had been expecting her. She should just walk in. The boss was sitting in front of his computer screen and did not react when he heard somebody entering the office. Missy opened the conversation:

"Good morning, Mr. Barnes. I know that I was 20 minutes late because I had a problem, but it does not matter because I see that you have already replaced me. I know, I am so ugly that I scare the customers."

The man suddenly stopped his movements and turned around without rising from his chair until he faced Missy.

"I am glad to see you, Missy. Please sit down. I wanted to talk to you. I did not know that you had been late this morning, but I have been reviewing your file. Here it is. Unlike most employees, you had never been late in two years. Besides, you may have noticed that I frequently inspect and walk around in the store listening to the way how my people interact with the customers. You have always been among the best. You give reasonable and helpful answers."

Missy was perplexed. The exchange was followed by a brief silence. The manager broke it.

"Why did you think that I wanted to dismiss you? I give at least two or three written warnings before firing anyone for cause."

Missy lowered her eyes before answering.

"You are a kind and fair manager, but I know that your employment depends on you making money for the company. I am now 29 years old and I know how and how much people talk about people like me. A long time ago, freaks were hired by circuses, but not anymore. I cannot be good for business because clients do not look forward to meeting me again."

The manager crossed his arms and pushed his chair backwards to win space. "Do you know what you have just said, Missy?" He took the woman's file again in his hands to gain time to think what he wanted to answer. The hunchback visibly had tears in her eyes.

"You still have not explained why I would want to terminate your employment, which I don't. I do not know how to tell people face to face that they must accept and make the best out of things they cannot change. You seem to view yourself in a light that is wrong and exaggerated. The keyword in your job description is assistance to the customers and you are intelligent and offer it better than most others. And you have always been punctual, unlike many others."

Missy still could not answer.

"Now I finally understand what is wrong with you. Can you imagine another world where most females physically were to look like you and women like Marilyn Monroe were despised as monsters? Would a visitor from Mars think that women are beautiful? We learn as children what to appreciate or want and what to despise. You seem to believe that it is logical and rational to judge the value of people by their appearance and you are dead wrong. You should simply consider a career or position consistent with your condition. Do not forget to include in your CV your education and intellectual level. It is always possible to find something good and great in people. Your Curriculum tells me lots of important things. In High School you always brought home excellent scores and graduated among the best in your class. You are intelligent and resolve well all situations. I have seen that you feel duty-bound and are trustworthy. Why would I fire you?"

"You don't understand what it means to be like me. I look at my mirror and I see a misfit. It will stay that way for the rest of life." She could barely repress a wail and lowered her eyes. Mr. Barnes remained silent for a while.

"I do not see a misfit in this room. Do you have a talking mirror like in Snow White? You are too old for that tale and are neither the fairest nor the ugliest. What you are is a good and valuable employee. Self-pity has never resolved anything or helped anyone. Go to a therapist capable of teaching you how to face reality as it is and to work to make the best of it. In life everything is gray, almost never black or white. Like everybody, you have both, assets, and less favorable sides. Exploit your assets and learn to live with what you cannot change. Observing you in the store, I thought that you should smile more, or make little jokes and look at people in the eyes. The costumers always got what they wanted and left pleased."

For one moment, Missy felt that she was in the presence of the loving father she never had. She was not used to human kindness.

"I once overheard a child in the store telling his mother to look at my hump."

"As all our employees, you have a health insurance. Do you go to your doctors?"

"I always go to the same. He is patient, always listens to the same complaints and prescribes pain pills. He says that it is late to resolve my little blemish. My parents should have brought me to an orthopedist when I was a child."

"Look, Missy. I am going to reassign you to a different job behind the "Pastry and Sweets" desk, next to where you have been working, and you will even get a small rise because of your increased responsibilities. View it also as a reward for the excellent work you have performed. More than selling, you will be packing and, in some cases, mixing or cooking some of our offerings."

Missy, surprised, smiled. "You mean, I will be doing Maria's job? Is she leaving"?

"She is. She believes that she has spent too many years with us and wishes to move to the competition. I am sure that you can cook, but here you will have all the tools and the simple, exact recipes used in all our stores. It is easy, pre-cooked. When done, you must only pack and label it. There will always be at least a new girl helping you, more than one for the holidays, so you will be a supervisor."

For the first time in a long time, Missy felt illusioned. "Shall I become a pastry chief?"

Mr. Barnes laughed. "Not quite, you will do only easy routine work, but it would be a way of getting started. If you make of it a goal in life, you might well be capable of reaching it. I am sure. We all need realistic dreams and objectives. There may be openings in our central bakery, but they would probably expect some experience. Check out the public library. You will find books on pastry."

"Will I have to come out and talk to the customers?" Mr. Barnes shrugged. So what?

* * *

Missy thoroughly enjoyed her new job and frequently arrived ahead of opening time. Maria stayed another week and taught her how to fulfill the simple regular duties and a few tricks. She found herself for the first time in a position of a certain authority and supervised a senior employee and a beginner. No, she was not required to come out from the back and talk in person to the customers. She occasionally did it and explored with anxiety the client's expression. Mostly she recognized either surprise or compassion in their faces, but many were great: they seemed to completely ignore her appearance. The children, however, artlessly hiding behind their Mom, always revealed concerned interest. Messy was used to all of this. During her occasional contacts with the drivers and delivery men from headquarters, she inquired about pastry chiefs. The company employed a few. The drivers thought that some previous training was probably required to qualify, but it was never wrong to ask. They had seen gifted beginners on the job and the bosses would do anything to save money.

Missy never met Mr. Barnes in private again, but she would never forget their brief conversation. He had saved her life and given her some motivation to stay alive. Every time he passed by inspecting the store, stopped near Missy, and smiled without saying anything. She worked hard to avoid mistakes. She really did everything right.

Missy felt inside a new voice telling her that her life was going to change for the better.

She had finished filling containers with locally made cream and was placing them in the shelves when her work colleague approached her repressing a mild laughter.

"Look out, Missy, and you will see something you have never seen before."

Missy washed and dried her hands behind the counter. She saw nearby a young visionless man with a white cane walking an aisle in the company of a mature woman, who had picked up an apple and was guiding her companion on how to recognize it by palpation. The blind man clearly felt insecure and asked numerous questions. The woman was encouraging him. After this they moved to the pears and the scene was repeated. Missy first thought that the visit was without purpose, as the items lacked a braille level throughout the store, and it would be impossible for the man to come alone and push the cart toward the checkout. Even paying for the purchase would encounter difficulties. The guide must have known all of this, but she continued offering to the man items for identification and cheered every time he identified them right. What about packed food? Missy thought that it was not hygienical. How would he check the sealed cans? Or the plastic-wrapped vegetables? She noticed that the woman and her companion were heading toward her pastry counter and decided to stay.

"Here is where we buy the sweet things, but they come always wrapped" explained the unknown woman. "You know, things like cakes, pies or cookies. Any kind of dessert. "

Missy decided to be friendly. After all, the young man was a disabled person. "Hallo. My name is Missy and I am here to serve our clients. Is there anything special I can do for you? We have many good and delicious things."

The blind man smiled in Missy's direction, but it was the unknown guiding companion who answered:

"Oh, thank you. I am only helping my friend Fred. He has started living alone and I try to describe places and make him familiar with everything. Excuse me, I forgot something that I need for myself two aisles ago and I must go back. Would you stay here waiting for me for a moment, Fred? Maybe this nice lady would keep you company for a few minutes. Is it all right with you?"

Missy nodded in the affirmative. She had never talked to a completely blind person and smiled. He asked:

"How do you bake your cakes? Do you also carry pies?"

"Of all sizes! We rarely bake them here. The company owns a big place that takes care of almost everything. Here we only make small and easy things, to make sure that our wares look fresh."

A brief but pleasant conversation unfurled. Both discovered and discussed things that had never occurred to them. Did Missy think that it had made sense to bring him to the store? The man explained that all cans and items received at his home were labeled in braille. He was sure that his presence in the store resulted in a spectacle that exposed him to the curiosity of others. Missy understood well what the man was saying but she could not easily find arguments. She did not have any for herself. The young man explained how natural and important above most other things the desire to be independent was. He became upset in his room when he forgot how to find something he needed or fell bumping into furniture. In the school for the blind, they claimed that these things happen only at the beginning. Missy kept her thoughts to herself. She was in a tough spot and had concluded that wishing to be accepted and helped by everybody was an impossible and absurd dream, but maybe one might succeed in being liked by somebody. One of the things she most admired in blind people was their memory.

"There is no choice. Many times, we must count our steps. Talking about memory let me ask you something. Ms. Hassie mentioned while she was guiding me toward this counter that you are a hunchback. What is that, exactly? If you do not mind explaining, of course."

"A minor problem with my spine, which is not quite as straight as it should. Not a big deal" was the answer.

* * *

Missy kept thinking at home about her encounter with the blind man. She had always complained so much about her unsightliness, but blindness was surely worse. She remembered something that her mother had once told to her: if you feel that you, poor girl, are in trouble and suffering, turn your head and you will see behind you somebody who is worse off. How many years would her torture last? But blind people could live even longer. And they needed some continuous help, whereas she could live independently. At this point of her discourse, she remembered the image that she was seeing everyday in the mirror and everyday the answer was "You are the ugliest of them all." "Yes, I am ugly. No doctor could have healed that as little as blindness; maybe they belong together" she answered. At this point, she stopped her elucidations, heated up a frozen dinner and tried to find something entertaining on TV.

But the memory of the blind man kept coming back and she was unable to dismiss it. Fred was too young for her, but would she not be the perfect life companion for a man of appropriate age with this condition? That man would attentively hear her voice and ideas and appreciate good will, understanding, companionship and compassion. Nobody presently cared for the many benefits hidden inside that she was ready to offer. She would finally achieve something good in life, accomplish her destiny, be remembered by a family. Maybe that was why God had made her the way she was, to prescribe to her and preordain the way to rightly act.

But what about the touch? Did blind people recognize the difference between beauty and ugliness? Should she explain to the chosen man

that she was ugly? Did he have something to compare? What would
the man's family think or say?

What was worse, what people thought or what they said? Doubtless,
what they thought, because, while it would be kept secret, it guided
Their attitude, and a hostile family member could derail her good will.
The power and sincerity of talking is limited by social rules and it is
difficult or even dangerous to tell the truth. It might be necessary to
sit down a couple of hours with the family. How would the parents
and siblings view her? She suddenly noticed that she was considering to
seduce an unknow man. But...but... Who was taking about seducing?
She would simply introduce herself and offer help and companionship, which the man would certainly need, but nothing else. Well, if
something else happened... she would let it happen. What other choice
would she have in view of her limited charms?

The more and more she weighed her position and possibilities, the
more convinced she became that she had finally identified the sole goal
and purpose of her life. A doctor had insinuated that her existence (he
meant life expectancy) might be briefer that that of other people. One
more reason to go ahead, to fulfill her destiny while she was able to do
it. People who knew her would cherish her memory.

Now she needed to figure out how to start. And find a suitable
person.

* * *

Missy started scanning adds in the left-over newspapers from the
store's kiosk, but she never found a relevant one. How would she get
started? Maybe she could ask an eye doctor... if she knew one. One
evening she stopped at the neighborhood's library looking for books
on blind people and noticed that they had organizations and beneficial
societies. How would anyone approach them? It would not be easy

to describe her motivation and it might be misunderstood. Whom might she ask?

The internet, of course! Her call-in Wi-Fi connection was slow, but she managed to log in for a search. She easily found the names and addresses of institutions. Refining her search, she looked for places within a short distance of her abide, and she found two. Both claimed to help, offer training, and independent living accommodations for totally blind or visually impaired people. She read everything she could find and chose one of the two places for a visit. Should she make an appointment? No, the low-level people who answer phones can easily say NO and hang up without giving good explanations. She would go in person. She arranged to take a free afternoon.

The *House of Light* was an old six story building. Missy found a small bronze plate at the entrance that read *House of Light* in English alphabet and braille without additional text. The woman felt the braille with her fingers and concluded that braille was very difficult. She had walked past the building several times without noticing what it was. She opened the door and found herself in a lobby with a large reception area to the left labeled with a name also in common alphabet and braille. She entered and found a middle-aged woman inside behind a desk. "Was she blind?" thought Missy. Not quite, but she had to be somewhat impaired. She was using strikingly thick and unusual spectacles.

"Good afternoon, Madam. How can I help you?"

"Good afternoon. I live in the neighborhood and passing by your entrance, I have thought several times that maybe I could be of assistance as a volunteer."

"Oh, good. We don't get many volunteers except family members of our guests."

"I have some free time and enjoy helping. I just wanted to enter and inquire about the possibilities."

"Great. What do you have in mind?"

"I am quite open to suggestions. I am not familiar with your needs."

"What training have you received, or what is your profession?"

"I am a supervisor in *Food Delight*, the large grocery store. You may have heard from it."

"Oh, yes, I have even shopped there. What is it you supervise?"

"I am in charge of the pastry and dessert departments, and I also run when needed the bread and baking items section."

"I see. Well, considering this line of work, I am wondering how you could be helpful. What additional training or skills do you possess?"

"Some days ago, we were visited in the store by a very pleasant young blind man in the company of a lady and I had a conversation with the man. He was leaving his parent's home to live independently for the first time, and he was being trained by the woman. I was pleased to make his acquittance. I did not see of what practical use his visit to the store was, but the incident made me aware of the plight of the vision-impaired patients and I thought that I had enough time and the patience to help. I am sure that I can contribute to resolve unfilled needs."

The secretary or receptionist asked for more information about the visitors Missy had mentioned and hinted that she might know both. Was she interested in the sort of work the training companion performed? She answered:

"I appreciate your willingness, but this job requires extensive training and patience. The education of a new trainee requires many hours of work. It cannot be done in your spare time or only on the weekends for a limited time. Besides, I do not think that we have openings. Those are paid jobs."

"Could you suggest something else?"

The woman withdrew to the next room to make a phone call. She came back a few minutes later.

"I talked to our Director. He says that he can receive you. I will bring you to his office."

Both women took an elevator to the top floor. During the trip, the receptionist had a warning.

"You probably will have to sit and wait for him. Many of our residents walk into this office by themselves. If one comes into the room, you must speak to him and identify yourself immediately. Never grab anyone by the arm and attempt to guide without asking for permission first. If he really needs to be guided, you should touch his arm lightly, just to indicate where you are and he will grab you, never the opposite."

"I did not know that. Thank you for telling me."

Missy did not have to wait long. A gentleman entered the room. "Good afternoon. I am Herbert Gerhardt, Director of this Institution. I understand you wanted to talk to me."

"Yes, Sir. I am Missy Bru."

Both entered a nice, but sparsely appointed office room.

"As your secretary may have explained to you, I feel that I have both the interest and the time for being able to serve in some voluntary capacity."

"Mm. I see. Of course, we welcome volunteers. Why are you interested in vision-impaired people? Does anyone in your family or do yourself have eye problems?" The man inspected her curiously. Missy thought that he was considering her little hump. She noticed that she was sitting in a chair affixed to the floor.

"I lost my parents a long time ago and I have no other relatives. The answer is no. By chance I met at work a blind man under training and I noticed that my heartbeat accelerated. I thought that it would be noble to devote spare time to help these unfortunate beings."

Mr. Gerhardt raised his eyebrows. "Well, Miss Bru, if you really join us, you will discover that these persons do not think of themselves as poor, unfortunate crippled beings. They are men and women who have been able to overcome great obstacles. Well the opposite, they are proud of being able to enjoy an independent and rewarding existence despite being aware that they will need some specialized and skilled support. Good will alone does not make a good supporter. You would need training first and a thorough understanding of many things you are probably not aware of. You would have to learn how to go to the park only to feel the sunshine on your face rather than to enjoy the scenery. I do not know if my secretary mentioned it to you, but we have in the administration an office dedicated to fund raising manned by volunteers with good eyesight. They make phone calls, keep lists updated and send letters. You are educated and seem to speak well."

Missy hesitated without knowing what to answer. She was ready to work for free, but only in personal contact with a different victim of misshapenness, to help a man who may have been waiting for her without knowing. Something was clear to her. She wanted contact with a man, not a woman. She needed to answer Mr. Gerhardt without revealing her true intentions. Was anything wrong with that? She recognized that in general men seek women and not vice verse. Her approach was logical because of the circumstances. No movie star would ever look at her. She met all the expectations of a blindman's heart and her appearance could be ignored as irrelevant. This situation and her real objectives did not need to be discussed with anyone. Missy attempted a daring try:

"I hear you and I am certainly open to the suggestion, but in the meantime, I think that I might be able to connect with some previously trained person. He or she would teach me and would not need the opposite. It would be a matter of spending some hours together."

"You mean a superficial, social get-together of benefit to both of you."

"Sir, you are not blind and can image that despite my good character, I do not find it easy to enter social groups and play games with somebody else."

A long silence followed. Mr. Gerhardt crossed the arms in front of his chest and sighed. He was weighing the young woman's intentions and their legitimacy, not to mention ethical implications.

"Well, Missy, I must say that I fully appreciate your openness. I do not remember receiving a similar inquiry in the past. Let me think about it. Leave or send me a list of references. I will discuss your request with members of my board and will get back to you."

* * *

Missy considered her visit to the *House of Light* successful. She had not lied. There was nothing wrong with her expectations, which she had come so close to disclose in full. If she found a suitable blind man, he would potentially gain a true and helpful companion. She asked herself whether she would like to have a baby. The hump was not hereditary, but could a girl be as loathsome as her mother? It was too early to entertain such thoughts. Maybe it would be a boy, and men do not need to be pretty to make careers, earn money and have social friends.

It was indeed too early for such considerations, but they returned each night in her dreams. She felt close to achieving her goal and ameliorating her future life, possibly climbing to a higher social stratus. She had once seen a musical ending in a great choral song with loud, enthusiastic music. It still sounded in her ears. Every morning, still fired up by her nightly visions, she vivaciously greeted all her colleagues in the store. Some thought that maybe she was in love, which in a way was not far from the truth. Illusions are much more attractive and perfect than real humans. She was filling with hot air a wonderful balloon that was always rising toward heavens high above the boring level of worldly meanness, unjust opinions and irrelevant trifles.

The phone call arrived two weeks later in the evening. It came from the receptionist or secretary who had brought her to the Director's office.

"Mr. Gerhardt was pleased with your references. He has been considering your request and has decided that maybe you could be socially useful to some of our residents, especially to those who are experienced and already well trained. He expects you to meet one in the company of a professional trained guide. You can all go out for a walk in the neighborhood so that you understand how it works. Then, if you have the time, you might join them for a game in the apartment and some conversation. Will this suit you?"

"Very much so. Can you tell me his name?"

"We are considering two persons, but we have not mentioned anything yet to them. One would be a young lady more or less of your age, a very pleasant, well-mannered and independent resident whose interest is literature. She gets a spoken tape chosen by her in the mail every week and has a program that reads aloud from a computer screen."

Missy was as surprised as disheartened. "And the other one?"

"That would be a gentleman in his mid-forties who has been living with us for a number of years. He had a family when he lost the eyesight, but he soon realized that, although they tried and loved him, they could not and were not going to be helpful. If I am right, he has kept some extremely limited residual vision. He also reads and likes computers, but he has repeatedly complained to the staff of boredom. Sometimes he is a little impatient an even a bit harsh. He has been counseled by our social worker about his realistic options. He has tried a couple of the suggested jobs, but momentarily he does not have one. I believe that he writes."

"He possibly may be complaining about lack of pastimes. It sounds intriguing and I think I might be able to offer him some entertaining challenges."

"I'll tell Mr. Gerhardt then and he or somebody else will talk to the resident and let you know what he thinks. His name is Chuck. Do you usually have time on Sundays? In the morning or the afternoon?"

"Anytime on Sundays" answered Missy.

She had to wait two more weeks. This time the call came from Mr. Gerhardt himself. "Hi, Missy. As you wished, I have been talking to our resident Chuck Nelson about you and your unusual proposal. At first, he was dismissive. I warn you that he sometimes may sound a little abrupt. You should know that blind people are fierce believers in their independence and in the satisfactory fullness of their lives. I started to point out at trivial things that could be improved if he had a helpful friend. He is being assisted by a woman, Julia, who is our employee, and helps him buying and bringing food, that he cooks himself, matching the color of his clothes, fixing broken things or cleaning. She is good, we had her for a long time, but she must take care of several residents including one who is not yet fully trained, does not read braille well and has emergencies. Somebody capable of spending some additional time might be welcome. And yes, Chuck likes to play games and her assistant rarely has time. Would you be willing to meet him?"

Missy was overjoyed. "Of course, I would."

"Let me explain to you something else. As you had requested, we can arrange to do this on Sunday afternoon. It will be a walk in the neighborhood. Chuck masters the terrain perfectly by using his stick and has gone out many times alone, but this has limits. He makes it to the park two blocks away, but probably he would like to go further, even taking a bus, and he needs an assistant to learn and try this. Since our regular employee is usually not present on Sundays and I don't want to involve anyone else, I have approached Chuck's sister asking her if she would be available next Sunday at 1 PM and she agreed. After the walk you could return to the building to talk some more or do whatever Chuck proposes. Remember: always identify yourself when you arrive; if needed, you offer him your arm but never ever grab him without asking for permission first. If you need his attention, you may lightly touch his arm. Something particularly important: if you view an unevenness or a step on the ground, you must stop and let him examine it with his cane before going ahead or otherwise he could fall. Never contradict him if he claims that he does not need you."

* * *

Missy arrived at the *House of Light* ahead of 1 PM. She entered. The door of the secretary was closed. The elevator opened and a blind man with a white cane appeared. Missy remembered her instructions:

"Hallo. I am Missy. Are you Chuck?"

"No, lady. Not my name" and he left alone. Missy moved close to the door and observed how the man safely walked away. The weather was pleasant.

Next time the elevator door opened, a man also with a white cane, well dressed and very upright, appeared in company of a relatively young woman who evidently enjoyed eyesight. She took an inquiring look at Missy and seemed displeased. One second later, however, she offered her hand and introduced herself.

"Hello. I am Lucy Robbins. I suppose that you are Missy. This is my brother Charles Nelson, better known as Chuck."

Messy extended her hand, but realizing that the man did not see, she tentatively reached to touch his. Chuck brusquely turned around his hand to grab Missy's.

"I don't know why you are here, but I am glad to see you. I say "see" because I have a little sight left. I can recognize some light and movements, but you are welcome to say "see" to me as frequently as you wish. I understand."

Missy smiled, a little amused or perplexed, but Chuck loudly laughed. "Shall we go out for a little walk? I hear the weather is great." As for Lucy, she grinned and opened the door.

The three walked slowly. Chuck, evidently familiar with the terrain, walked alone. Missy noticed how he was counting his steps, but he safely stopped at the edge of the sidewalk. There was little car traffic, but any automobile would stop at the sight of a white cane. Hopefully.

Lucy explained that she had accepted to come because Julia, Chuck's regular caretaker, was not available on Sundays. She was usually busy with her husband and the two children, but she was pleased to have made an exception. Missy answered that she was glad to have met her, but Chuck said nothing. No easy conversation was developing. The hunchback, however, was curious. How was the relationship between that unpleasant woman and her unfortunate brother?

"How long have you been visually impaired?" asked Missy. Lucy, visibly upset, made signs with the two hands requesting an immediate change of topic. But Chuck intervened:

"Why are you moving your arms, Lucy? You remind me of Don Quixote and the air mills. Don't you remember that I can see movement?" He received no answer and he went on "Well, Missy, it was long ago but I started developing problems during my last two years in High School. My dad wanted me to become a physician like him, but it was not God's will. I was able to start College but did not make it to the first-year final exams. Dad was more disappointed than helpful. But I have been happy to develop a full and happy life."

Missy had a proposal "I do not know how far you come by yourself, but would you like to take a bus and go somewhere else, farther away? Maybe to a park?"

"Why not! Yes, I have been wanting to do that."

"The stop is across the street, some 10 or 12 steps to the left. The line number is 32, direction Auburn. Do you want me to guide you?" Missy extended her arm that was immediately grabbed by Chuck. Lucy did not look pleased but said nothing relevant. The group approached the edge of the walkway. Missy remembered her instructions and stopped at the edge without saying anything. Chuck immediately explored the floor with his stick and walked down to the road level. The play was repeated in reverse order at the other side of the street. The man turned to the left and started counting the steps. They were fifteen. It was Sunday and the bus of the line 32 did not arrive immediately. There was no bank to sit.

Missy noticed that Lucy appeared increasingly unhappy. Why? She decided to speak:

"Where did you grow up?"

"In Big Falls Township. It is a suburb. Do you know it?"

"Yes, yes. I may have been there one or two times. Did you go to school there?"

"Of course. They have a High School" answered a scoffing Lucy. "Our Dad ran a big medical practice."

"Oh, well" answered Missy. "We lived in the city, but we were a modest family. I could attend a good Catholic School, though. I find a good education is important."

It was Chuck's time to scoff. "They did not teach braille in ours."

Finally, the bus arrived. Missy thought that the driver had seen Chuck's white cane because he stood up ready to assist the blind man boarding. The three passengers sat together with Chuck between the women. Again, no interesting conversation developed. Lucy inquired where and in what capacity Missy worked. She listened to the answer with an inscrutable facial expression. She clearly was not pleased.

The bus was almost empty. The driver announced that the next stop was Riverside Park. The tercet descended and walked toward the water. The weather was truly splendid with a mildly chilly breeze and Chuck for a moment looked, smiled to the sunshine, saw light, and sounded happy.

"I have been trying to come back to this place many times. Are there any flowers?"

"If you wish, I will help you to come here as frequently as you wish. I know well this park. And... There are still few flowers. It is not quite the season."

"I knew. I would have smelled them."

"Tell me, Chuck. How do you spend most of your time in the apartment?"

Chuck shrugged. "There are many things I can do. I can play tapes, I read a sort of newspaper in braille, I listen to music or radio, I go outside for a walk. Sometimes I write articles that have been published. I have domestic chores to do, like everybody else. Dr. Gerhardt's office sends us circulars. They have in the office a big braille printer."

"Then you must always be busy."

Lucy looked at Missy with contempt but did not comment. She was giving her the silent treatment.

"Can you cook?"

"I sure can. An assistant delivers the stuff labeled in braille and I can do things like boiling, microwaving, seasoning, even frying in a pan. But I also get sandwiches. Only easy stuff."

"Except for the braille labels it is not hugely different from what I do. Do you like sweets? I could bring you something from work."

Lucy inhaled air into the nose and warned:

"Watch out, Chuck. There are stones to your left and the floor is uneven."

They had to return after only one hour because Lucy needed to go back home to bring her children to a music lesson. She was unable to accompany Chuck to his apartment because she was late, but he did not need help for that. She took her leave at the *House of Light* entrance, kissing the man on the cheek and shaking hands with Missy.

After some hesitation, Chuck asked Missy to enter and join him for some chat inside. The community had a large social room on the ground floor. Missy went along but she thought that the walls were dull-brown and had not been painted for a long time. There were few garnishments. The window was relatively large, but some lamps were available. The chairs were big, old, and ugly but amazingly comfortable.

Chuck loudly inquired if somebody was there. Nobody answered. He safely advanced toward two chairs near a club table and signaled to Missy to sit in one in front of him.

"I wanted to thank you for coming, Missy. It was a great afternoon.'

"Thank you for telling me. I am a lonely young woman always interested in contributing social service. I have thinking about it and that is why I came to speak to Mr. Gerhardt."

And she repeated a lie "I had been considering it for a long time."

"Although I am very independent and really do not need anything I do not have, I could imagine some advantages and improvements to be gained from a sincere friendship. I am not talking about obstacles, because these have been taken care of. What do you have in mind"?

"Nothing in particular. I was hoping that I could offer something you identify as missing. The trip to the Riverside Park was an example, but we can discuss anything you want. I am available almost every Sunday."

"Well, Missy, I see that you are a very educated woman. Do you play chess? I can scan text in English letters and have the computer read it to me, but it is not perfect. Maybe you could scan a few things for me, or read to me something or describe images."

Missy was joyous to hear that Chuck wanted to meet her again. They exchanged phone numbers. Chuck would memorize hers and print it later. They would meet again next Sunday afternoon.

* * *

Early in the following morning, Chuck's phone rang in his apartment. He retrieved it easily. It was his sister Lucy.

"Did you get rid of that horrible woman yesterday?"

"What are you talking about? Missy was kind and intelligent. We had a brief conversation and we'll meet again next weekend."

"When Gerhardt called asking me to come yesterday, he failed to mention that she was a hunchback, ugly and small."

"Really? I could not see much of her, but these attributes mean little to me, as you probably know. I liked the way she talked and her wish to help me and possibly become my friend."

"Don't you have your assistant Julia, me, my husband and children for friends?"

"I have all of this but when I still lived with Mom and Dad in our old house, you were of help only for brief periods of time when you had nothing else to do and now it is the same."

"I am terribly busy raising my children, but we come to visit you and I call and if you need something we are always here."

Chuck smiled to himself contemptuously.

"Do you remember how I asked you to learn some braille to help me?"

"I meant to, but it is difficult. It will take time, but I will do it. I know the essentials."

"You will have to show me sometimes."

"I had to warn you because we don't know what this Missy really wants. She has a miserable job in the grocery store"

"I will ask to bring me there."

"Try to find out what she knows about the endowment that dad left to you. Maybe she has smelled money."

"Dad left it to me and not to you. For now, it allows me to live decently but it is not a lot of money to be smelled for profit."

"My husband makes enough money for my whole family. I need nothing. But you watch this woman."

"Thank you for calling. She was not ugly for me. When are you going to have time to bring me to the Residence to talk to Mom? She never picks up the phone."

"She is all right."

* * *

Missy called Chuck on Friday to make sure that the Sunday appointment or date was still on. It was the first time.

"Of course, I remember" answered Chuck. "We shall meet at 1PM in the lobby, like last time."

"Is your sister also coming."

"No, she is always too busy. Last time she came only to meet you."

"Did she like me? She did not talk much."

"Because she never talks much. It is the same when we go somewhere together. I don't care whether she does or does not like somebody. She never likes anyone."

"But she has two children and a husband. I am sure she loves them."

"Maybe, because they never dare to talk back."

On Sunday, Missy arrived ten minutes too early. She was joyous when Chuck appeared almost at the same time. She made her presence known. Should she hug him as young men and woman frequently do? No, too early. Besides Chuck did not expect it and might think that he was being under attack.

"If you like parks, I could bring you today to the Duck Park. There are many nice walkways and probably still some flowers and on Sundays it is full of families with children. We need to take a different bus and the next stop is a few blocks away."

"That will be great. I need some exercise. Just show me the way. Do you think that the flowers will smell?"

On the way to the bus stop Missy was tense, concentrating on guiding the man and preventing mishaps. She was so worried that she could not sustain or initiate any conversation. Finally, they climbed into the bus and a passenger immediately made a seat available. Missy began to relax.

The weather was again truly radiant, pleasantly warm. The couple was surrounded by families with children. Chuck could hear their voices. One asked her mother why that man was wearing a white cane. The answer was that he was blind and was in the company of a nurse.

"You said that you developed your vision problems when you were in High School."

"Yeah. And my dad who was a physician did not take it seriously at the beginning. Me neither. After a few months, I started complaining about serious problems reading and playing at school and he brought me to an ophthalmologist. I did not understand what he said but Dad was clearly upset, and he brought me again to another one in his Hospital. He told me not to worry and added for the first time that I would be a great physician like him. He had never said that before and his voice sounded unusual. He actually had meant that I would never be a physician."

"Did you get a treatment."

"Sure, many, but it got worse and worse and finally most of the light went off. I can still see some and movement of shadows, which is not much, but I wouldn't want to lose it."

After a while, Chuck carried on:

"I stayed home. Sure. I could even register in a modest College near our home, but I had to quit after a few months. My parents at first were supportive and they enrolled me in a school for the blind. It was located far away from our home, though. My mom wanted to move closer, but dad said that he did not like the school's neighborhood. One of the two first and later Lucy had to bring me in by car and pick me up in the afternoon every day and I know that they did not like it. Except for mom, Lucy and dad had other obligations. Many days I had to wait a long time for the car. Some days in the morning my dad called a cab to bring me to the school and prepaid the fare. I already was able to walk from the car to the entrance. Some drivers offered to assist me, but they always grabbed me without permission. Then there was the story with the braille. Somebody in our home should learn braille too, but all found it too difficult. I tried to convince Lucy, but she did not have the patience. He learned only a little."

He again made a pause, that Messy did not interrupt.

"My dad was watching sports on TV all the time. I sat next to him and asked him to describe the events. Why were people crying? He tried a couple de times, but I noticed that he did not want to be disturbed and his explanations and comments were short and not helpful. I was no longer a joy to my parents, just an unpleasant burden. Or a disappointment. Only my mother and Lucy were understanding and tried to help me but didn't know how. I had learned to move around in the house by myself and found most items I needed but my father did not pay attention and misplaced many things. One day I couldn't find my little radio receptor although I knew exactly where I had left it. It was especially important to remember the exact resting places of my items, as I had learned in school. It turns out that dad had taken it and put it in a drawer. I was so upset that I was in tears and started complaining to him. He loudly answered that he was in his home. He would buy me anything I needed but he could not be responsible for me all the time. I remember that I cried a lot. He suddenly died of a heart attack. I remember how I felt touching for the first time the cold face of a deceased human. I recognized his traits, but the coldness felt very strange. Shortly after the funeral, I told mom that it would be better for me to move to a residence for people like me. Two years later she herself left our old home for a suitable Residence. Whenever Lucy says that she has time, we visit her together. Like good siblings, Lucy and I fight all the time, but she really cares about me and she is the only one who fully accepts what I am. I can and have had a few times a paid occupation, hardly sufficient to make a living. There are places which hire people like us, as all social workers explain, but these are horrible jobs. A well-educated man expects something better."

In an unexpected way Chuck had opened himself to a stranger. Missy understood, or at least believed to have. Chuck was also an innocent reject of society like herself. She felt hope rising in her chest. They would work together to heal their pain and score a victory over a cruel and unjust world.

"I appreciate that you have explained to me all this, Chuck, and I think that now I know you better."

"What about you?"

Yes, what about Missy? What was she going to explain? That she was an ill-proportioned and ugly adult woman, with a good brain, but desperate to find understanding, warmth, and companionship in this world? That she had come begging friendship?

"It is a complicated story and I will tell you, but our bus runs on an hourly schedule and if we fail to catch the next one, we'll have to wait for a long time."

"Let us go to the bus stop then. If you still have no other engagements, we could carry on this interesting conversation in my building."

Yes, thought the woman, that was what she wanted. She would have extra time to prepare her story. She concentrated on the issue during the entire return trip. She did not want to lie but proper embellishment is one of the necessary resources that make social life pleasant and promote friendship. Consider for instance a painter on the job improving the color scheme of an apartment. She had to think...

Chuck invited her again to join him in the *House of Light*'s building reception. It did not go well because Chuck immediately heard the voices of two individuals using the room. After some hesitation, he lowered his voice to make a different proposal:

"Sorry, Missy, but as you can see, we would not be by ourselves. Would you be willing to come to my apartment for a while? I know, one should not invite a woman."

Missy stopped him "Of course I would be willing." She laughed. "We are both of age."

"People sometimes are foolish and talk about things that are neither true nor a concern of theirs. I have no hidden intentions; I only need a place to sit down and carry on our pleasant private conversation a little longer. I enjoyed the afternoon."

Missy did not like the small apartment, nor the color of the walls. Everything was orderly and appeared to be in a fixed, easily reachable place. There were two large, comfortable chairs in the center of the room placed around a large working and eating desk with instruments. In a corner, a small open door led to a second minute room, clearly a bedroom. She recognized a walk-in closet without door, a medium-sized computer with an unusual keyboard and a music player with a loudspeaker. Upon entering, Chuck placed his white cane in a container on the left of the apartment door. He knew exactly how much he had to lift the stick to exactly hit the mouth of the container. He had a second cane in reserve. The woman thought that she would not like to live there but maybe it all suited Chuck perfectly.

Missy re-opened the conversation trying to stay away from what they had come to discuss.

"How come you don't have a service dog?"

"Oh, I have been trying for a long time. A puppy that might be available for me is being raised and trained. They say that I should go there soon to meet it and get acquainted. It is expensive but it may last more than 10 years. It would make it possible for me to walk much further away. In the meantime, as you can see, I have a nice apartment and everything I need. What about you? Do you have an apartment?"

"Yes. It is a studio in an old building about the size of this place. It is very convenient. I even know some neighbors, in particular Mabel, who has a small child and lives next door. She is black."

"It makes no difference to me. Do you have family?"

Her father had run away because he was disappointed with the daughter that he found home every evening. He frequently came home intoxicated and had beaten her mom. Missy was afraid of him and lied, which was a straightforward way of reconciling herself with her past.

"My father died while working in another city and we never knew what had happened. I stayed with my mother who was a lovely woman and constantly gave me advice. I could enroll in an excellent Catholic High School in the neighborhood thanks to a stipend. Then mom was diagnosed with cancer and died leaving me alone. I don't know whether I have relatives or not."

"It must have been a great school. I noticed how well you speak. It will be a magnificent pleasure to talk to you from time to time. Can you stay for a little board game?"

* * *

Missy and Chuck continued meeting regularly for several months. They went to parks, to a concert and the man finally learned how to find and use the city bus. One time the bus came late, and Chuck grew so impatient that Missy used her phone to call a cab. He was just too tired and explained that he carefully considered the distance he walked to avoid feeling too tired on his return. Missy noticed that Chuck could be irritated and raise his voice when something displeased him. Missy had learned to describe the place and scenery, but Chuck had interrupted her a few times. He did not care about what she was saying but he craved the warmth of sunshine and the breeze in an open space.

They frequently returned to Chuck's room. Missy considered inviting him to hers, but she thought that there was no point to be made. Should she limit her visits to Sundays, or should she extend them to a weekend afternoon? She was sure that at work she could trade a weekday for a Saturday. Was it time to attempt a move forward?

Missy thought in increasingly unrealistic terms about his relationship with Chuck. She memorized, reviewed, and attempted to interpret every single word he had spoken. Things were going well, she concluded. Many evenings she watched TV from her bed, and she envied the characters shown. They lived in rational family and friendship relationships and were able to conduct serious conversations on matters of interest, but nobody talked to her about anything that was not work. She admired the frequent happy ends. Why was such an outcome unavailable to her? She was sure that most women experienced it and that she was being deprived of what was her human right.

While she was entertained by such promising thoughts, the telephone was ringing in Chuck Nelson's apartment. The caller was again his sister Lucy.

"Hi, Bro. How are you doing?"

"I am still blind."

A brief silence followed.

"Chuck, you are becoming a terrible man. Do you also bite?"

"Only to people who try to penetrate the depth of my eternal darkness." And he laughed.

"I'll stay away from that, then" answered Lucy. "Listen, next Sunday we have time and the entire family is planning to visit mom in her community. Would you care to join us?"

"Oh, sure. I was missing Mom. In recent weeks I have been going for walks and discovery trips with Missy. You may remember her."

"I sure do, but I don't want her with us on Sunday."

"Would you care to explain why?"

"You don't see her. I do not mean to sound cruel, but she is mishappen. She has an insignificant job in her store, just like a plain worker. I went and saw her discreetly the other day. But when she speaks, she sounds conceited and very self-secure."

"I get very bored on Sundays and appreciate some company. She is very well educated. I'll start watching her to discover, imagine and enjoy the marvelous attributes you describe."

"I wish you would take it seriously. I do not want her to meet mom. I don't know what our mother would think or assume. She cannot always think straight."

Chuck did not answer, but his sister carried on:

"Let me tell you something else. You are a grown up now. One of these days, she is going to try to go to bed with you if she has not done it already. She probably cannot find anyone else."

"She would be one of the many sexy women who solicit me every day. Come on, you are insulting her and me. She has not done anything to you, and what you are hinting at is none of your business. You have never bothered to show me new accessible parts of town like she has, and she gets nothing out of it."

"Are you going to come with us or not?"

Chuck did not have to consider her sister's offer for a long time. He had Missy's phone number stored and dialed it. A delighted voice full of illusion answered.

"Hi, Missy. I am calling because I have a change of plans for next Sunday. My sister is going to visit my mother, with whom I have not spoken for a long time and I would like to go along. I miss her. She is old and rarely picks up the phone."

"I see. Would it be possible for me to join the group and meet your Mom?"

"It would be great but this time it is impossible. It is a long car trip and Lucy's car is small. We are going with her husband and two children and there is no room inside for more than five people."

* * *

Time went by and passed as it always does, sometimes slowly and other times dizzyingly fast. Missy was running out of novel places to find for her Chuck and she was not experiencing the search with the same interest. Did it matter to Chuck where they went? He could not see the scenery, the lakes, the floral trees. They could simply go to the nearest place with sunshine and flowers every time. Maybe it would be easier if she owned a car. Would it be? Maybe they could go and visit his mother. He had never wanted to talk about her again.

She had been able to obtain some free afternoons from the store. One time, however, she had to renounce to her salary for the day.

It did not matter, but she got nothing out of it. Chuck was in a bad mood. It was not the first time. Missy had tried to calm him down but achieved the opposite. He had been listening, that is reading from the computer, but the voice rendering was deficient, and he felt irritated. He took several pages of braille text, but he soon discarded them. He always placed previously used items very carefully, to be able to retrieve them, but this time he was not successful, and the sheets fell to the floor. Missy rushed to pick them up, but she collided with Chuck's arm. The man loudly showed displeasure and pushed Missy's hand away. He did not want Missy interfering with anything he was doing. Missy did not know what to do or to say. "I will tell you when I need something" he added.

It was his first outburst in Missy's company and Chuck had scared her. Realizing this possibility, he smiled and invited the woman to play a game on one of his special table boards. She agreed, but it did not amuse her much because she found the pieces too big and the plays too slow and easy to evaluate for a person with vision. Chuck, however, needed time to figure out by palpation Missy's moves.

Earlier, she had been considering the possibility of giving her friend a hug or even a kiss on the cheek to further develop their relationship but there had been no chance. She deeply sighed. She left for home early. On her way back she thought that both had a difficult day. She remembered fights between her parents, the only role models she had. They cried and pushed each other. Furthermore, she had to learn a lot to be able to penetrate the world of a blind man and anticipate his needs. She was not quite there yet, but she would achieve it. The woman smiled thinking of her friend's face. She liked serious men with a superior air. It was so sad to be disabled and need other people. She knew from her own experience. It had not been such a dreadful day after all.

Next Sunday, on her way to the *House of Light*, she was wondering about Chuck's mood. Had he maybe received sad news from his elderly mother? She would ask. A blind woman coming from the basement was already in the elevator. Missy remembered the requirement of introducing herself at once.

"Hallo. I am Missy and I am headed for Chuck Nelson's apartment."

The unknown woman smiled

"Chuck is really a great guy. Isn't he?"

"Yes, I like him too" confessed Missy.

"Are you being sent by the administration to help him with the computer problem?"

"No, we are personal friends. I am no computer expert."

Upstairs, the man appeared to be well humored.

"Hi, Chuck!" said Missy. "I rode the elevator with a young woman who said that you are a great guy and she knew about your computer troubles."

"What is her name."

Missy was embarrassed to recognize that she had not asked.

"She must have been Lisa from the fourth floor because I had mentioned the computer to her. She has the same set-up and it works perfectly, but we are unable to deal with this kind of problems. She invited me to come up to her place with my tape and listen to a few chapters, which we did together. Afterward we had two little wine drinks."

Missy immediately felt jealous. He had never offered her a drink. Chuck wanted something else:

"Tell me what is the color of my shirt? I spent time looking with my little bit of vision and thought that it is red."

"It is bright red."

"That's what I was afraid of. I have spent the week wearing a blue light jacket. It must have looked horrible, but Julia did not warn me."

"I will find another one" And she entered his bedroom.

"Chuck, I found a grey and a white shirt. Which one do you want?"

"Pick your choice. I don't see any difference."

Missy was jubilant over this answer and chose the grey one. Chuck, before entering his room to change noted that the red shirt, which he would never have selected, had been a gift from Lucy. To spare himself such problems, he said, he wanted that all his clothing, weather purchase of gift, be of the same color. Missy smilingly offered to go to a clothing store, and she would help him.

"Another day, Missy. Stores are crowded on Sunday. Too many people think we the blind are curiosities and they gaze."

* * *

On that day, they had agreed that the woman would teach and explain to him how to reach the entrance to a second residence for vision-deprived people within walking distance. Chuck's original trainer had not done it apparently because of the existence of at least three construction sites. Missy's good judgment had left her because it had heavily rained the preceding evening, and she failed to report the soil's condition to her companion or to draw any consequences. She worried only about a near intersection with the traffic light flashing in yellow. How would she explain that and what action would she recommend? What could a disabled blind person do about blinking lights? It was a puzzle.

She was walking alongside Chuck. His arm was placed inside the woman's, and he completely relied on and followed her guidance. Suddenly the man tripped, attempted to regain his balance assisted by his stick and ended with both hands in a mudpuddle and with the stick lost, in the remote world outside of the man's reach.

Chuck was silent but very upset. Missy, even more distraught, was breathing heavily. Chuck had raised from the floor, his clothes soiled, while Missy had retrieved the stick and was attempting to clean and remove the mud. Her heart was beating fast. What had she done wrong? She was terrified. A passer-by stopped to offer help. Not needed, thank you. "It was my fault" explained Missy to the stranger. Chuck, enraged, was thinking the same thing.

"Did nobody explain to you how to guide a blind person? When there is an obstacle on the ground, you are supposed to bring the arm to your back and I would have moved behind you and followed you step by step. It was an unexpected fall and now I am dirty and could have been hurt. It is a matter of common sense and responsibility! If you don't know how to do something, do not offer to do it."

"It rained a lot yesterday and you slipped over a little puddle with some mud, which I had not noticed."

"I do not believe you. You had noticed but it did not occur to you that it was dangerous to me."

Missy could not repress her tears. She moaned:

"How can you say that! Please forgive me. I have learned my lesson. It will never happen again."

Chucks facial expression remained hard, unfriendly, unforgiving.

"Let's go back home. I need to clean myself and change my clothes. I feel that my pants are wet."

The way back was silent. Missy made an extra effort to avoid a new incident. In the lobby of the House of Light, Chuck suddenly announced "Thank you. From here I can do by myself. Goodbye" And he took the elevator.

Missy reached her apartment and started crying again. First, she felt dumb, clumsy, useless, and undependable. She feared to have jeopardized, maybe lost her relationship with Chuck. Why did he not show more understanding and tolerance? Nobody is perfect and she had spent many hours trying to help him but was not being rewarded with gratitude. After all, the accident had not been so serious. Nobody was hurt. He was harsh and punitive, like her father had been.

She tried to sleep but could not. All dreams and expectations of being able to reach a more acceptable existence were already associated with Chuck, and she knew of no alternative. He was a serious and handsome man, more than her father. Men have a way of being loud and tough and Chuck had good sides. She would try to be more careful next time. She decided not to call him that evening.

But she called the following Thursday at noon. Could they meet again? What about having lunch together? She would bring two sandwiches and soda drinks. Missy felt hesitation in his voice, but he surprisingly answered in the affirmative. Missy again asked to be forgiven for the past incident and Chuck responded that it was forgotten.

Was it? The woman entered the apartment joyfully laughing. She had meant to smile but remembered that Chuck would not notice.

"Look, I brought four fantastic chicken tacos."

"All the same? Quite frankly, I don't like chicken too much. And the Mexican stuff is too hot for me."

Missy was taken aback. The reason she did not bring more variety is that the tacos were unsold, and she got them cheap. She felt dumb. "These tacos are not hot unless you pour in the sauce in these little plastic bags. It is true that they are made of chicken, but it is ground and mixed with cheese and tastes differently. I also brought two pastries from my department. I was hoping you would like it."

"I would but I am used to the kind of stuff that my assistant Julia brings me every week. I know that you do not read braille but go to the left pantry and get some boiled rice and one egg and heat it up for me. Everything is open. Just heat it up in the microwave oven."

Missy felt a little offended but pleased that Chuck would entrust her with the responsibility of cooking for him. Caring for somebody was one of the things that she wanted to do her whole life. She found several cans, all of them labeled in braille. She opened several and finally found boiled white rice. In the refrigerator there were some middle-sized eggs and sauce bottles.

"I got the rice. What about the eggs? How do you want them?"

"Is there a choice? They are all boiled. Just remove the shells. They won't hurt my teeth" the man sarcastically answered.

Missy laughed loudly. "Well, if you want, I can learn all of this in time. One can figure out whether an egg is raw or boiled by spinning it. I could also bring you fresh fruits and vegetables from my store."

"Thank you, but I need all of this every day."

Missy bit her lips and did not answer.

Chuck was not in a good mood. He said that his sister Lucy had upset him on the phone, but he would not go into the details. At least he had seemed to enjoy the dessert. Missy ate her two sandwiches and decided it best to leave early. More would follow on better days. She had much to learn.

Missy could not meet the man the following weekend. He had decided to join a group of residents and attend services in a certain Church, to be followed by lunch and a small concert. They had a little bus for transportation.

Missy had fallen victim to suspicions that Chuck might no longer like her. But she would persevere, it was only a matter of getting used to his roughness and tantrums. It was difficult to enter the mind of a disabled person. Was this not the way it was with her? She knew that she was different, and that people disliked her and that she was unable to get out of the tangle. Chuck was probably quite different when talking to other blind people because their problems were shared and he did not desire to lock horns with others under the same predicament. Besides, everybody respects the visionless and nobody laughs at them. Missy was not always able to understand him. She was going to try harder.

She came to the next meeting again full of illusions and happy expectations. Missy was ready to pay attention and work. She had brought again some sweets. She found Chuck as always in his living room listening to a recorded book. He had been smiling but did not look happy when he noticed the hunchback entering his apartment. He stopped the playback.

"Hello, Chuck! Did you have lunch already? If so, we could eat together some delightful cranberry and blueberry pie that I brought. You had mentioned that you liked berries."

"Alright" said Chuck smiling. "Bring them here and get a small spoon for me."

A spoon? She did not know how or where the man kept them. Everything looked so different in the kitchen. Nothing was loose on the bench.

"Tell me where the silverware is, and I will bring it to you."

"What? You don't know where to find it?" Chuck stood up. He never used the cane at home. He took two steps to his left from the chair where he had been sitting and walked straight to a drawer hidden in the bench. He found it immediately. Missy was forced almost to jump away to avoid a collision. "Here they are my spoons. Do you need one too? What about dishes? Don't touch the dirty ones. I prefer to handle them later."

Missy sat next to Chuck to consume her snack. The man appeared pleased. She attempted to start a conversation. Was Chuck interested in politics? Did he vote? Yes, sometimes, a method existed and they enjoyed special assistance. Everybody had the right to vote. He would not mind telling her for what party he voted, but blind people did not get any electoral ads. It was only a make-believe game for him, although he recognized that it was the same for every individual citizen. His sister Lucy said that the Republicans are always better. Missy explained that she always looked-for third-party candidates. Chuck was entertained.

Next, Missy inquired about the religious service, but Chuck only shrugged. It had only been a way of doing something else. He did not care much about sermons, which in his view were always too long. And always about the same."

Missy laughed and nodded in agreement adding "Yes."

Did Chuck plan to spend his entire life in the *House of Light*? He answered with a shrug. His options were sort of limited. It was a "wait and see" game.

Missy brought up her key proposal for the next encounter, which in her mind was a date. Would next Sunday be all right? Sure, it would.

Missy spent days thinking about ways of deepening the relationship to her friend, which was becoming a more and more principal issue in her life. Should she become bolder and directly address the issue explaining to Chuck the nature of her growing feelings? Sometimes the man looked serious and unapproachable. She had to wait for an opportunity, for an occasion when he looked happy. Both were crippled, although in separate ways, both cruel and difficult to bear individually. They would make each other's misfortunes supportable and stay together never minding the world's opinions. The planned union would be a win-win for both. She spent the week planning her approach and felt sure of her success. Did women frequently solicit men? She laughed at the thought. Only when the anticipated lover deserved it!

The much-expected Sunday arrived. Missy provided herself with desserts and even with a little bottle of sweet wine to celebrate her entrance into womanhood.

Chuck was not good-humored and did not receive her with joy.

"Are you Missy? Do you remember what you did in my apartment, I repeat: in MY apartment, last Thursday?"

"Hello, Chuck. What is it? What did I do?"

"You moved the chair where you were sitting and left it on the way I always use to go to my kitchen. I bumped and knocked it, lost my balance, and fell to the floor. I hurt my left leg and my right arm, which are still hurting."

"I am so sorry. I must not have paid attention."

"Indeed, you did not, because not being blind you do not understand how important these things are. I always need to feel safe and at home. You disturbed my peace."

Chuck had spoken loudly in an almost menacing tone. Missy was shocked and close to tears.

"I am deeply sorry, I apologize, there are so many things around you I do not understand yet. Please do not raise such a fuss. I meant well."

Chuck briefly altered his facial expression upon hearing these words. But then he resumed his string of reproaches.

"Then you changed the settings of my radio and I could not listen to my usual station in a different wavelength. I had to give up listening and had to wait until somebody could come to help me next morning."

"I am so sorry."

"I bet you are. There is more of your mischievous and disorderly conduct. You left the two dessert dishes on the bench, I touched them without knowing, one of them fell to the ground and broke. The other one was smeared with food and I had to wash my hands. You claim that you want to help me but look at the things you do to make me furious."

After this outburst, Missy was so terrified that she was unable to speak.

"You know, Missy, I understand that you wanted to help me pass the time, but it takes a lot of learning and experience before you are able to do it in an acceptable manner. With my sister Lucy it was the same. Finally, we were tired of each other and had to separate."

The unexpected direction of the talk was scaring Missy.

"If I knew how, I would drop on my knees asking again to be forgiven and you would notice the tears in eyes. I understand what you are saying but I tried to be good to you in good faith. I will keep trying until I succeed."

Chuck raised one of his eyebrows.

"Maybe it is more complex that you think. My Mom and Lucy are the only people who really tried what you mean and both failed. Lucy always was complaining about the braille. She was unable to learn it beyond a few essentials and claimed that her fingers were not sensible enough to identify with certainty the position of the dots. When we were together in the same room, she tried watching and weighing every movement she did as to avoid disconcerting me. She sounded upset every time I tripped or failed to locate one of my items. We started fighting and sometimes our Mom had to intervene. Lucy complained that she was trying her best, sacrificing her social life because of me and that I was ungrateful. We agreed on staying completely out of each one's room. It did not work, because from time to time I need assistance. After Dad passed away, I saw the writing on the wall. No, it was not in braille, but it was telling me loud and clear to move away. I had never expected that Lucy would give up her life to help me. I learned to socialize only with my equals."

Missy had listened in painful anxiety. Chuck was revealing to her emotional episodes of his life and personal family history. It should have been a good sign, but he was projecting his past negative experiences with well meaning caretakers on her. Missy falsely interpreted Chuck's opening as a green light and decided to act boldly. She planted a brief kiss on Chuck's cheek. The man, surprised, stiffened his back.

"What was that Missy? Did you give me a kiss? I never authorized it. Except for my Mom, I do not remember anyone ever kissing me. I cannot interpret your meaning."

Missy swallowed hard, lowering her head.

"I only wanted to express how deeply I value our friendship and how far I am willing to go to make your life easier."

"Do you want to make my life easier? Ha! What about yours? Lucy told me that you are a hunchback. You never talk about your friends. Do you have any? Why are you here? Do you believe that because I cannot see I can be manipulated as if I were mentally retarded? Do you believe that because we are both disabled you would obtain from me an attention that nobody else is willing to dispense on you?"

Now the woman was openly crying and was almost unable to formulate her thoughts.

"Chuck, why do you talk this way to me? Being a hunchback has created a problem between me and the entire world. I grew up and nobody let me forget it for a single moment. My father hated me, my mother did not, but she lamented my existence. Why so? I was a good kid, I brought home good scores and was willing to accept everything as it is. I was the only one excluded, all others were in. I started thinking, but I could not figure out what to do. Is it not so that many humans can demonstrate their value by working well and acting like decent humans? I was judged by my appearance, not by my deeds, no matter what I did. If my parents had had a health insurance, maybe a doctor could have helped me and I would not be a hunchback now, but I never found in my entourage anyone willing to help me. Some people tolerated me despite my disgrace, but nobody loved or was willing to help me. Why do they teach to children that all humans are equal?"

"Missy, I believe I understand your personal tragedy and I am sorry. I know well that many must carry a cross and that there is no way out.

It does not explain, though, why you came here. I can only accept in my surroundings skilled and trained helpers. You were right thinking that your physical appearance would mean nothing to me. I am a grown man and I am not so naive that I would not have understood what your target and expectations were. You are an intelligent woman. I would accept your intentions and the implied proposal as reasonable and it does not offend me even as I reject it. I am even proud of having caught your eye, but in considering the probable consequences, I must remember the negative evolution of my family's attitudes. At the beginning, when we all were forced to recognize the magnitude of the impending disaster, the first reaction of my parents and my sister was to offer unconditional support for my entire life and they hoped against reason that the advances in medicine would sometime soon restore my eyesight. They all became less friendly, loving and concerned, especially my father, as the situation evolved and the future became clear. My parents had been planning a happy retirement surrounded by grandchildren, like one sees in the movies but everything collapsed like a house of cards and my dear Papa hated it. The accommodations needed in our home bothered him and he frequently ignored them. But I am convinced that he had loved me before the disaster. The new situation was too much for him and he could not accept it. He seemed to be permanently enraged. Mom and Sis Lucy were better, but they could not learn braille."

"It would not be the same with me, Chuck" replied Missy. "I approached you with references and a realistic vision of who you are and what your situation is."

"And I am telling you what our situation would be in a few months or years. Now you could learn a couple of things and you might feel joy trying to enlighten my day, but it would soon change. I am a fiercely independent man and everything surrounding me is carefully planned and memorized. That is the way I want to keep it. You would try to make first little, later major changes and you might start finding me harsh and unreasonable. I don't need and I don't want to go through any such trial. I don't accept anyone's charity. Thank you, but Goodbye, Missy."

"And my soul? Don't you like my soul? I have a beautiful soul" She received no answer.

The woman was speechless and profoundly afflicted. She slowly picked up her desserts and turned against the door. She was thinking that Chuck had only spoken about himself and had never cared about her. Her beloved had been aware all the time that she was an ugly mishap and had not expressed any concern or sympathy. She was a useless freak for the entire world and now she had to return to her isolation and solitude. She walked slowly home. Very slowly, thinking. Her world had collapsed faster in one afternoon than in the previous 29 years.

* * *

Mabel was a single black woman who lived with a small child in a one-bedroom apartment next to Missy. The building was old and neighbors frequently overheard other people's loud television or angry fights. It was pointless to complain about noises, but sometimes she listened to amusing discussions of certain couples.

When Mabel and her child returned home that Sunday afternoon, she was surprised to hear moans and cries coming from Missy's apartment and she became first curious, later alarmed. The neighbor seemed to be crying in pain. Mabel worried. They did not live in a good neighborhood and she had heard stories of single women being raped or murdered. She paid more attention and the cries seemed to get worse. She grabbed a heavy frying pan of cast iron in the kitchen and knocked at Missy's door. Getting no answer, she tried to open the door, but it was locked, and the cries from inside intensified. Missy did not respond to her calls. Mabel ran to the superintendent's apartment and reported the situation demanding that the man immediately open Missy's door, which he did.

They found Missy lying in her bed. Next to her on the floor they found a bottle of bleach that Messy had emptied over her eyes and face and she was crying in pain. For a moment, she stopped and mumbled in tears:

"Now I am like him and he will not reject me again."

THE RIDICULOUS DUEL
THAT ENDED A CIVIL WAR

T HE TROUBLE STARTED ON a cold evening in the late fall. A thin layer of dry snow was already on the ground covering the Marktgasse, when a happy, young couple strode toward the Lindenhof Restaurant. The air was cold and pure, the sound made by the carriages was dampened by the snow flakes, and the light coming out of the lampposts was exceptionally bright. The Lindenhof establishment was one of the best dining accommodations in the city, renowned for its exquisite cuisine and outstanding service. Kurt and Helga Kirschner would normally not have been able to afford the stiff price tag, but on that faithful evening they were celebrating the first anniversary of their wedding. The young and beautiful woman was wearing a full winter dress and she almost had to drag its long, wide skirt over the snow. Kurt was dressed in a black suit covered by a long grey coat and wore a tall top hat. Both smiled when the head waiter took their coats and respectfully directed them toward a table with flowers situated next to the window. It was going to be a merry celebration. They ordered some domestic wine from the eastern region. Helga chose to sit by the window.

"Do you remember what your father said?" asked Kurt. The young wife merrily laughed. "I will never forget anything that happened one year ago."

"Mr. Schwarz was worried about our finances. Now he no longer is, and I am the only one who is." Helga immediately objected "Oh, no, Kurt. You always have and will be able to provide for me."

Kurt was happy. "I hope so, my dear. I was lucky to meet you" His eyes met those of Helga. "Let's eat and not worry about money" Kurt smiled. "Yes, darling, in the news paper's office I spoke to Editor Meyerhof. He does not quite see an immediate raise, but he feels that my future is bright."

Helga was going to respond, but she was interrupted by the head waiter, who was being followed at a distance by two expensively dressed elderly couples. The man appeared troubled. He spoke:

"Madam, Gentleman, I must humbly apologize but I have made an unforgivable mistake. This table by the window was reserved for another gentleman and his guests. We will immediately make another one ready for you and to signify how much we regret this misunderstanding, the house will offer you free drinks, whatever you and the gentle lady may desire."

Kurt felt stung. "You want us to spring up, leave this table, interrupt our conversation and go somewhere else? Many tables are empty, you had no reservation place holder on this one and we were guided to sit here. Maybe your other guests would be willing to sit elsewhere" The face of one of the two severe gentlemen in the background turned grey. His wife spoke:

"Sir, I advise you to watch your manners. We are aristocrats! You are in the presence of important people of national prominence with access to the Court. We have had this table by the window for years and everybody knows it. Yield the table and take the free drinks."

Here Helga jumped on her feet, with Kurt immediately following. "Madam, madam, I beg you. We are not acquainted with each other and we are all reputable people", objected impulsively Helga. Kurt added: "Madam, Sir, I am Kurt Kirschner, a respected journalist who publishes a daily column in the *Nation*. I respectfully object to your language as inappropriate regardless of your motives." The unknown woman inhaled deeply and raised his hand to her mouth, turning around in a spin and facing her husband. The previously grey face of the husband, an impressive tall man, turned red. He shouted:

"A scoundrel from the *Nation*! Maybe you are also Jewish. Since you don't respect the King and his Government, it is no wonder that in your shamelessness you dare to address an aristocratic lady who has not been introduced to you in an insulting manner. It will not be tolerated."

Kurt was more surprised than shaken but he suddenly felt that he had to start paying attention. "Well..." he murmured. "Sir, it has been a dreadful day. For my part, I prefer to withdraw without offering explanations. Come, Helga, we are leaving."

The tall man was decidedly not willing to let it go. He planted himself in front of Kurt, his head high and bent backward. He removed one of his gloves and spoke loudly and clearly:

"Sir, I am Field Marshal von Steinsiepen, Baron von and zu Dillenburg, and I demand satisfaction for the disrespectful utterances you and your wife have addressed to my spouse" Having said so, he hurled his felt glove to the face of the stunned Kurt. Helga opened her mouth and covered it with her hands.

* * *

Kurt was worried. His anniversary celebration had been thoroughly ruined. The couple returned home in silence. Helga had not spoken much, but she spent the evening crying. The following morning, Kurt had tried to reassure her that the incident was not half as bad as it looked like and that he would find a satisfactory resolution. Nobody would want to kill anybody over a table in a restaurant. But the Field Marshal was such a prominent man, she protested! They should have recognized him. "I would not even recognize King Friedrich Wilhelm in a Restaurant. Even if he is who he says he is, I am not going to kneel in front of anyone and apologize. We gave him no reason to insult us. He called me a scoundrel, and you were entitled to address his wife", murmured Kurt. The doorbell rang. Their maid, Kati, opened the door. Kurt suspected at once what it was. The girl entered the living room and announced: "Sir, two gentlemen to see you" Helga stood up and ran toward the bedroom.

The two newcomers were formally dressed in black. They greeted Kurt by bowing their heads and introduced themselves. One of them, who shall be called "Number One" spoke: "Mr. Kirschner, we shall be brief. We are the seconds to Field Marshal von Steinsiepen and we are here to report that he feels aggrieved by your reckless insults to the Baroness. He gives you the choice of either formally apologizing or accepting his terms for a duel"

Kurt turned pale. This was too much. "Gentlemen, I am only a modest citizen without the record of service to the arms, the King and the Country of the Field Marshal but I can assure you that I would never willingly offend anyone, much less such a distinguished member of our national nobility. Yesterday's incident is not worthy of a follow-up. I understand that it was all a misunderstanding. I was celebrating our wedding anniversary with Mrs. Kirschner and I was not prepared to start an argument."

"Will you then offer a general, unqualified apology recognizing your offense?" asked the first man sternly, with raised eyebrows.

"A general apology? I? I did nothing to require it" protested Kurt.

"Sir, The Field Marshal has gallantly fought for and saved the Monarchy, and the freedom of our nation from chaos and barbarism. He cannot accept being ignored by plain citizens or spoken to without proper respect. He insists on requiring a formal public reparation from you to restore his wounded honor. A man with his record of service to the Country and the King can tolerate no casual offenses."

"He also offended me without sufficient reason. He called me a scoundrel."

"I see no alternative to a duel in the field of honor. The Field Marshal has chosen pistols at 20 feet."

"Pistols? Gentlemen, I have never served in the army. I have never fired a pistol in anger" Kurt recognized contempt in the faces of the seconds.

"Sir, if you decline to defend your honor, you will be posted as a dishonored coward."

"I am no coward, but I will not allow anyone, even the Field Marshal, to kill me in cold blood. More so, considering how absurd and disproportionate the incident is and that the responsibility was shared."

A pause followed. The two visitors looked at each other and exchanged a few inaudible words. Finally, visitor Number 1, the evident spokesman, replied:

"Sir, nothing of the kind was shared. We shall report to the Field Marshal your lack of familiarity with pistols and your refusal to issue a formal apology. We shall return with further proposals if instructed to do so."

"No need to return, I beg you" thought Kurt without saying anything.

* * *

Kurt rang the doorbell at the apartment of his brother-in-law and closest friend, Dr. med. Peter Schwarz. Unexpectedly the doctor himself opened the door.

"What is that? Can you no longer afford a servant to open the door?" asked Kurt.

Peter laughed "Come in, Kurt. I was expecting you. Everybody was talking in the Hospital about your encounter with the Field Marshal. I knew that you would come to see me. Helga must be dismayed."

"I did not know that the unknown person was the Field Marshal. I had never met him. I was merrily enjoying an anniversary dinner with your sister and then he appeared and charged against us."

"Are you going to kill him? It would make you famous."

"Peter, I really need your advice. Your patients give you access to higher circles of society. He has already sent me his seconds and proposes a pistol duel. I cannot believe that he is serious. The matter was only a minor incident."

Peter led the way to his consultation room where both men sat in comfortable chairs. Peter produced a box of Havana cigars; two of them were selected and lit. Peter requested to hear a description of the whole incident. Then he thoughtfully commented:

"I am sorry that it happened in the presence of Helga. She has always been a sensitive girl. Let me think. It is not the same story I heard this morning. They told me that Helga and the Marschalin had exchanged angry words."

"You know that Helga would never raise her voice nor offend anyone. It was that atrocious woman who insulted us. Peter, please, listen to me and tell me what to do."

"How good are you with pistols?"

Kurt was flabbergasted. "Me, with pistols? I have barely seen them and never shot one. I did not serve in the army. I may have gone hunting a couple of times with a musket, but I never killed anything except the time."

Peter assumed a practical air. "Well in that case I can help you do some practice shooting with my weapons."

Kurt was terrified. "Are you nuts? I do not want to fight a duel, much less with this man. It is all an absurd event. I have no reason to wish to kill a Field Marshal and he has no right to kill me."

"I will take no sides, but you should recognize that a man in his position has a strong need to defend his honor and reputation. He is a national hero. In a moment of danger, he led the armies of our nation to the victory thus preserving our statehood, our monarchy, and traditions. The King thinks highly of him and frequently invites him to his palace. He is an old man, but his pulse is firm. You could not have sought out a worse enemy."

"Peter, I do not challenge his right to be the object of universal deference and it is quite natural that people yield to him in everything, but in this case, I did not know who he was and the whole incident was finished before I could grasp the situation. Now, for no reason whatsoever, he is demanding an unqualified public apology, which would make me a coward and an unworthy husband of Helga."

Peter shook his head.

"You are in a quandary. I think, though, that you should not be forced to a fight with weaponry that you don't master. In a duel, both parties ought to have the same chances. There are other choices."

Kurt shuddered with terror. Evidently, Peter thought that the duel was unavoidable.

"But, Peter, is it not possible to find a mediator? The Field Marshal, if given explanations, maybe would understand that I am among his most fervent admirers and that there is no reason to fight."

Peter thought for a moment ,"All right, let us try it, but I am afraid
he will only conclude that you lack courage. I attend services at the
Memorial Reformed Church. A few times on Sundays, I have seen the
Field Marshal talking to one of the Pastors, the Reverend Messinger,
who happens to be my patient. He is the one who preaches when Pastor
Meyer is not around. Go and speak to him. I will write an introductory
note for you on my stationery."

* * *

Kurt passed his visit card to a clerk seated at the entrance of the
Memorial Church Parish. The man was alarmed to read that the visitor
was a journalist.

"Is Pastor Messinger expecting you? May I inquire as to the purpose
of your visit?"

"I wish to speak to the Pastor in a private matter, Sir. It is unrelated
to my work as a journalist."

In a transparently suspicious demeanor, the clerk led Kurt to a
small waiting room and closed the door behind him. Several minutes
later the door opened and an overweight, elderly cleric appeared. Kurt
rose to his feet.

"Mr. Pastor Messinger, I thank you for the kindness shown in
receiving me. I am Kurt Kirschner and I bring you a note of introduction from my brother-in-law, Dr. Peter Schwarz, whom you may
know." Kurt gave him the paper, which the Pastor read slowly. After
finishing, he signaled to Kurt one of the seats and he deposited his
voluminous rear in another. He invited Kurt to speak. Kurt related to
him the incident with the Field Marshal and his wish to find a peaceful
and mutually agreeable resolution of the absurd but embarrassing and
dangerous situation. Pastor Messinger listened in silence. Then he
started a conversation:

"You say that the Field Marshal had noticed that you work for the *Nation*. Are you Jewish?

"No, Sir, I am not, although I fail to understand why he made any such assumption, nor of what significance that would be. The outburst of the Marshal in this matter was completely unprovoked and unwarranted. There is no difficulty between the two of us."

The Pastor raised his eyebrows in disapproval but changed the topic.

"Well, Mr. Kirschner, my first comment is that the owner of the Lindenhof is at fault for not having immediately identified to you the Field Marshal, whose identity must be well known to him."

"I do not disagree" commented Kurt, who had not considered the angle.

"A man who is national hero has certain expectations in his social interactions, the same as the King and his Ministers. He will not be treated like a commoner. This would humiliate the entire nation. If he wants a table, he should get it."

Kurt listened silently. Hope was growing in his chest. The cleric sounded reasonable. The old man's eyes wandered aimlessly though the room.

"I understand that you found his reference to your Journal and the well-known religion of its editor unpleasant. There was, however, a day when we all feared the worst for our country and the king. I still remember the dirty, filthy crowds descending through the streets of our capital, claiming to be hungry and exploited but as well fed as you and me. They were dressed in disgusting, dirty rags and not like the men of decency and education who naturally have the responsibility of leading the ship of the state. The clothing of their shameless women was even more repulsive. And they wanted to destroy the principle of private property and claimed that we are all equal, and that the Religion is the opium of the people and that the country should be ruled by common elected men and not by our King, enthroned and exalted by God himself for the duration of his natural life. I still remember those days with horror. I had to hide in my sister's cellar in the countryside; churches were burned, and we had all lost hope. Many pastors of mine and of other denominations were cowardly murdered. The Field Marshal rose against the chaos and the crime and assembled from nothing a powerful army and defeated the rabble and shot the leaders of that canaille. He restored our country to peace and honor and the King to the place that he occupies by God's pleasure. I mention those unforgettable days of epic because sometimes it seems that your newspaper has forgotten them."

Kurt almost jumped in his seat. It became clear to him that the Pastor was identifying the *Nation* with the past failed revolution. Now, it made sense. Maybe the same thought had crossed the mind of the Field Marshal. Kurt Kirschner finally understood the motivation of the old military man. The Pastor was being helpful.

"Mr. Pastor Messinger, I feel touched by your ordeal and suffering during those years. I was myself too young to have kept any memories, but I can give you my assurances that the *Nation* does not in any way condone revolutionary attitudes and only supports the Chancellor, democracy, social justice, and rule of law. We do not sponsor criminal activities and would be the first to denounce any terrorists to the royal police."

The Pastor was not convinced. Kurt tried something else.

"Nobody has more respect and admiration for the Field Marshal von Schlingensipen than me and my spouse. I am here to ask if you would kindly be willing to convey to this great man that I and my wife Helga would be proud to emulate him. It was all the consequence of an absurd misunderstanding resulting from the failure of the Restaurant owner to identify him. I could not bear the thought of harming or offending him in any way."

Kurt carried on:

"You are a man of the cloth. I am sure that the Reformed National Protestant Church disapproves of civic violence and that the thought of a duel which shares the malevolence of suicide and murder attempt is condemned by the Theology of your Congregation."

The Reverend did not respond as fast as Kurt had hoped.

"You are right, the Church does not approve of duels… as it does not approve of many things that happen daily and it would be impractical to try to avoid. Our world is not perfect, the customs are deteriorating. I do not know how I would choose between honor and cowardice. Our Lord Jesus Christ did not leave guidance in matters of honor and reputation. Sometimes…" He did not complete the sentence. Kurt had turned speechless.

"I am a hardworking, respectable man and I hope to have a child soon, Mr. Pastor" He was talking about his future expectations. Helga was not pregnant. "I am also a man of honor. Honor is not at stake here. I would like to put an end to a senseless, ridiculous incident and I was hoping that you would help me."

Pastor Messinger agreed to pay a visit to the Field Marshal.

As he left the Church, Kurt felt wounded and threatened. For the first time his mind was occupied by dark thoughts that he was unable to repress. The duel had become a distinct possibility.

* * *

Kurt and Hilda were having a pillow conversation.

"No, Hilda, do not feel that way, I beg you. It was not your fault. I repeat that you could not have known who this man and his wife were. It is intolerable that a gentleman in company of a lady is asked to yield a table without explanations."

"But I have instincts, Kurt. I should have guessed. I remember how in school we learned about the Field Marshal's battles and how he saved the country. We held him in high esteem."

"Me, too, I have always admired him but don't worry, I do not want to explain once more that Pastor Messinger will take care of everything and the case will be resolved discreetly and with honor. Do not think about it anymore, Helga, my love."

"He must be a master sharpshooter."

"I am sure, but this is of no concern to me. Even if I had to duel, which will not happen, I would never agree to do it on his terms, with weapons I do not master."

"What weapons do you master?" asked Helga, somewhat intrigued. "You have never told me."

"I have gone hunting a lot with your brother."

"With Peter? You never brought me home anything. What will my father think of?"

"The same as mine! Let that rest, please. I would like to sleep. Good night, Helga. Everything is going to be alright. Everything...."

Before falling asleep Kurt imagined himself facing the Field Marshal with a slingshot, as David did. A slingshot...

* * *

It was almost noon in the redaction of *The Nation*. Kurt was seated at his tall, inclined desk writing. Sources had reported that the Chancellor was considering territorial negotiations with the French Imperial government, but was it true? Kurt was debating the case for and against, but he was dissatisfied. His comments were too transparent, lacking the irony and subtle double meaning that had earned him reputation. He heard steps on his back, but he did not pay attention because people were moving up and down around the office all the time, but this time they were of Mr. Jakob Meyerhof, publisher and editor of *The Nation.*

"How are things going, Kirschner?" he said. "Yesterday's article was full of vagaries and grammatical errors. Your sentences were too simple, the words poorly chosen, your meaning unclear. I barely recognized your style. You can write German very well when you want."

"I apologize, Sir. It will not happen again. I hope that today's piece will meet with your approval. I am not finished yet but if you wish to read it now..." He did not add ...go ahead, but he instead carried on: "It is about the alleged project of negotiations with France."

With a sarcastic tone, the editor responded, "This time you are not going to insult the Field Marshal again?"

Kurt sighed deeply and turned toward his boss.

"No, Mr. Editor Meyerhof, not today. I never did it. I know that I should have talked to you. The incident is in everybody's mouth."

Meyerhof signaled him to follow him to his office. Behind closed door Kurt once again described the incident emphasizing the Field Marshal's reference to *The Nation* and its Editor's religion and reaffirmed his good will and innocence. He was expecting much of the mediation of Pastor Messinger of Memorial Church.

The old newspaper man thought over the case at length, but he did not know what to say. Finally, he asked:

"Well, Kirschner, what are you going to do if the mission of Pastor Messinger fails?"

"It will not fail" protested Kurt. "It will not fail. I have a young wife and this whole incident is a monstrous absurdity. I see no reason to fight with any such man as the Field Marshal. Or with anyone else, for that matter. What a horror!"

"Yes, we are pacifists in this paper but you are in trouble, Kirschner. As I see it, the challenge is an abuse by a powerful aristocrat, whom you did not mean to offend. Our national history is full of such incidents. If you apologize you will be a coward. This would harm this paper. You must find another solution."

A coward? He? What had Kurt done to deserve that label? He had nothing to apologize about. A silence followed. The eyes of Kurt fell on a Menorah standing on a side table.

"May I ask something, Mr. Editor?"

The boss raised his shoulders. "Absolutely, Kirschner, if it is pertinent to the issue at hand."

"How does your religion view duel?"

An embarrassed long silence followed. Finally, the old man shrugged.

"I have no idea. I will have to ask my rabbi, but, in life, you are always allowed to do whatever you must to survive. Our faith places the highest value on the preservation of human life and on humanity but if you are cornered and they give you no choice, you are entitled to try to save yourself and restore your good reputation. Honor is something that you need in our society. Without honor you cannot work, you cannot show your face among decent people, you cannot sit at the table of the righteous. And you should not raise children."

Kurt had the feeling that he had been given a warning. Maybe he would have to flee to a republic with his wife. The editor went on:

"He is a bad enemy and a son-of-a-bitch, but he is no fool. A single human life does not mean much to him. He has caused the death of many. He crushed the noble cause of the working class."

Kurt looked up. The leftist that he had known for years was in front of him. Meyerhof was not finished:

"The Revolution was a spontaneous uprising, poorly planned and disastrously executed and these circumstances, rather than the Field Marshal's military skills, caused its downfall. But the repression was brutal and heartless; the participants were not treated as human beings, just like beasts who had threatened the way of life of their overlords and bitten the hand that fed them. Their cause was just, because despite their arduous work they could not earn a living nor were they allowed to negotiate better salaries. I was only a minor and very young chieftain and that is why I escaped retribution but at trial my friend Karl Marx said it best when he was being judged: "There is no common law between this court and me. Kill me if you have the guts, but you have no right to judge me." The executions of combatants and their leaders and the torture were criminal murders. This man is a butcher."

Kurt would never have gone that far, not in thoughts, much less in his speech. "I understand you, Kirschner. What you asked before is whether I have found myself in a situation where without fault of mine I had to fight to resume normal life. It is a ridiculous question to ask a Jew. We are recognized by our clothes and there are always people who hate us without reason and wish to harm us. I am clever, and I stay away from sharp confrontations. I wish you had known how to do the same, too, but let me tell you something: A civil war never ends while participants of both sides are alive. Never! The struggle goes on by different means until death. A political butcher is linked to his victims and their families by indestructible ties."

* * *

Kurt was resting at home shortly after dinner. He had already read all the city's newspapers at work and he had now time to read some books. Helga was finishing in the kitchen. The maid had a free day.

A loud and firm knock came from the door. Kurt's mood changed. He hesitated for an instant. Then he jumped out of his fauteuil. It was too late; Helga had beaten him to the door. The two seconds of the Field Marshal again appeared under the frame. Helga showed them in and darted to her bedroom. Kurt faced the two visitors and without offering to shake hands, he bowed his head. The gesture was corresponded.

Visitor Number 1 spoke:

"Mr. Kirschner, we are here once again on behalf of Field Marshal von Schlingensiepen, who has given us plenipotentiary authority to make whatever arrangements are needed to resolve this matter and restore his honor."

Kurt did not like the sound of it. "Gentlemen, I don't know if you are aware that I recently charged Pastor Messinger from the Memorial Church with certain mediation endeavors pertinent to the matter at hand because I never violated his honor."

"We are aware, Sir, and we are bringing you the Field Marshal's answer. The honored Pastor approached the Field Marshal with your pretension that the slight had not been intended and that the occurrence might well have been the responsibility of the waiter of the establishment."

Kurt nodded. "That is correct. Said employee failed to make us aware of the presence of the Field Marshal, whom we regretfully did not recognize."

Number 1 countered: "Only few people fail to recognize him. I am sorry to report that the Field Marshal has fully rejected your argument."

A subdued cry was overheard behind the closed door of the bedroom. Kurt hesitated. Should he go and comfort his wife? It was not the time.

"May I inquire as to the reasoning behind His Excellency's decision? The offer had been presented in good faith."

Number 1 carefully weighed his answer. "The Field Marshal, listening to the words of the Pastor, considered that you were not offering an unqualified general apology, which would have been required to fully dismiss the incident with all its consequences."

Kurt shook his head. "The Field Marshal wanted an unqualified apology? There was no occasion. What we offered, while expressing regrets, was an explanation of how a ridiculous oversight of a third party had grown to the point of creating a dangerous incident."

"An incident…" countered Number 1, "…which was incompatible with the honor and veneration to which a man of the credentials of the Field Marshal is entitled and was tantamount to an outrage."

Kurt was growing nervous. "It is sad that the Field Marshal felt offended, but it was never my intention to cause him distress and I see no occasion to apologize. Furthermore, Messieurs, I am not willing to exchange fire with the Field Marshal, neither to put my or his life in jeopardy."

The countenance of Number 1 and Number 2 became serious. For a moment Kurt thought that Number 2 was finally going to speak but it was again Number 1 who responded:

"Nothing is more important to a citizen than his honor and reputation. Since you will not restore the Field Marshal's honor by an apology, he calls you to the field for fighting to the death. Otherwise, Sir, you will not be able to escape the label of cowardice that will descend upon you and your family."

Kurt stiffened his back. "Sir, you are insulting me in my home. Enough!"

"Mr. Kirschner, we have been authorized by the party we represent to negotiate with you and possibly accept whatever terms for the duel you offer."

"I will not accept pistols, because I have never handled one."

"It is understood, Sir. Do you prefer a musket? Swords? Mention your terms."

Kurt was recomposing himself. "What is clear, gentlemen, is that I insist in a means of confrontation such that both I and the Field Marshal will stand the same chances of death or survival."

Kurt did not know what to propose. Editor Meyerhof had told him many times that he was a crafty man. Where was his ingeniousness now?

Finally, he spoke:

"Intent on restoring my honor by means which give to both of us the same chances of survival, I propose to the Field Marshal that we meet at sunrise in the middle of the Bridge of the Prince and we both jump into the waters of the river and try to reach without assistance the right riverbank."

The two black-dressed gentlemen looked astonished at each other. Number 1 protested: "Sir, I beg you! I was expecting a serious proposal. The custom requires that the two adversaries face each other armed with a weapon and fight following ancient chivalrous rules. It is a mandatory code that needs to be respected."

Kurt was implacable. "You told me to choose and I have chosen. The rules only require that both combatants expose their lives. The waters of the river are extremely cold this time of the year and most people who fall out of the bridge will die of exposure or drown, but not everybody. I am an excellent swimmer and I presume that as a soldier, the Field Marshal also is. Either one may survive or perish. The proposal is suitable and honorable."

Dumbfounded, the two men withdrew promising to make the old nobleman aware of the proposal. Kurt stayed home. For the next hours, he would be busy calming down Helga. Don't worry, my love, everything will be fine. There is a God in heaven that will save me and protect our marriage. We shall grow old together surrounded by our children.

* * *

"Peter" said Kurt. "I do not know what else to do."

His brother-in-law was thoughtful., "Me neither. When I first heard of the challenge, I found it funny and laughed. It was too absurd to be taken seriously. I failed to recognize the danger for you and my sister. How is she taking it?"

"Not well. Do you know anyone at court who would have influence on the old man?"

"I do not. Only Pastor Messinger."

Kurt sighed. "I still have no children. Promise me that you will watch over Helga. Will you be my second in the duel?"

Peter shook his head nervously. "It is not time for self-pity. Do not talk that way. Nothing has been decided."

"They are going to come back anytime and reject my proposal."

Peter had to repress a laughter. "They probably will. Let us talk business. Do you have friends in the press who would write articles denouncing the challenge?"

"I have numerous friends, but none that will write articles denouncing a matter of honor or attacking the Field Marshal."

"I hear you. Who told you to work for a Jewish editor in *The Nation?*"

"Well, Peter, I could not find any other work. Your father would never have approved of my marriage to Helga if I did not have a steady job."

The physician raised his hands to his head in exasperation. Everything was wrong.

"Listen to me, I can teach you how to fire pistols."

"How long will the instruction last? One week? Two?"

"Do not be pessimistic. Look, these weapons are most inaccurate. The judge and the seconds will be in more danger than you or the Field Marshal."

"But he has been at war. Probably he can shoot well."

* * *

Emissary man number 1 reported "We have submitted your offer. Your proposal is not sanctioned by the code nor accepted by current usages. The Field Marshal urges you to fight by means consistent with the restoration of the Field Marshal's honor." Kurt stiffened his back "You heard my offer, Sir. I am willing to restore the immaculate honor of the Field Marshal but not by means that leave me no chance of survival."

"Then, Sir, choose the weapons. Make a reasonable offer."

Kurt approached Number 1. "I did not injure the gentleman's honor, Sir. I enjoy living with my wife, giving her support, and providing her with an honorable existence. I have no wish to destroy our family because the Field Marshal despises Editor Meyerhof. Be advised, Sir, that my views differ from those of my excellent employer, for whom I have the highest respect and admiration. Let me live my existence in peace."

Number 1 could not show restraint. His eyes rolled wildly. "That is intolerable. You entertain doubts as to the motives and the honor of the Marshal." He went on: "You are referring, Sir, to a decorated national hero, who is honored with the royal friendship."

Kurt decided to end the argument: "Sir, everything has been said. As to your challenge, I choose life and peaceful resolution of all conflicts, while repeating that we are not in the presence of a serious conflict."

Number 1 fixed Kurt's eyes. Then, he slowly uttered the horrible damnation:

"Sir, if you do not offer satisfaction and ignore our field challenge, we shall be compelled to publish you a coward."

* * *

Helga finished wrapping the beautiful woolen scarf she had herself knitted for her father-in-law's 60th birthday. The couple left their apartment and walked in silence toward Mr. Kirschner's elegant residence. Helga was Kurt's fragile porcelain doll, a frail, pale and beautiful woman in need of protection. She was mumbling: "...and yet he is such a national hero and a savior of our country. How can he do that to us?"

"An old demented reactionary bastard is what he is," thought Kurt. "He and Meyerhof should fight it out and leave us in peace"

The elderly Mr. Siegfried Kirschner resided in a magnificent grey town house of stone near the park. "Welcome, my children!" he said. "It is good to see you."

Kurt responded, "We came to convey our best wishes on your 60th birthday, father." Helga advanced smilingly and offered her gift "It is for you, father. I knitted it myself."

"Then I am sure that it will be magnificent, dear" Having said that, the old man pushed the present aside. His wife took it and deposited it on a table that was already covered with better gifts. Siegfried had never liked his daughter-in-law because her dowry had been small. She blamed her for his son's financial constraints. "Please, sit down and join us for coffee and cake."

Siegfried Kirschner stared at his son and said:

"You remind me more and more every day of my venerated father. He was a man of honor, a great merchant, a solid column of peace and prosperity in this Kingdom. Our family owes everything to him and his straightforward principles."

Kurt braced himself for the worse. Would he have to argue in front of his mother and wife?

"When your grandfather spoke" added the old man "I listened, harboring no other desire than to grow and be like him. One day..." he grasped air "...one day in my youth I was working as an assistant with him in the shop. He was the age I am now, a senior textile dealer respected by the entire community. We heard noises, cries, and gunpowder explosions. Father ordered me and all other clerks to stay put until the forces of order reestablished public safety. After one hour, the human riffraff appeared on our door: poorly dressed men, foul-speaking women, dirty children, repulsive geezers without teeth. People of education do not come to the city dressed like that. They had no manners, and no shame, yet my father had donated money to charities to run Christian schools for their progeny." Siegfried hit the armchair with his clenched fist. "They did not want to be civilized humans. They despised everything that was good and wholesome. They had heard the voice of the prophets of Satan. Ours was the only open shop in the square. They entered and ransacked it. Father stood in their way. A filthy womankind pushed him. He was outraged and beaten. They called him fat pig. I ran to assist him, but he signaled me to stop and stay behind. No, son, it is not our time, the gates of hell shall not prevail, but they are now open, he said."

Kurt's mother had tears in her eyes, "Please, Siegfried, do not upset yourself. It is your birthday." The man was not finished:

"We had to hide in the residence of our servants, who were loyal. We heard about the young Field Marshal von Schlingensiepen, hero of the first war against Russia, that he had assembled a group of loyal soldiers, armed them, and restored order and provided exemplary punishment for the bad apples. One day he entered in the city again and was received by the King at the doors of Palace. Father was crying of joy. He pointed with the finger to the Marshal and told me: Never forget this man. Learn from his sense of duty and patriotism."

Half an hour later, Kurt and Helga were putting on their coats and getting ready to leave. Kurt noticed that the old man was alone and decided to approach him.

"May I have a word with you, father?"

"Speak, son" answered the old man.

"Father, you obviously know about the event that unwillingly confronted me and my wife with the Field Marshal, whom we had not recognized."

Siegfried did not answer. He knew. Kurt made a break and deeply sighed:

"You obviously feel that I should fight. I am not knowledgeable of weapons and he would likely kill me. I am your only male heir and still have no children. Yet you want me to accept the challenge. It was not my fault. I stupidly mentioned that I worked at *The Nation* and that set him off. He hates our paper."

"You should not be working for that godless Jew."

"Thanks to Editor Meyerhof I have had a dependable salary and I have been able to sustain my family. I was well treated and could practice my trade. Do not speak against him, I beg you."

"Will you now impart lessons to me? Think about your heritage and the faith and sense of honor of your ancestors. Only God knows who shall live and who shall die, but a man needs to be respected or else his life is worthless."

* * *

Kurt thought that he was meeting his brother-in-law for the last time.

"You should not think, Kurt, that my father would have answered differently. Both are old and their uprising was tough. You are a man of high intellect, a true analytical person with common sense and I enjoy talking to you and reading your articles. There must be something that I can do. Could I write a medical attest? It would have to be something that has a base in truth. They say that unless you take the field, they will post you a coward. It is an outrage worthy of them, but it must be easier said than done."

"Not so, Brother Peter. They have papers that compete with us and hate *The Nation* as much as von Schlingensiepen. They will publish letters to the Editor misrepresenting the facts and making the charge. I will be finished, and my entire family dishonored. What is even worse:

Editor Meyerhof will have no choice but to fire me, or else he would lose the readership of his paper."

The physician shook his head. He felt in front of a dying patient. Kurt had a request:

"Will you second me? The judge will be Attorney Guslow. Maybe Pastor Messinger would be so kind as to come and bless my remainders." Kurt nervously bit his finger but kept talking.

Kurt was ending the conversation. "I hate him. I understand now that he is a man full of hatred and resentment."

"Wait, wait a moment. What weapon are you going to choose? Not a sword or a pistol. He would have the advantage."

"I already proposed jumping into the river."

"Don't be a fool, this is serious. Choose a loaded musket. You have hunted with me and understand them. It is exceedingly difficult to aim at anything. If some little amount of blood flows, the judge will declare that everybody's honor has been restored and you will go home."

"I expect that we both have the same chances of surviving or dying."

"I will go to see them. I will propose that you shoot at each other from a long distance with a musket and you will really stand a chance."

* * *

In the dawn hours of December 15th, carriages drove to the Neuenburger Field.

Kurt was upset. He had tried to keep the matter secret from Helga, but he had failed. He had slipped out of his bed silently and dressed himself in the drawing room, while hearing the loud sobs of the woman. He had tried everything, he thought. He drafted a brief farewell letter assuring her or his continued love and hope of triumph, and because of this, he was obliged to defend the honor of all his family. Neither Helga nor her family could survive without honor. He closed and signed the letter assuring her of his never-ending love. He deposited the letter on a table and he rushed out of the apartment avoiding to see Helga. At least, he was leaving no infant child behind. His eyes swelled with tears and he thought of the Helga that he was in danger of losing. He would never meet the daughter he never had.

The Neuenburger Fields were covered by few centimeters of dry snow. Kurt thought that it would be enjoyable to walk in the forest near the almost frozen brook. It would be his final pleasure.

Kurt had been the last to arrive. Attorney Guslow, the judge of honor, came forward to greet him before delivering the last instructions. He had chosen a suitable flat spot for the encounter. At a distance, Kurt recognized the odious figure of the Field Marshal. He was a tall man, strong for his advanced age, dressed in a heavy brown long coat. Like everybody else's, his head was covered by a black top hat.

Despite the low temperature, Kurt removed his coat, his jacket, his tie and stripped down to his white shirt. He even rolled up his sleeves. He tossed his clothing on the ground without folding it. He looked in the direction of Peter, who would pick it up and bring it to his widow. The brother-in-law understood and sighed.

Guslow instructed the seconds and witnesses to move back to the top of a small nearby bluff and invited the combatants to follow him to the chosen area. He was carrying two muskets. He advised the two adversaries that the muskets were loaded and had been inspected but that the combatants were free to check them again before choosing. Only the Field Marshal did so. The men took possession of their weapons. It felt so cold that Guslow and the Field Marshal were visibly shaking. Kurt only thought that it was the wind of death.

The judge asked the two men whether the possibility of a reconciliation existed. Both denied it and were advised to make themselves ready.

The Field Marshal was shaking. He advised Guslow that he had chosen to keep his long, unbuttoned winter coat on. Guslow nicked.

The two adversaries positioned themselves in the center of the chosen field of honor, back-to-back, with the musket in the right hand and the barrel pointed toward the ground. The judge started to count. The contenders would walk ten full steps forward. At the voice of FIRE, they would spin around, raise the arm and fire at their discretion. Guslow started: ONE. The men walked one-step away from each other. TWO. The two adversaries walked another step from each other. THREE, FOUR... NINE and TEN. Both were at less than twenty meters from each other when they turned around. The judge then shouted: FIRE!

The Field Marshal started to lift his right arm, but the skirt of his heavy unbuttoned coat was very long and the bottom became entangled with the barrel of his gun during the rotary movement needed to face the adversary. With Kurt already in his sight, the old Field Marshal attempted to lift the musket but the gun's long barrel was caught for a moment by the bottom of the coat, and was delayed. It did not matter, thought the old hero. He would lift it again. A bright lightning appeared in front of his eyes and he felt a thump in his chest. Unable to stay on his feet, he fell backward. He moved his right hand, which strangely was no longer holding the weapon and felt a warm fluid running over his chest. His days of glory reappeared in front of his eyes and he relived them, thinking of a glorious entry in paradise in company of the King. Then the darkness and the silence came and surrounded him for all eternity.

The Field Marshal's party and the judge rushed toward the body of the fallen Marshal. Peter, unable to control himself, yelled, jumped, and ran toward Kurt. The journalist was astonished, paralyzed, and had also dropped his musket to the snow. With patent incredulity, he contemplated the corpse of his enemy laying flat on the snow, covered by blood. He checked himself. He had no blood and felt no pain. He had experienced one of the ultimate thrills in life: A man had come straight to him with the intention of taking his life but he was the one who walked away.

The affair, the judge announced, had been honorably conducted and the honor of both participants had been fully restored. Regrettable as the tragic outcome was, no one was to be blamed. The King would undoubtedly agree.

In the evening, the Royal Household announced that the glorious Field Marshal Baron von and zu Schlingensiepen, pride and savior of the Country, had suddenly passed away because of an unexpected heart attack. His Majesty had ordered three days of mourning and a State Funeral.

Editor Meyerhof's sarcastic, joyful, and triumphant eyes greeted Kurt Kirschner the next day as the old man smilingly placed his arm around Kurt's shoulders. He surprised Kurt with the unexpected offer of a raise. Kurt first wanted to reject it as blood money, but he had asked for it long before and he needed money for Helga and the baby girl they were planning. Meyerhof, always smiling, hugged the journalist with enthusiasm.

Before leaving, Jakob Meyerhof asked him whether he cared to write the Obituary.

BAD PEACE FOLLOWING A BAD WAR

B ARCELONA HAS NOT MOVED away from the Mediterranean shore, but the city and its residents have evolved in different forms to the point of making it unrecognizable.

Why do people feel that it still is the same city of similar name mentioned in history books? Hannibal and his elephants passed through. Sometimes one could imagine Roman soldiers on the same site revering the pagan gods. A few Roman columns and ruins are still preserved. After the Roman Empire, the medieval knights came. And the Arabic army of Al-Mansour burnt the city to the stake. It was here that Ferdinand and Isabella welcomed Admiral Columbus, who had brought to the city, to its denizens and to his sovereigns nothing but a few enslaved Indians. Don Quixote was finally defeated on its beach and had to relinquish his marvelous madness. Does this city return common sense to those who have lost it? Not all its occupiers recovered it.

The civil war was underway in the late summer of 1937 at the time when Roser started feeling unwell. Her husband was Jordi Foguet, a tall and proud municipal Police officer in charge of overseeing food distribution to impoverished war victims and refugees in the neighborhood of Sants. He had set up his headquarters in Les Corts, inside the then soccer stadium of the FC Barcelona and had responsibility for the daily feeding of women and children. They were the wives and widows of the brave men who were defending Catalonia and the Spanish Republic in an attempt to stop the unstoppable advance of General Franco and his fascist army, supported by superior German and Italian units, aviation, and equipment. Like modern Quixotes, these men and women fought on in a futile attempt to avoid the unavoidable disaster, and like Don Quixote they were destined to be defeated on Barcelona's beach. Revolutionary fervor was on the streets but the city was peaceful. Jordi had been clever to stay away from affiliations. A police officer could only belong to the city, never to a party. He had once gone for lunch to the popular kitchen set up by the anarchists in the old Ritz Hotel and he had liked the ambience, the camaraderie, and the brotherhood, but as a municipal employee, he explained, he should never join an organization. Recently the Stalinist-supported Government of Madrid had forcefully routed its Catalan adversaries, an event viewed with horror by George Orwell, who developed the understandable permanent hatred against communists so well described in his book *Homage to Catalonia*. But let's go back to our story.

Roser would become seriously ill and her husband Jordi had reason, but not time, to worry.

Officer Foguet continued his work under the current authorities with success. Many women and children showed up in his dining rooms, or rather dining spaces, to be fed. He encountered many transportation problems trying to bring in the food supplies, but his superior had been able to appropriate some old trucks no longer suitable to go to the front. All he needed to find was gas. The Honorable but badly battered and powerless Lluis Companys, President of Catalonia's Government, named *Generalitat* since immemorial times, had visited the facility and congratulated the staff on their efforts and dedication. But Jordi was increasingly worried about his supplies. The fascist armies occupied the granary areas of Castile and the soldiers and Spaniards in the occupied territories enjoyed all the food they needed while the democratically elected Republic had little or nothing, except for the miserable help delivered by Stalin with ominous attached conditions and generously paid for with the gold reserves of the Bank of Spain. And France and Britain were doing nothing for Spain, except maybe crying in pain. And the fascist Nationalists were advancing and advancing.

"Don't worry. They will be stopped soon enough. The people hate them because they are assassins and they are disunited", said Roser reassuring her husband. Jordi was not so sure. He hated them, but he knew better about the Spaniards in other territories. The famous "black Spain" was easily recognizable in all fascist territories. He had listened to some of their radio broadcasts in short wave. "But think of their savagery, the crimes and mass executions they have committed" added Roser. "Even if they win, which they will not, they shall not last." But the Republicans had also killed people. Revolutions are cruel and civil wars especially savage. The winner would wipe out the memory of his own crimes and punish those of the enemy. Roser was a progressive woman who also worked in City Hall. She insisted: "Spain and Catalonia are poor countries but the achievements and progress of our people in the last years are irreversible. Remember how the Spanish people defeated them in the outskirts of Madrid. They will not be able to turn back the clock." Irrational hope survived in her heart.

On Sunday, Jordi and Roser left their apartment and walked toward the mountain of Montjuic. They reached a steep street that led to the park. They meant to climb it all the way to the National Palace to enjoy the views of Barcelona and the beautiful gardens. Jordi dressed at all times in uniform for security reasons. He saluted men in several uniforms and armed militiamen on their way, but nobody stopped and bothered him.

The couple was only halfway up the hill when Roser stopped complaining about shortness of breath. "I cannot go on. Let me rest. I need to catch my breath."

Jordi was more surprised than worried. Roser had always been a strong woman and looked healthy.

"What is wrong, my dear?" He looked around in search of a bank but he did not see any. Roser once again surprised Jordi by sitting on the curb. She was breathing heavily and was moving her arms and shoulders as if wanting something to grab. Jordi, visibly worried, sat silently next to the woman. What was the matter? She had never done anything like that before. He watched Roser in silence.

"Darling, do you want to go back home?" he asked.

"No, no, just let me rest a moment and I will be alright."

Finally, both got up and resumed their walk. But Roser was walking very slowly.

Jordi noticed a police vehicle approaching. Without much reflection, he flagged the vehicle down. It was occupied by two Mossos, the policemen of the Catalan Generalitat. The men appeared to be of mature age. Jordi was happy that they were no militiamen.

"What is the matter, Comrade Policeman?" they asked.

"Health and Republic, Comrades. My wife who also works with the city administration is feeling sick. She did not have much to eat."

Actually, Jordi had enough food but he thought that the two men probably had not. The Mossos understandingly nodded. Same thing with everybody, they answered. We'll see if Stalin comes through soon. Of course, he will. He has promised.

"Are you going in the direction of the National Palace? Could you give us a ride, please?" asked Jordi.

* * *

Next day, a Monday, was unusually tough. Officer Foguet had a difficult day. He was running out of food to distribute. His commanding superior, Sergeant Roure had openly told him to fasten his belt tighter, because things did not look good. The promised Soviet boats with solidary assistance from abroad had not arrived and whatever they had was needed for the soldiers at the front.

Foguet shook the head "But Roure, we already have so little and we get every day more and more people asking for food. Most of them are the wives and mothers and widows of the soldiers at the front. We have promised them that…"

"You and I have promised nothing, Foguet. They should complain to the Government. It is a disaster. I don't know how we are going to survive without food. How could we win this war?" Foguet murmured "We are not going to win this war" The sergeant ignored him. He knew how severe the punishment for defeatism was.

Jordi had ordered to cut again the individual rations. On his way home he was still hearing the bitter complaints of the women: "Comrade, how am I going to feed my child with what you are giving me?" Maybe Stalin will give you something, thought Foguet bitterly. Well, at least he would be able to bring home enough. He had a right to provide for himself and his wife. The requirements of his job were terrible. He had to face hungry people who believed him guilty, grind his teeth and bear their disappointment in silence.

It was the evening and he felt exhausted. He had already forgotten Roser's indisposition. Jordi came off the city bus. He passed a group of boys and girls waving the flag of the Republic and singing patriotic war songs. A wall painting read "Union of Proletarian Brothers." They were collecting coins for the Red Secours. How many coins would they be able to eat when they were hungry? There was nothing to buy. The songs would keep their empty bells warm up to the time of the unavoidable disaster. A few weeks ago, Jordi had been able to briefly tune over short wave a fascist radio station. The hosts talked loudly, sounded terrible and were threatening. In his hour of tribulation, he was grateful to have Roser's support. Was it true that the Nationalists had the latest German and Italian tanks? How frequently would they bomb the city from the air? The dark clouds that he was seeing, were they in the skies or in his mind?

Jordi climbed up the stairs to his apartment. Roser did not immediately come to hug and kiss him, as was her habit. Maybe she was not back. The policeman found her in bed, in the bedroom leaning over several pillows.

"What is the matter, my dear?" asked Jordi tenderly, sincerely worried. He remembered the incident the day before.

"Well" answered Roser, "I was working and I felt tired and short of breath. The feet were hurting because they are swollen. I talked to Empar and she felt that I was hot and should come home."

"Of course, you should have. Why did you not send me word? I am easy to reach" objected the husband.

"I had much work. You know that several of our girls joined the army as nurses last week. There was a line of citizens waiting for the coupons."

"If you get really sick it will be worse because nobody will be there to distribute the coupons."

"Ay, Jordi, if you could have seen their faces."

"You are telling me? I distribute thin loaves of bread to hungry children every day and milk on weekends. And we had to cut the rations. But when did you come home?"

"At noon. And I lay down and here I am."

"You haven't eaten anything the full day. Weakness is bad. I will prepare something warm. I am going to take real loving care of you. I will bring as much food as you need. I am sure that it is a cold", sentenced Jordi.

In the following weeks Roser did not get any better. She was short of breath at all times and could not sleep. It had to be the winter. Barcelona had a mild climate without snow or ice except on rare occasions but if you have no heating, you can feel cold in winter. Jordi found an old electric space heater with an incandescent resistor in the center, surrounded by a radiating screen. Roser resisted using it, as the electricity (the "light" as the power was commonly called), was too expensive but finally she was compelled to submit. She felt cold.

This disease lasts too long, thought Jordi after two weeks. Finally, he announced that he would try to bring home a physician. He had already made inquiries and he might be able to pick him up tomorrow.

Jordi and the Doctor arrived in the early evening. The physician was wearing a white coat over his jacket because it helped to protect against hidden snipers. He was old and people respected him but nobody knew who the snipers were. All young doctors were at the front.

Both men entered the bedroom. Jordi noticed that Roser had managed to stand up and replace the linen. The room looked neat.

"Good evening, my dear. This is Dr. Jubany, from St Pau Hospital and he has come to make you healthy."

The Doctor smiled broadly as he shook Roser's hand. Walking alongside the husband he had listened to a description of the "cold" and was worried. "Do you prefer to stay in the room or go outside?" he asked Jordi. The man answered without hesitation that he would wait outside and left the room.

Dr Jubany came out half an hour later and was not happy.

"What do you think, Doctor?" asked Jordi anxiously.

* * *

Doomsday was around the corner, almost in sight. The army of the Republic had launched in July a desperate attempt to survive by crossing the River Ebre into the Fascist-held territory. At first, the Republican army had been successful but the joy did not last long. The news from the front were unclear but the rumors said it all. The Republican army was retreating in defeat in front of the fascist army units led by the insurgent General Yagüe. The offensive and the ensuing massacre had been in vain.

Jordi was fearful. He knew that there were no natural barriers between the Ebre River and Barcelona and that the Republic had no army left. It was all lost. It was all the fault of the inept Communists who had taken over. Their Stalin was to feed and arm all of Spain. Where had he been all the time? And now he was signing a pact of non-aggression with Hitler! And the events of Munich! They still had hope that France and Britain would save them, but everybody had sold out to the Nazis. The entire world was going to become fascist. He thought with bitterness that maybe he would prefer to die with Roser and leave this cruel world.

Caring for Roser had become increasingly difficult. Nobody was helping him at work. Roser was chronically short of breath and in pain. Dr. Jubany was no longer of much help. He had neither time nor could he offer medications but he kept visiting. He said:

"It can last months or days, I do not know. Let me try to puncture her belly again to extract fluid. Maybe she will be able to breathe better."

"I really thank you, Doctor"

Dr. Jubany weakly smiled. "You are right. Both Catalonia and Spain are almost dead. And we shall be, soon. I have never done anything bad in life, my friend but I am going to be punished. Have you heard their radio?"

Jordi felt tears in his eyes. "We have been screwed by many people, Doctor."

The old man answered "Yes, we have, you can say it again. Did you hear the latest about the Ebre battle?"

"Do you mean that the Republic had nothing to oppose the German airplanes?"

"And worse" The Doctor was tossing his instruments into a pot of boiling water. "The nationalists opened two upstream water reservoirs to drown our men and destroy all bridges. And they released barges with explosives to blow up everything in their way. Another physician has told me that our men were slaughtered and that all is lost. Unless of course a big international war starts."

"Oh, sure. After the treaty of Munich, the Europeans are not going to fight a war against the Nazis, I assure you. It is over." Jordi thoughtfully added. A silence followed and Jordi added: "Before I forget it, I saved for you a large roll with some sausage inside."

Jordi turned his back to the doctor and went back to Roser's bedside. He mumbled:

"My love, Dr. Jubany is in the kitchen and will be here right away to perform another operation. You will feel better and I will give you some food" The sick woman did not answer. In despair Jordi added "I do not know how I can leave you alone the full day."

"I am not alone. Montse looks me up all the time."

The neighbor? She did not come more than once every day, if at all. But he had nothing else to offer.

* * *

Jordi recognized or knew most of the people who came to his lunch kitchen between 1:00 and 3:00 PM. They were a sad and growing aggregate of old men, women, and children, many of them in rags. Two employees took out of the kitchen a big smoking soup kettle with some floating bits of potato, meat, and white beans. Little as it was, the people in line were more than eager to get it. Children got half a serving. That day, there was some bread distributed with each bowl of soup. Foguet had long lost his last security guards and he had to stand in the dining room by himself. How could he discipline hungry people? He mostly looked the other way.

He noticed in the line a woman with two small children, maybe 2 or 4 years that he had never seen before. Another widow with infant children, he thought. His eyes crossed with those of the woman. When her turn arrived, he saw her pleading with the kitchen aid to give her something extra for the children. Jordi did not want to hear it and turned his back.

At home, he found Empar, who had been Roser's section chief at City Hall in the apartment. Apparently, the patient was having a good day. She had opened the door herself and was now seated in the dining room with the visitor. With mocking deference, Jordi said:

"Pleased to see you, Comrade Empar."

The woman smiled and answered in the same tone: "Happy to see you, Comrade Agent. And even more happy to see that your wife is doing so well. I brought her some food. We miss her very much at work."

"How are things going, Empar? Are you already learning how to do the fascist salute? Just raise your right arm."

Empar made a grin and twisted her mouth with disgust. It took her a moment to respond: "I will salute them with a raised fist."

"Not good for your health" objected Jordi. "You may get a lead indigestion" Upset, Empar countered:

"They are all criminals. I have heard that they are shooting all the town majors and republican officials that they find. This man, General Franco is…."

Roser shook her head. "They can come and kill me. I am dying anyway."

Jordi intervened "Do not speak that way, Roser. I don't like it. I was too old to be drafted. We have nothing to hide and nothing to fear. I have never killed or harmed anyone. I was never involved in politics, I did not serve in any militias and I have spent the war feeding hungry people."

Empar knew something. "Do you know that many are planning to flee to France? It is only temporal. Once the big World War II starts, Franco's regime will be overthrown and everything will be over."

Jordi warned her "I know that many are escaping to France but watch where you speak. Would you leave with them?"

Empar shook her head. "Vengeance in a civil war will be terrible. I don't know if you have heard, but your Sergeant Roure is one of the people meaning to escape to the French border."

Jordi was surprised. "Roure? Why? He is a good man and never harmed anyone."

Empar laughed: "Was he not a member of Esquerra? They are shooting all Catalan separatists."

"What! For being a member of Esquerra like President Companys? It is a legal and constitutional party."

Empar grinned. "They said that he is in the Palace of the Generalitat helping them pack the files. And you know what? Spain's President Azaña is also making the suitcases."

"This does not surprise me. They day he brought the Government of the Spanish Republic to Barcelona, I knew that we had already lost"

Jordi could not dismiss the thought of Roure leaving him alone. He lacked the Sergeant's connections. How was he going to get any food for his charges?

* * *

Jordi helped his two last women employees to set up the distribution center for lunch. Miraculously the soup included a little beef meat, fat, and bone with marrow. Was it a holiday?

He noticed again on the line the woman with the two children.

The line was longer than ever. Jordi knew that he had less food than the day before. What a disaster. Maybe the fascists should finally arrive and put an end to their miseries.

Jordi saw a car stopping outside and noticed Sergeant Roure getting off and walking toward the office with a large basket. Many eyes looked in his direction. The policeman went to meet him.

"Hi, Roure. What is up? Did you want to rub your food in their noses?"

The Sergeant was irritated and in no mood for pleasantries. "I was with the militiamen in the Vallès trying to get a truckload of vegetables. I also found some assorted things. I have fresh eggs. The problem is that few farmers have more than 4 or 5. I will give you two for your wife."

"Is it true that you are going to flee?" asked Jordi suddenly.

Roure looked intensely at his eyes. He feared indiscretions "Yes, friend Foguet, we have lost and I want to save my skin. The entire Catalan Government is going to leave into exile. But keep it a secret, please. What about you?"

During the morning, Jordi had been thinking of arguments and recriminations to submit to the Sergeant, but now he dismissed all as absurd. Only one thing came to his mind:

"What will you do if the Nazis come to France?"

Roure did not hesitate "Oh, then they will have to fight directly against us and we shall not leave one of them alive, I swear you. They will pay us back. And then we shall return."

Jordi shook his head.

"Alright, Sergeant, I will miss you."

"You should come, too, Jordi. It is very dangerous to stay."

"And what do I do with Roser? She is very sick and cannot walk. She needs care that I am not giving her now."

"She will be worse off as a sick widow."

Upset, Jordi turned his back to the Sergeant and left the small office slamming the door behind him. He took his place again behind the big table. The unknown woman of the previous days and her children had just been served but the smallest child, still an infant, was crying. Jordi decided to approach them.

"Hi, little comrade. What is wrong with your son?" he asked the mother.

The woman did not hesitate "He is hungry and dirty. I have no money and no clothes."

Jordi shook his head in sympathy. He understood. Many women were in the same situation. She spoke in Spanish, like many other refugees.

"Did you lose your husband in the front?" he asked. He feared that she was going to answer that he had been shot by the militiamen. It did not matter anymore. But the mother did not answer at once and continued balancing the child in her arms. Then she raised her eyes toward the policeman.

"No. The bastard put me on the street weeks ago. He said that the world was coming to an end and that this meant that until then, it was free love and the marriage was abolished. I hear that he has fled to the French border."

"He left you on the street with two small children and disappeared?" inquired Jordi.

"Yes. A German airplane destroyed our home behind the Cathedral. We had gone to the refuge and were not injured. We slept that night in the refuge but next day he said that he no longer had money to find another apartment because he could not pay the rent or feed us and that he was leaving alone. Did I have the money to pay the rent or to feed our children? The bastard!"

Jordi agreed. The man was a bastard. He felt sympathy for the poor woman. But he wished he had children himself.

"I am Officer Foguet, but people call me Jordi", he said. "What is your name?"

The woman was surprised. She answered: "Maribel Olmos Romero, at your service. My children are Pedrito and Iris."

Jordi did not have anything else to say and started retreating "Enjoy your meal" But the woman moved a step closer to him.

"Officer, please, may I ask you something" Others were watching nearby and she lowered the voice. "Please, Sir, you see my situation. Could I do something to help here? Anything at all. Cook, clean toilets, saw, sweep the floor, whatever. Tell me and I shall do it for whatever you can afford to pay."

"Are you asking if I have a job? No, I don't. You know in what situation we are. Soon we shall not be able to pay or feed anyone anymore. I am sorry."

Maribel grabbed his sleeve. "Nothing? Nothing at all? Give me a place to sleep, please. We are spending the nights in a corner of the municipal parking garage but it is noisy, there are too many people and it is becoming dangerous. And a German bomb missed us already. There are many rapes. Please, anything. I have no pride. Do it for my children."

Jordi was touched but he had nothing to offer and walked away.

One hour later, he saw Maribel leaving sadly the place with Pedrito in her arms and Iris in tow, their bellies nearly as empty as before.

Jordi suddenly yielded to an impulse and ran after the woman.

"Maribel, listen. Here I have nothing to offer but at home I have a very sick wife and nobody to take care of her while I am at work. If you were to care for her, you and your kids may sleep in some place in our apartment and share with us whatever food we have. So far, I have been able to bring home food. Later, we shall see."

Maribel brought a free hand to her breast and opened her mouth. Tears flooded her eyes.

Jordi added: "I have no money. I am offering only a roof and some food for the three of you in exchange of care for my wife. Assuming that Roser agrees, of course. She is a good woman. She is dying. Yes, she is dying." Now, his eyes were also filled with tears. She was really dying. What was he talking about? He had recognized it for the first time.

Jordi stopped. Maribel was moving her head up and down in the affirmative "Yes, yes, yes, I will do anything you say, anything. Thank you" She even attempted to kiss Jordi's hand.

* * *

January of 1939 had been a mild month. Jordi no longer had any food to distribute, and many of his friends had fled to France. Many thought that it would be better to have the Fascists finally occupy the city than to continue the slow agony. Where was the Government? Jordi had left his service gun in the drawer in the office. What was the point? It could only get him killed. It was all over. The policeman had succeeded in bringing home some cans and food preserves. He, Roser, Maribel and the two children had been able to eat, but what would the future bring? How would he be treated by the new masters? The rumors about their conduct with the defeated were terrible. But no matter what people said, they had to be human and the victors

sometimes are merciful. Aren't we all countrymen? It was said that
General Yagüe's men were mostly Moroccan Moors.

Maribel was a hit in Jordi's home. She was an excellent and reliable
helper and a lovable friend. She had immediately become a member
of the family. And the two children were funny and beautiful. They
were dressed almost in rags but Maribel said that it did not matter,
that children do not understand anything about clothes and that only
the food was important. Milk was very important. She always had a
smile in her face. She slept on the floor wrapped in her children. Even
the patient seemed to adore her and sometimes invited Maribel to lie
next to her in the bed. Roser's condition had visibly worsened. She was
losing weight and her belly was full of water. The doctor did no longer
come to visit. What for? And where was he? Jordi felt that the entire
world was falling apart. He did not want to think about the impending
catastrophe. "Don't worry, God will provide", said Maribel with her
marvelous smile. "You and Roser have been good to us and you will
be rewarded" Jordi was not so sure. Next day he scraped together all
the groceries he could find and brought them home. He saw starving
people outside of his door but he no longer had any tears left for others.
He had found a can of condensed milk. Roser was not eating anything.
If she was not able to swallow fluids, the children would appreciate it.
Yes, the children! Roser viewed them like her own.

Jordi entered the apartment without making noise. He heard
Maribel in the bedroom talking to his wife. "Come, Roser, try. Sit
up and I will help you with the toilet. Jordi will be here in a moment
and you must look good, so that he does not think of other women"
Jordi walked into the kitchen. A profound sadness overtook Jordi
and he sank his head in the chest. He had to wait and collect himself
before meeting the women. He was a beaten-up man. Everything and
everybody was dying.

Roser was in bed and Maribel was holding her hand. The patient tried to smile when she saw her husband:

"Come to me, Jordi, give me a kiss and a hug" After a while she collected herself and spoke:

"I know that I am dying and although I am sad that I cannot grow old at your side, Jordi, as I had wished with all my heart, I feel comforted because I am ending my days in the care of two such goodhearted people, the best I could imagine. And the two children that I could never have, are beautiful and bring me the joy that I needed. Thank you to both of you for everything."

Jordi and Maribel, both with tears in their eyes, were going to interrupt her, but she raised her hand signaling them to stop. Roser was not finished:

"I have been thinking. Jordi, you are still young and need a woman at your side. After I am gone, you must rebuild your existence. The war will soon be finished and maybe, if they let you, you will be able to make a new beginning. I have had an opportunity to know Maribel well. She is a truly good person, lovable, selfless, dependable, and beautiful. She is blessed with two adorable children. The three have been treated like dogs. Please, Jordi, please Maribel: when I am gone, marry each other and live happily together for many years. Jordi, be a father to the children, because they need one. Maybe the heaven had denied us a family so that we would be ready for them. Promise me, you both and I will die in peace."

* * *

The Nationalist army made a triumphal entry into the city through the Diagonal Avenue, soon to be renamed Avenue of the Generalissimo Franco. Many of the soldiers were Moroccan Muslims under the orders of General Yagüe. The Catalan radio stations went off the air. Another radio started playing unfamiliar military music. Many people had gone to the street to greet the victorious army with wild enthusiasm and raised the right arms in the fascist way. There were so many of them among us and we did not know, thought Jordi. But maybe they showed up because of the exhaustion and frustration of the last three years. They were not that many, after all.

Barcelona had entered what would be a very long period of forced stupor, of grey survival, of living death. Our hero decided to wait for the new masters in his primary office and in uniform. They did not come until next day.

"Por Dios y por España! Viva Franco! Arriba España! De pie, rojo-separatistas!" (For God and for Spain! Long live Franco! Long live Spain! Stand up, red separatists!)

The conqueror had arrived. Jordi and ten of his colleagues, all of them impeccably dressed in the uniform of the city police stood up in silence and saluted. The newcomer was a young man dressed in the fascist uniform, wearing blue shirt and red beret. Attached to his belt, Jordi could see a large German-made handgun. Behind him, four nationalist soldiers in campaign attire armed with rifles were suspiciously looking around and had an unpleasant smirk in their faces. The boy approached one of the policemen and shouted to his face:

"Speak, who is in charge here?"

"Sir, it was a Sergeant Roure, but his whereabouts are currently unknown."

"Another Red coward, running like a chicken! Are you armed?"

"We don't know if the Sergeant was killed. We have all old guns which we keep in our drawers."

"Out with them, Reds! And watch what you do. You Catalans are a treacherous people. We shall teach you to love Spain. You shall remain here at my disposal until further notice."

Jordi remembered his wife and dared to object. "Sir, with all due respect, I have home a very sick wife. She is dying and I am her single caretaker", he lied.

The newcomer laughed "What do I care about your shitty whores! Many good Spanish patriots better than your wife had to die because of your persistence in the ways of the evil and your fight against God and the Motherland! I do not wish to hear anything. You will stay here locked up until I interrogate you; when I finish reviewing your files, I will decide what to do with every one of you. Some of you will be jailed and presented to a war council, others put on probation. High live Spain!" The men repeated for the first time the fascist salute.

The eleven men were brought in a truck to the City police head-quarters and spent there three full days in cells, subject to questioning, harsh treatment and unable to communicate with their families. Despite the danger, Jordi could not take Roser off her mind.

He finally was released and allowed to walk home. He would not be sent to a concentration camp. His heart was beating fast. It was the 31st day of January of 1939 and the sun was shining but Jordi felt that everything was dark, threatening, and hopeless. Above all, he worried about his beloved Roser.

He climbed the stairs of his apartment. The moment he reached the entrance of the building, he knew that Roser was dead. The stairway was eerily silent. A neighbor greeted him with a nod of his head. "I am sorry for your loss." Jordi had to fight a sob. He climbed the stairs. His door was open and he overheard crying women. He ran to the bedroom. Roser, dressed, lied peacefully in their bed with her hands crossed over the chest. Jordi turned around and saw Maribel with the two children. Impulsively he moved toward them and hugged them as strongly as he could. They all cried.

* * *

Foguet was finally allowed to keep his job as a member of the Urban Police, which had lost almost all its power and attributions to the "grays", Franco's centralized State police. These would now veil for public safety and for the safety of the Dictator and his new Regime. The "grays" were invariably non-Catalan immigrants who spoke no Catalan. This language had been strictly banned. Jordi had been warned never to speak it in the headquarters with anyone, even not with old friends, under pain of dismissal… or worse. The newspapers were all printed in Castilian, the Radio spoke only Castilian, and new teachers in the Schools spoke only Castilian. Did it mean the end of the Catalan nation? Like most other people, Jordi was mostly concerned with his own and his family's survival. Everybody had been forced to translate his given name. Jordi was now Jorge. Empar became Amparo. Maribel, however, was fine.

Jordi and Maribel had accepted the advice of the moribund Roser and were looking forward to getting married to each other. Even the two children accepted the man as a new father. How really great had Roser been, by giving them her blessing! Jordi had refused to initiate matrimonial relations with the woman before they were married. He still was in awe of Roser. What a personality she had! How could anyone take her place?

After two months, the two decided that they had waited long enough and that it was time to get married. Jordi did not know what formalities were required. He collected his wife's death certificate and went with Maribel to the same office in City Hall where he had been married to Roser years ago. In his uniform nobody bothered him and he easily found the office. The war had not caused too much damage to the magnificent civilian gothic building. Jordi, however, found that the room was nearly deserted. Only an old man sat at a desk.

"Sir, I am Officer Jorge Foguet Puig and this is my fiancée Maribel Olmos Romero and we are here because we wish to be married to each other."

"Then go to a Catholic Church", answered the man.

"But we are not religious people" objected Jordi "We would prefer a quiet civil wedding."

Now the man was irritated. "Ha! That is finished. If you wish to be married you have to go to your Parish and do so according to the rules of our Holy Mother the Church and with her Blessing."

Both Jordi and Maribel had opened their mouths. "Do not understand me wrong. We respect the Church greatly. But do you mean that we do not have the option of being married by a judge instead?"

"Such are the orders of the Glorious National Movement and the Caudillo of Spain. The devilish Godless government of the Republic has been defeated and now law and order have been reestablished and everything is as it should have always been, as it always was before your impish Republic. Go to your Parish" And the man went back to reading the paper. The conversation was ended.

Still dumbfounded, Jordi and Maribel exited the building toward Sant Jaume Square (now named Plaza de San Jaime). "Well, where is your Parish Church?" asked Maribel.

Jordi sighed. "I have never been inside, but a city officer knows everything. It is Saint Eulalia. Let's go right away."

In the Parish office, the climate was quite different. The priests were not militants from the Regime and spoke Catalan. They could relax, but Jordi and Maribel knew the need for prudence.

"You say what you are members of this Parish?"

"We never came to the services."

"I see" The priest was indifferent. "Did you spend all the time of war in the City until our Liberation?"

"Yes, father. I distributed food to women in children at the Les Corts Field of the FC Barcelona."

"I was hidden in Sant Boi", countered the priest. "The Reds wanted to kill me. They probably were the same ones you fed."

Jordi did not answer, but Maribel responded "I know. It was a terrible time" Maribel also assented with a movement of her head. She explained that she had no political interests but had been hungry and on the street with two small children before she found Jordi. And she had met Jordi there. The priest seemed to calm down.

"What can I do for you?"

Jordi took over again "Well, Father, I lost my dearest wife at the time of the... liberation, three days after. This Angel" he said pointing at Maribel" came to our home and helped her and me. Before she died, my Roser asked both of us to marry each other."

The priest raised his brows but did not seem moved. He had heard too many stories.

"We went to City Hall but with the new Regime it seems that everything has changed and the procedure is now different."

"Of course. Before the Republic, Spaniards had always married in Church. Anything else is akin to living in sin."

Jordi and Maribel made long faces but quietly assented. If these were the orders from Madrid, that is what they would do.

"You say that your wife is dead? Show me the certificate?"

"Yes, Father. Here it is."

The priest inspected it. "Very good. And you, Maribel? Are you single?"

"No father, I was married to the father of my two children."

"Was he killed in the war?"

"He escaped to France" explained Maribel.

A silence followed. Then the priest placed his flat hand on the desk making a loud noise.

"Is he alive or not?" he asked

Maribel and Jordi looked at each other helplessly. Jordi spoke.

"We don't know. He was a shameless and irresponsible man. He abandoned his family in the time of their greatest need and we don't know where he went. Neither are we aware of his whereabouts nor of where he has been buried. Nor of whether he is dead or alive."

Now the priest was angry.

"What you are telling me is that Maribel's husband is alive, and that she is therefore still married, alright? And you come here to get married again? Are you a bigamist? Why do you think that we condone bigamy?"

Jordi protested. "No, father, I work for the City, please" The comment was superfluous, since he was in uniform. He pressed on "But father, we did not view this situation as in impediment, since Maribel and this cruel man who hit her and abandoned his wife and children on the street to starve had only been married in City Hall, not in any Church. We should be able to easily get a divorce."

Now the priest exploded. "Divorce!!! You want a divorce? And you have the nerve to come here to tell me to my face? Take notice, once and for all, that the red domination has ended. The divorce law of the Republic was a devilish attempt to undermine the family values on which the fabric of Spain rests, to transform Catholic Spain into a cesspool of heresies and crimes ruled by irresponsible minions of Stalin and the Communist International."

Jordi and Maribel were speechless, fearful. "But father" dared Jordi to object, "surely some form of marriage termination will still be feasible. We all know of things that...."

The priest pointed at him with a finger "Not again, not again. Spain shall be Catholic or shall not be. Our war, the Glorious Crusade of National Liberation, was about this, about rescuing Spain. Holy

Matrimony is a sacrament, a sacred institution instituted by our Lord
Jesus Christ. What God has united, man cannot let asunder."

"But father, Maribel's husband was a godless and cruel man...."

"Like all the Reds" interrupted the cleric.

"...who did not have religion or went to Church. And he failed to care
for her or their children. Why should his civil marriage be indissoluble?"

"Because..." was the slow, loud answer, "because marriage is
marriage. You should not have married one of them. It should be
contracted in front of the altar although to become a valid marriage it
only requires the mutual expression of commitment in front of witnesses.
With or without church, she is married as long as her husband lives.
The Caudillo Franco has ordered that henceforth all family matters are
settled according to Canonic law of the Holy Church, as it behooves
to a Catholic nation that has been born again, reverting to what we
were in the times of the Spanish Empire."

Jordi could not answer. He would have to wait in silence almost 40
years before he could freely do so. But on his way home he remembered
what the priest at St. Eulalia had said: To become valid, a marriage
only requires an expression of mutual commitment in front of at least
two witnesses.

They would do just that, express commitment in front of witnesses.

* * *

Jordi called his few relatives and friends to his home. Maribel
served two bottles of wine, glasses and cake slices arranged in a circle
around a black and white picture of the couple. Even the two children,
now nicely dressed, looked at them and laughed. Maribel had found
a white veil to wear.

And in everybody's presence, Jordi spoke: "I, Jordi take you, Maribel,
as my legitimate spouse to love you and share my life for the rest of our

lives. And I will care for you as my wife and partner and I will raise your children as if they were my own. And we will commemorate this day every year as our wedding anniversary which it truly is."

"And I Maribel accept you, Jordi, as my beloved husband and true father of my children for the rest of my life."

The guests and witnesses applauded. The sun should have shone outside, and the moon that followed, too. But preferred to hide under a covered sky. The skies refused to see what was going on in the city.

* * *

Maribel had relatives in Palencia, in the heart of Castile. The wheat-producing region had lent support to the fascist uprising and subsequent war. At the first opportunity after the end of the hostilities she expressed a wish to visit her father and siblings along with Jordi and the two children, who had never been outside of Barcelona. Jordi made his calculations. If the children could stay with relatives, he had saved enough money for a railroad trip and finally at the same time the two adults would be having a honeymoon trip. To be sure, he reworked his financial calculations. They confirmed that he had enough money to pay for a second-class railroad couchette in one way, which at night allowed turning the seats into a bed. There was no bed lining, but the passengers could throw some covers or coats on their bodies. The return trip would have to be in the third- class, because the funds available reached no further. Maribel had never been in a couchette nor traveled in second-class and she regarded it as an enormous luxury. The children however would have to stay back in Barcelona with a friendly relative. Jordi and Maribel were going to have a real delayed honeymoon.

Maribel received a letter from her sister Gregoria, who lived in Palencia with their old parents, which would spoil their joy:

Gregoria had been very happy to learn that she had survived well the troubles with the Reds before and during the liberation of Barcelona. The entire family had been from the beginning with the Glorious National Movement and both their father and Gregoria's husband, Teodomiro, were proudly wearing the blue shirt of the Phalange. They were somewhat unhappy that Maribel had joined her fortunes with a former Catalan Red, but they knew that such unions frequently were the result of the hard circumstances and human weaknesses and that they needed not be permanent. (Here Maribel had to read twice) Both were of course welcome to stay in his house, but not being married, father would not allow them to sleep in the same room. Father had consulted with the Rector of their Parish who praised us for being tolerant but reaffirmed that Maribel and Jorge had to sleep separately. Unfortunately, she could offer no second room and father did not allow people to sleep around on couches or straw because it interfered with his work. She was really sorry. Maribel would of course always be welcome if she came alone. If she wished to confess her sins, their Rector was the proper priest for such cases. She had attended to the spiritual wellbeing of interned prisoners in a nearby concentration camp. But if she insisted on coming with her Catalan lover, they would have to be housed in the Fonda (cheap, family run hotel) on Main Street.

"Then, we are not going. The Railroad will refund the tickets", said Jordi/Jorge. Maribel, who had read the letter three times before showing it to Jordi, did not answer. She was upset but she had been looking forward to meeting again her family. She remembered her childhood playing in the streets with her two sisters. She said, however, what she had to say and Jordi understood well the unspoken conclusion:

"If you don't want, maybe we could go to the beach. I understand" and she unexpectedly hugged her man. Jordi felt Maribel's emotion and added:

"It is no good to take decisions when you are upset. Let's wait until tomorrow. We must get used to facing this problem. When I married you, I accepted it for the entire duration of the regime. Things are as they are and nothing lasts forever" True, nothing lasts forever, but some things may last for a long time.

* * *

The relative who very unwillingly had agreed to take care of the children during their parent's absence was Cristòful (now re-named Cristóbal). He had three children himself and he ran some irregular but rewarding business involving black food acquisition and distribution. He felt that Jordi's apparent police protection was invaluable to his illegal business, although in fact it was non-existent or assumed only of the basis of the family relationship. In Cristòful's opinion, he was helping the people of Barcelona by procuring them the decent food that the Government could not. He was not altogether unhappy with the new National Movement's ideology and he had never concealed his admiration for Mussolini. With Hitler, however, he was not altogether happy. The trains arrived and departed on time in Italy! That is what they needed in Spain too.

The day before the departure the two children were ceremoniously brought to Cristòful's fanciful apartment and dropped there. "You will see how good their food is. And they will be brought to the movies as frequently as you or they wish" explained Jordi to them.

But Jordi had asked him for something more important: Letters of introduction for him and his wife and travel documents. As a city policeman he needed such documents as much or more than any other citizen. Besides, Cristòful's business was no concern of him. He regarded it as unfair and dangerous, possibly even corrupt. The general public opinion was that he and his colleagues were all participants in the chain of abuse and exploitation of hunger and human misery that was the black market. Who was he to pass judgment? He did not ask him for anything. Times were very hard. And Cristoful could write his letters in paper with the head of the provincial Secretariat of the National Movement for Barcelona, an excellent endorsement. Jordi and Maribel went to the France Station with everything that was needed by the couple neatly arranged in his pocket. Jordi was at all times careful not to compromise himself as a collaborator in the case the regime was soon overturned.

Maribel had long argued with Jordi whether or not the children should come to the station for the farewell. Actually, she was anxious to experience the drama of the kisses and hugs of the last moment and the last embraces of her children, not to mention her tears, vows, and last-minute reminders. The kids came alongside their host.

* * *

The train departed late and had to stop underway on numerous occasions. They had reached the endless plains of Northern Castile when they finally decided that it was time to prepare the modest couchette bed and retire as if they were in an expensive Hotel. Maribel was literally cracking out of happiness.

The door of the small train compartment opened up and a small, dark man with an artificial leg entered. He could not smile. He had forgotten how to do it in the Francoist foxholes and later in the hospital ward where he had been amputated. Jordi at once displayed his travel papers and his police shield.

"You had been a police officer under the red domination?" He omitted inquiring for what reason he was not in a concentration camp.

"I was only an urban policeman. My job was not political or military. All I did was to feed people, especially women and children in a soccer field. It was the stadium of the FC Barcelona" The man did not seem convinced, and Jordi additionally explained: "Following the Liberation, my whole unit put itself at the disposition of the new authorities and the National Movement. As you can see, they recognized that I would be useful keeping my previous position" Maribel had been warned not to speak in any such situation. She stood by and smiled. After a brief silence, the inspector spoke again:

"Alright. I have no problems. At any rate, you were lucky to have survived it all. Are you two married to each other?"

Big problem. Ay! Jordi Foguet attempted to give his explanation. They had no wedding certificate. Terror had appeared in Maribel's still smiling face. The face of the mutilated inspector had darkened and was now threatening, as if he were awakening from a nightmare. His eyes had turned piercing and would hurt any casual observer. He was standing at the door, no longer listening.

The unknown policeman appeared very bored and uninterested. "Well, are you married or not? I will tell you why I am asking. My instructions are to arrest and bring to the nearest police station any couple found using this facility without having been previously blessed by our mother the Catholic Church. You see how simple my obligation is? And instead, you tell me all kinds of stories that I don't understand."

Appeals to camaraderie, humanity and understanding followed. After dropping a couple of demeaning comments on "certain women and whores" "a designation which of course did not apply here" Jordi and Maribel were allowed to continue their journey under the condition that they opened the door of the compartment and restored its day-time appearance, without couchette.

After the train left station, an overweight, smiling train inspector with a moustache came by. "The old man with the wooden leg is off the train. There will be no more controls before Palencia, so do as you please. Before the war I spent three years living in Catalonia and it was great. We are turning more papist than the pope and it is the fault of Mussolini! Aren't we all human beings?" Not for everybody, evidently. Nor every living human was a human being. "Go back to what you were doing and forget the trouble. We get nothing out of judging other people."

* * *

The city of Palencia, one of the provincial capitals of Old Castile, was a paradise for antique and antiquity seekers. Its streets, like a museum, exhibited Roman, Visigoth and Christian remainders and churches.

"The city was founded many centuries ago. It was always welcoming for Moors and Christians and it even had some Jews, but not many" said Micaela, Maribel's baby sister. "But if you are interested, you should ask father. He knows everything" Unfortunately, it was no longer as welcoming for alleged Reds and Catalans "but the Caudillo" she added "saved us from becoming a concentration camp full of starving people like the Soviet Union" Jordi remembered how much he had always disliked and mistrusted the communists who had taken over for plenty of reasons. They had not won any elections and Jordi never voted for them.

It turned out that Gregorio himself, Jordi's putative father-in-law, had registered his guests at the Fonda on Main Street. He viewed his situation as a tragedy and he was not in any way unfriendly. He had hugged Maribel merrily, laughing, with tears. He was tolerant and forgiving but in the current tough times, hard points of view were unavoidable. The instructions of the Movimiento and the Caudillo were clear and represented a national priority in this dangerous moment of reconstruction and nationalcatholicism. All new laws were to be followed without excuses despite of the lies and the usual anti-Spanish mendacities of the Masonry and the Socialist International. False piety with the defeated enemy could only lead to the waste of the sacrifice of those who gave their lives for God and for Spain. Why should anyone share the table garnished with the bread earned with so much sacrifice with the murderers and criminals at the service of the Kremlin and the International Anti-Spanish conspiracy? In Spain the fight was won, but the German Youth was at the time still in the process of fighting its historical effort for a better order in a clean Europe. How could Gregorio be lenient with Spain's enemies and those who wanted to break her? Like a Spanish Cavalier of the glorious imperial times of America's discovery and civilization, he would put his sword to the service of the King and the Homeland while cutting with the tip of his weapon a rose to be offered to the bosom of his beloved Dulcinea. A new world and a new era were opening up in front of him, a word without materialism who had found the third way between capitalism and socialism. Jordi listened patiently to his possible in-law and did not answer. He remembered what he knew about brain washes. But he understood.

Gregorio, a man with a sturdy frame like most farmers, insisted on carrying one of the suitcases himself and to speak to the Fonda's owner, as he had done two weeks earlier. Jordi understood that his in-law believed that this step might be helpful. It was already the afternoon. The two men, loaded with multiple suitcases and bags advanced on Main Street toward a simple building labeled with the word FONDA. Gregorio rang the bell and a middle aged, sturdy citizen opened the door. Gregorio greeted and attempted to explain:

"Hola, neighbor. Here is my friend Jorge, who has come to visit us after we had been separated for years during the Crusade of National Liberation from him, and our dearest daughter Maribel, who in the meantime had two beautiful children, my only grandbabies. They were trapped in Barcelona with the Reds and we even did not receive news from them for a long time."

The man at the door was discreetly trying to hide his boredom.

"Then enter, seat in the parlor and you can explain the whole problem to my father. He will be back soon."

Jordi thought: "He has said "problem" This means that his father has given a negative answer. We are in for a long time" He sighed.

It was already dark when Nicomedes, the owner, returned to the house. His son met him at the door and evidently briefed him on the situation. Nicomedes made with his mouth signs of deep displeasure "No quiero problemas", he was overheard saying to his son. Finally, he acceded to enter the waiting room and listen to Gregorio. When the farmer was finished, he responded speaking in solemn tones:

"I have heard you, Gregorio and I have known you my whole life and there is nothing I would not do to help you when you are in need. But you put me in an impossible situation. Do you want me to show you the pile of papers I have received prohibiting that hotels and inns be used for sinful meetings between men and women?"

"It is not for the purpose that we both understand, Nicomedes. The war was cruel and did not discriminate. What support does the son of a bitch who abandoned my daughter and her children deserve?"

"None, I would shoot him on sight. This is not the issue. The issues are the papers from the Government prohibiting me, as a condition to keep the business open (a business which is my only means of sustenance) to use my hostel for prostitution (and please, amigo Jorge, forget the language which is not mine). The fact is that one makes lots of money at a time when we are all short. We were and are all here staunch supporters of the National Uprising from day one. My son is a militant of Phalange and fought in the foxholes for the Crusade of Liberation. We have won and opened the door to a new Spain, the same as Hitler and Mussolini opened the door to a new Europe. True, some things do not work well but they will improve under the guidance of the Caudillo Franco. We need to have patience, not to increase the chaos that would sink us into the anarchy if we were to go each his own way. The Caudillo will show us the way. And I have told you what his orders in this matter are."

There was silence in the room, which was finally broken by Gregorio. "So, you are telling me that there is nothing that can be done?" He made a sign of standing up and leaving. Luckily for him and Jordi, Nicomedes' economic situation was really bad. His Fonda had only one guest, a mutilated gentleman (war mutilated) to whom he was forced to grant a heavy discount.

"Wait, Gregorio, wait. I only wanted that you understand the situation. If they stay in your home, it is your conscience; if they stay here, it is the law. Our motives are in both cases honorable."

Finally, Jordi though it appropriate to intercalate a word.

"Why don't you tell us what to do? The fact that I am an urban policeman approved by the National Movement is not of any help?"

Nicomedes sighed deeply "I was thinking the same, amigo Jorge. The police commander of our ward is a man of mature age and you could talk to him. He has common sense and is always helpful. It is still 8:30 PM and people rarely dine before 10:00. Why don't you go? You may leave here your baggage... waiting for your return" He wants to keep our luggage here? thought Jordi. A good sign.

The Police Precinct was only a few houses away. The two solicitants were at once led to the boss, a middle-aged man of friendly appearance who greeted them: "Good evening. So, you must be Gregorio and here is our Catalan friend *Txordi* " He pronounced the name badly.

"Yes, Sir."

'And I am Lieutenant Pedro Santamaría, to serve you. I stayed several times in Catalonia before the Crusade. My family enjoyed it. Many people, of course, abused the liberties that the republican government granted them and tried to break the sacred unity of Spain" Here the

Lieutenant stopped, waiting for an answer. Jordi looked at his face. He would not trust him. He looked so friendly but if a wrong word escaped his mouth… "I fully agree with you and I am happy that they have been finally defeated and that my children will grow in a Christian Nation" Santamaría smiled in a way that denoted irritation that his play had been discovered. He found himself the official language stupid. It would be useless to continue playing with Jordi.

'Tell me, Txordi, how do you think that your situation with this Castilian woman will evolve and end" Jordi knew that it was no time to reveal his hopes regarding the short duration of the Regimen. He rather responded:

"In my family, lieutenant, I am proud to say, there has never been a single divorce. Maribel and I have been married in front of witnesses and will stay together until death does us separate."

This time the lieutenant laughed uncontrollably. One of the best answers he had ever heard. If it was not so late, he would enjoy continuing the interrogation. But his wife had been cooking something special for him and besides, Jorge was also some kind of policeman. What was an urban policeman?

"I will tell you what, Txordi. The rector of this parish is a saintly and compassionate man who fought in the National Army during the Crusade and now shows a fantastic common sense and as he says, lots of evangelical piety. Why don't you talk to him? If he agrees with your demand, I will not disagree. And I am sure that Nicomedes could use some extra money. Do you see? Everybody would be happy. His Parish house is in the big square next to the Church. He is almost always there. I will call ahead of you."

Jordi was thinking that next they would have to talk to His Excellency the Civilian Governor of the Province. In the meantime, Maribel was probably getting tired of waiting.

The two men arrived at the Parish building in a few minutes, almost at 9:45 PM. They noticed a weak light at the entrance. They had no need to ring the bell. The door opened by itself. Hidden behind was the dark, pale, skinny, and pious figure of Father Jesús, the Rector. The man did not look at all like his Redeemer of the same name, but he occasionally dared to reproduce without enthusiasm or life the words of the Master in his priestly mouth. He rarely looked at people in their eyes.

"In the name of our Lord Jesus Christ, who died in the Cross for all of us, I will forgive all the sins you may wish to confess and bless you. Come inside, my friend."

"I will, Father, although I did not intend to confess any sins at this late hour" At this point, Gregorio kissed the saintly priest's hand "Father, we are seeking advice from many honorable people of the town and everybody has advised us to seek your opinion."

"I can give to you my advice; forgiveness, however, which is the real issue here, belongs only to the Lord and to those who live in Communion with him. Come inside, my Brothers in Christ."

Obviously, the priest already was aware of the situation. The three men sat in a room of the rectory. Father Jesús raised his hand. "I have heard and people in my confidence have told me everything, not today, but long before you, Jorge, and those in your care, came here."

"Those in my care, father, will have assured food and drink during our brief stay thanks to the kindness of this good man here, but we need a place to stay" Jesus shook his head in the affirmative. Jordi could speak very well.

"Have you considered leaving your companion and the innocent ones in the care of their father and you, as a Catalan, seek somebody else's understanding and hospitality? Because we are all Brothers in Christ and you could not choose where you were born."

A silence followed. Gregorio interrupted it. "I have told him the same, Father. I would easily have directed him to appropriate addresses" Finally Jorge exploded.

"I won't do it and Maribel, the one whom you properly call "my companion," and my companion for life she is, will not do it either. And we won't because it is an insult and a capitulation to insults, prejudice and lies. To us and to her children which are also mine."

Desperate, Gregorio signaled the Urban Policeman to close his mouth, lest their last chance be lost. But the priest once again signaled to be silent and looked with his eyes to heaven. He might have seen the skies if the rectory had not been platooned.

"You know, Jorge, I started the Holy Crusade of National Liberation in the Basque Country, with the Reds, close to my brothers. After the assassination of many priests and believers by the Reds, I decided to cross the line and join the Nationals until God granted us victory over our enemies. I though that I could better serve my nation and my fellow humans by joining the Christian army of my resurrected Nation led by the Generalissimo in agreement with the principles of the nationalcatholicism. Maybe I was thinking of moments like this one."

"If you wish to shoot anyone, father, kill only me, not my wife or children who are innocent, I pray you" commented Jordi.

"Jorge!" moaned the old Gregorio. But once again Father Jesús insisted in being recognized.

"Here I am. I love my enemies, I will set right the enemies of the State, who are also the enemies of God, I will suppress the Catalan and Basque Separatism that has already almost once led us astray. All of this, reinforced by the force won by those who fell for God and Spain and never forgetting that the error may have almost the same rights as the justice. The lieutenant assures me that, using proper discretion, there is no danger for the public morals and he expects discretion from all who know. And he adds that Nicomedes could use some additional earnings. In other words, I give you my blessings under the condition that you introduce yourselves as husband and wife. I wish you and I find the opportunity of meeting again until you understand us better."

"I already understand you well, you are a mild, nearly harmless fascist" thought Jordi as he smiled.

That evening, for the first time, he and Maribel would sleep in the fancy main room of the Fonda. Maribel had never been in such an establishment and was anxious to inspect and try it out. She declared that it was three times larger than their bedroom in Barcelona. And the bed was also much more comfortable. Then she added loudly, almost laughing: "What a clever and well-spoken husband I have! You are going to take care of us very well! Come here"

Jordi had made peace with the entire family and had found an affordable place to sleep. As for the others… suddenly it occurred to him that they were also human beings.

From that evening forward, the vacation trip became a joy. Jordi had some time to think about his future.

* * *

The Francoist Regime was going to last a long time, over 40 years. And after the Dictator's trespass in 1978, his lackeys succeeded in getting hold of all the control buttons to seduce the regime's enemies enrolling them in a well-paid transition with mandatory amnesty for everybody. The new rulers would be chosen by elections which would never lead to real changes. And Catalonia's expectations would be once again frustrated.

The nineteen fifties came and went, the sixties came and went. In January 1970 still in the Dictator's lifetime an airmail letter from Paris had arrived. The secretary of one of the still surviving refugee organizations in Paris notified Ms. Maribel Olmos Romero of the sudden death of her husband and former anarchist comrade Miguel Prieto Fernández of a heart attack in the care of her companion Louise. He had been cremated and his ashes dispersed in front of a monument to the freedom fighters in Spain, as he wished. She was being sent this notification in case that she required a death certificate appropriate to the existing Francoist legislation, since she had legally become a widow. If this document was important to her, she should contact a M. Martinot, officer in the French Consulate General in Barcelona, who had been helpful in the past in similar cases that still needed regularization.

So, Maribel and Jordi were now able to get married according to the rites of the Holy Catholic Church. Maribel read the letter again and again and commented "Miguel Prieto Fernández was his name. Did I ever tell you? Who is this Louise? They must have been enjoying themselves and here we could not get married." After a break she added "And my father almost cursed me as a public sinner."

Jordi tenderly looked to her eyes, which were showing some contained rage. He would immediately start with the formalities. But he also phoned both his children, who were of mature ages and well employed, but still single, asking them to meet him alone in a bar at the Rambles, the famous street in the old city, after work. Both had learned on the phone of the news he was bringing with a worrisome silence. Pedrito had asked before hanging up: "Had this individual a real name, like humans do?"

"You should not say that, Pedro. After all you wear his name" (They had tried in vain to change it twice).

"Maybe so", added Pedrito "but you and Mom have been married for many years. What do you need this wedding theater for? First, they slap you in the face and now you are going to kiss their hand. I won't be there. It is even an insult for our mother. You should have more pride."

* * *

Jordi found the two siblings seated at a table of a popular Café. They did not look friendly. In fact, they were clearly annoyed and combative.

"What music are you going to play, father? Wagner's or Mendelssohn's Wedding March?" They never had called Jordi "father" but always "Papa." They were making their attitude very clear. It was going to be a fight.

Jordi objected: "My dear children, I have called you both to discuss a very serious matter that affects us all. I understand that you are entitled to express your views. Me and your mother, too."

After a silence Iris spoke: "Father, we both strongly feel that you both have been *really* married for more than 30 years as you have told us many times and we do not understand what this comedy at St. Eulalia's church will achieve. Are they not the same who treated you both, us included, like garbage?"

"You know that I agree. You will never know how I felt at the time. Our mother thought that the Catholic Church had betrayed us. We were insulted and vilified and called names that we did not deserve"

Pedro interrupted. "Yours is a fine church. The sinners do the clever work and donate money, but they crucify the innocents. Once in school I beat up a boy that had said to my face and in the presence of witnesses that my parents were public sinners."

"It is not the proper time to remember, Pedrito. And it serves no purpose. You know that we were no public sinners. After all, the times of the dictator are coming to an end and the mess he imposed will disappear with him. For Franco the time to die has arrived. I mention it, because you have never known anything but the tyranny, the lies, and the threats of his dictatorship. Beneath the sheath of opportunism, many human beings are hiding. Maybe we shall see them surface after Franco is gone."

"Father, father, und three times father" Pedro said while Iris was assenting with the head, "you and you alone picked up mother and ourselves from the street where we were starving. You gave us a home and an education. Without you, maybe we would have died. I even don't know who this son-of-a-bitch who kicked the bucket in Paris was."

Here Jordi had to intervene smiling "To find you was my great luck, not a virtuous deed. Don't thank me for that. It was my happiest hour. Besides, I did not bring you here to cry, just to decide how we should act. It is your mother who wants to get officially married. Her wedding with the anarchist had meant nothing to her and now she wishes a real wedding in the church surrounded by her children, as she has always wanted. I think we should fulfill her wishes. I went yesterday with her to the store to choose a beautiful black dress. I almost was embarrassed because sshe started dancing in the store. She deserves it. You must grant her this joy. Next September 14th, at 12:00 o'clock, at St Eulalia's, you both will be our witnesses. Maribel says that it is alright if you bring your boy or girlfriend, should you have one. If you wish, of course. We know nothing of your lives."

Nobody wanted to cry but Iris started. And the tears in Pedro's eyes were now apparent. Jordi extended both hands across the table and they were grabbed.

Seizing the opportunity, Jordi added: "There is something more I must ask you. Would you both buy our wedding rings? It is also an idea of your mother. She tells me that she would be very happy. They should not be expensive. Your Mom is running the show and I don't you dare to contradict her!"

THE WAY IT SHOULD HAVE ENDED

The church was not very old but had some interesting gothic motives. It was dark but light entered through several windows and white beams of light bathed the seating area. They had not paid much money and because of that only the altar and some small nearby areas were garnished with flowers. Pedro and Iris had been able to get two cars. The young man and a hitherto unknown young lady sat in the first one with the two main persons, Jordi and Maribel, in the back. Iris showed up with an equally unknown gentleman sitting next to her in the second vehicle. Inside the church in the first two pews a few people, all of them close friends and relatives, were waiting. Maribel was beaming in a ray of happiness. She was carrying a white bouquet of flowers that contrasted well with her dark dress. Jordi was wearing a tie. The couple approached alone the altar, slowly and smilingly .They did not want that the priest celebrated a mass. The officiant appeared dressed for the wedding only. He was a young priest and had spoken several times to Jordi and his bride. He knew nothing of the events at the end of the war, which was common among young people, and had found that the elders refused to talk and they had lost the memories of Franco's nationalcatholicism (in place of nationalsocialism) and the evident impending dismemberment of the regime. The memory, explain the psychologists, always prefers to remember the good and represses the troubled times.

The ceremony ended. **"I declare you husband and wife..."** *pronounced the priest. The bridegroom kissed the wife, decently, on the cheek and all other attendees started hugging each other and shaking their hands. Then the priest started his sermon:*

"*My brothers and sisters. I beg you to thank God for the privilege
we had of seeing these two becoming husband and wife, as they
had wished for so many years. Normally after a wedding we speak
to remember them of their obligations toward all the children the
Lord may grant them . In your case, you Maribel and Jordi, you
have already fulfilled your duties and may now rest and celebrate
your own love of your children and maybe grandchildren. I am
aware of your complaints against my Church and I know what
happened to you and how unjustly you were treated. And yes, your
matrimony in your apartment surrounded by your friends was a
good one in the eyes of God. Among those who had survived the
horrors and the passion of the war, there were some who believed in
Love and Justice as our main precepts ordered by Jesus Christ. For
what others did and in the name of this Parish, I wish to apologize.
You do not need my blessing but please, forgive and bless me.*"

ADVENTURES OF THE ALIEN SHIP THAT DISCOVERED THE EARTH

Dedicated to the unforgettable
professionals responsible for
STAR TREK and STAR TREK New Generations
which did so much to
enlighten the youth and later life of
millions of worldwide TREKKIES

Brief Information on the
Nature and Life of the Namuhs

NO ONE WHO IS aware of the size of the World, of the limitless validity of the Einstein findings and of our knowledge of the universal physical laws and planetary chemistry will be surprised to read this report, but what it is not yet generally know is that we have already been once visited by a ship occupied by intelligent beings from a star system located several light-years away from us. Knowing that the speed of light is 100.000 km/second and that it cannot be surpassed (nor probably equaled) by any intelligent live civilizations, it seems to be a foregone conclusion that the distance to other inhabited planets is an unsurmountable traveling obstacle. There are however conceivable, still untested theoretical means around it and the civilization present in the fifth planet of the star named Zircon34 unexpectedly succeeded in part. Its astronomers discovered in their reachable neighborhood that a novel, unexpected item suspected of being a new *wormhole* had come into view. They knew about remote wormholes, but this time the unexpected item was not only close but revealed a clear entrance ring within reach, which made it potentially penetrable and navigable. The intelligent scientific population had never been able to come close to one or inspect it. The entirety of the planet's residents was excited and celebrated the open possibility of new explorations of remote civilizations. A *wormhole* is a possibly cylindrical tunnel developed at the edges and contacts of separate time-space sequences but outside of both, which connects two remote parts of the universe with each other regardless of the distance. The best learned groups of scholars could not in any way estimate the location and distance of the exit, if one existed, or even if it might narrow or end in a blind sack. Some wormholes in the universe are stable; others are not and appear and disappear on their own for unknown reasons.

The star Zircon34 belonged to what for us would be a remote galaxy and was the equivalent of our Sun, but it was surrounded by eight planets of varied sizes that rotated in orbit. One of them, of dimensions similar to those of our beloved Earth, had a flat surface, was surrounded by a thin atmosphere of hydrogen, and was inhabited by several live species, one of them being the highly intelligent and developed *Namuh* creatures, comparable to some extent to our humans. Evolution had taken place in this as in other planets for billions of years and had brilliantly culminated in the current creatures after innumerable annual cycles (which are twice as long as our years). All namuhs received at the end of their childhood an electronic medical enhancement of their central processing units, comparable to our brains, in the form of implants of a quantum computer widely capable of connecting or disconnecting language transmission at will and from the youthful age of only 40 years. The intelligent creatures required nourishment at least every second day and needed to breath nitrogen frequently, no later than at two- or three-hour intervals. Oxygen was harmless, but useless.

The namuhs were parthenogenic, which means that they reproduced asexually and were all of the same genre. For thousands of years reproduction had been left to their discretion, but their leaders had introduced improvements to better organize their society: all citizens would have equal rights while recognizing that they evidently were born with different capabilities. Upon determination of their individual potential the new citizens were assigned to learn an identified skill or profession to fulfill for their lifetimes existing needs at one of their different communities. Some of them were chosen and assigned to fill replacement needs of their nation whenever the leadership requested it; others would be trained as technicians, astronomers, flyers, laborers, food and nitrogen suppliers or whatever other collective need was identified, inclusive leadership positions. The new youngsters would be released from training as useful, fully educated community members at which time computers programmed to assist in the assigned intended function of the new citizens would be implanted in their brains. Their life expectancy, to be reached almost always, exceeds 120 of their years. It was all very rational. Violence was banned from the planet although some discovery and meetings with supposedly intelligent species of other planets had required brief wars and their superior spaceships were equipped for fighting. Namuhs were invincible.

For a terrestrial creature, the most shocking characteristic of these intelligent beings would have been their physical appearance. They were regular spheres, mostly of a 1,5-meter diameter and, although they had a smooth external surface, the individuals could at will push outside four limbs or extremities equipped at the edge with finger-like mobile extensions capable of supporting slow walking or performing delicate work like typing into computers or assembling instruments. If the Namuh required for any reason rapid motion, which a sphere with short extremities could not reach, he could morph and flatten by compressing the sphere and shifting his previous body shape into a regular large wheel capable of spinning over its edge to be able of moving on the ground at higher speed. All Namuhs were happy creatures who lived and worked in peace for the length of their secured existence, always working with each other for the common good. Communication among them was assured by their electronic brain additions which they could connect or disconnect at will to exchange or receive spoken or unspoken information from only one colleague or from all other congregated individuals or authorities. Most Namuhs lived almost constantly connected with colleagues. This connection realized for the leadership the objective of immediately obtaining the result of votes on relevant issues; it was frequently required by the leaders when they needed to learn the opinion of all or a selected group on any issue. When a Namuh so desired, he was allowed to disconnect from all others and temporarily retreat into his privacy.

The Namuh Adventurers
Depart and Discover Earth

The Namuh High Council had determined 200 years ago that their technology allowed them to undertake spatial explorations. They first built missiles and later ships that were launched toward neighboring planets. They found in these targets some plant and animal life but the conditions did not support Namuh colonies and their land was irregular with undesirable and bothersome mountains, rivers, and valleys, also populated sometimes by residents of inferior intelligence and without scientific knowledge. They considered whether these worlds could be exploited for mining, but it was discarded. Why not check other stellar systems with different planets? It was easier said than done. The distance was prohibitive, and the fueling, feeding and survival of the aeronauts uncertain. Even the transmissions of spatial communications might take many days to be received.

Finally the entrance to a huge wormhole at a short flying distance of the planet appeared to open unexpected possibilities. The physicists and astronomers had built and immediately sent probes to the interior of the wormhole, which either never returned or were damaged in the attempt. How deep was it? So far, all wormholes had been recognized only in remote, unreachable areas, and seen only outside of their entrance. Was the present one stable or would it disappear as fast as it had appeared? Their knowledge of the precise causes of wormhole formation was nil. To what part of the Universe would it bring any ship who dared enter? Could it be traversed by the astronauts to an ultimate destination? Would they be able to come back? The scientists had not learned anything from their probes. Where did the wormhole end? Would it possible be to find other planets capable of supporting Namuh life?

The most daring navigator among the leadership Namuhs, named Krik, came forward: he was ready to fly inside the wormhole as Skipper with a crew of his choice in a new, properly fitted spaceship. The Council, as required, submitted the matter to immediate universal vote. Many Namuhs expressed concern about the future of the astronauts and the peril of vanishing without leaving a trace, but the enterprise was approved. Krik was appointed Skipper by the Council and put in charge of the mission. He chose his old friend Kcops as his Vice-Skipper and a crew of twenty people with different specialties was assembled.

They were all aware of the dangers and death peril and had accepted. The entire Namuhkind of the planet had enthusiastically followed the enterprise and on the appointed day thousands came to the launching area to bid the heroes farewell. The spectators shifted shape from spheres into spinning wheels and joined several joyful moving circles around the spaceship. At the appointed time the vessel lifted off and disappeared into the thin hydrogen atmosphere.

Inside the ship, Skipper Krik watched the approaching opening of the wormhole jointly with his entire crew. They aimed for the center. As they came closer, they all considered and accepted the possibility of an immediate death. It did not happen. The ship, once inside of the mysterious cylinder, seemed to have accelerated but all the instrumental readings became absurd and useless. The artificial gravity inside the ship was lost and the Namuh navigators, all of them in the community room and connected to each other, started flying and bumping on the walls in their spherical shapes. A few among them had exteriorized their extremities in an attempt to grab something and stabilize, but it was in vain because the walls were smooth and the astronauts normally rested on the floor without having or requiring chairs. They decided to spend the entire transit time together communicating with each other, watching the strange views outside and the absurd instrumental readings rendered by video screens.

Finally, all ceased. The wormhole had maintained its caliber all the way to the exit and the spaceship was not crushed. Having just passively emerged out at an unknown destination, urgent questions had to be answered and the instruments required resetting. How long had the trip taken? They all knew that it was useless to consult their clocks. Time had lost its meaning. What time or year was it in the home planet? The spaceship's engine, a matter-antimatter device controlled by a fusion nuclear reactor, was functioning normally.

Relieved, the crew emitted an electronic noise that was the equivalent of what humans call a happy laughter. Their anatomy did not permit hugs. Everybody was alive!

Vice-Skipper Kcops upon completing a check of his instruments, announced to the general delight that they had reached Galaxy F567, which on Earth is referred to as Milky Way. And he explained:

"We are some two light years away from home," to what Skipper Krik added:

"Let us hope that when we want to return, we can enter the exit opening of the wormhole in the same place we are leaving it now. But for now, let us start our travel of discovery of new worlds and civilizations!" The crew exploded again in the collective electronic noise equivalent to human celebration.

* * *

The early observations of the first encountered star systems were not interesting. A few were surrounded by orbital planets which occasionally revealed either plants and vegetation or strange non-stationary beings of limited intelligence, comparable to what humans call animals. Others consisted only of gases or ice. It was all similar to what they already knew because they had seen it elsewhere. The crew was disappointed until a crew member made an announcement:

Uluz mentioned, as everybody already knew, that they were close to the star S234, better known by humans as Sun. He had observed in the atmosphere of the third planet, clearly already in open space filled as always with black matter, fabricated structures of uncommon shape and appearance that may well have been small spaceships with primitive technology. Scanning the planet, he noticed something extraordinary: it was surrounded by thousands of mini satellites, some of them stationary that had to be necessarily the work of intelligent beings, but whose purpose was unclear. The temperature range on the planet's surface was similar to their own but their atmosphere did not contain enough hydrogen to support their lives, at least not without industrious adaptations. He had identified no visible ships capable of long-range stellar flights, but the planet was undoubtedly inhabited by intelligent creatures still at a lesser developmental level.

The explorers expressed joy. An inhabited planet that supported and harbored intelligent life was exactly what they had wanted to find. If the unknown creatures were less technically proficient that the Namuhs, they might even be able to help them. The Skipper, however, warned that this would be inconsistent with the Prime Directive of not interfering. They had come only to observe and report, not to assist, destroy or assuage.

Skipper Krik immediately ordered cloaking their vessel to avoid detection and to cautiously approach the third planet of still unknown local name. Uluz complained about the thousands of minute satellites and pieces of broken equipment visible orbiting the planet. Why did the people downstairs cause that level of space pollution? Weren't they not able to clean it? The Skipper and his entire community were anxious to see the physical appearance of the inhabitants. Aruhu, the crew member in charge of communications, scanned the surface observing the numerous video signals that he was receiving. The first moving item he could see was an elephant. The community, always connected to watch everything, was surprised. The elephant was in company of four additional beings of different dimensions. The travelers had never seen anything alike. How could these beings build spaceships? Aruhu showed to everybody the existence of vast areas of dry land separated from each other by huge water amounts, never seen in other known planets. The water consists of hydrogen and oxygen, remarked somebody. He even identified structures floating on top of the water and moving while releasing some kind of fume to the atmosphere. All wanted to view greater enlargements of the floating items. They found one that consisted of three levels with a pool of water on the highest. Something else excited the newcomers even more: there was movement on all levels of the cruiser. Very excited, they all requested larger magnifications and Aruhu complied. The first observation revealed beings lying flat on some piece of furniture facing the ocean. Their exterior surface was pink but they had covered parts of their body with materials of assorted colors, in some cases one piece, in others two. Were these the inhabitants of the planet? Their anatomy was completely different from that of the Namuhs. All visible creatures were topped by a relatively small spherical differentiation covered with some hairy-appearing material. Fascinated, one of the navigators commented that these structures might well be animals capable of movement, but their activities were possibly limited to the floating structure. Only intelligent beings would have been able to build any such floating structure with people inside, commented Vice-Skipper Kcops. He wanted to widen the search before drawing conclusions. The Namuhs observed people of different skin colors found walking in the ship, some were covered by white materials (uniforms, probably), others were displaying variable clothing of multiple colors. Nobody seemed to be doing anything useful. The observations made were stable and lasted hours. The travelers finally relocated their observations to targets far away, discovering big and small cities on the dry lands, large and small buildings, lit towns at night and saw thousands of creatures walking on two legs, with a solid trunk, two upper and two lower extremities and on the top a fast spherical structure with two eyes, a mouth, and a nose of unknown function. In their first approach the Namuhs missed the ears because they were frequently covered by hairs or hats.

The Skipper joined everybody else in their excitement and joy and announced that a culture capable of shooting satellites should possess means of aerial communication and linkage and ordered Aruhu to search for them. This yielded many channels of what humans call radio and television, which confronted them with a genuine problem: they could view many human activities but were unable to understand anything they heard or saw. They were shocked the first time they recognized on TV an image of violence with a killing with blood spilling and noticed that the event was somehow associated with an explosion and that the victim appeared to fall to the ground, apparently dead. Not one of the crew members had ever witnessed any violent acts. The perplexity grew among the travelers. How could they communicate or study these beings without understanding the language or exposing themselves to danger?

Skipper Krik remarked that evidently it would be necessary to send something or somebody to the surface, but he deemed to be too dangerous to send any of them considering their very different requirements to survive. What would be the reaction of the inhabitants when encountering such strange creatures? It might have dire consequences. He thought it best to utilize the technology of using *physically enhanced projected holograms* of human appearance controlled by individual members of the crew, as it had been done in the past in other worlds. The enhanced solid holograms in the shape and size of the creatures would be projected on the surface and one of the tripulants would act like a puppeteer continuously in charge of each image, attempting to interact or at least watch any humans that came close. The entire crew would stay connected, view, and listen to everything without interfering. They would take it from here. This approach would be safe without jeopardizing anyone.

The group enthusiastically acquiesced and Yttocs immediately displayed his four extremities and started working with his keyboards to retrieve the required technique to make the holograms and announced that with the Skipper's permission he would like to pilot the first hologram to descend to the surface. It did not take him long. Aruhu, who had transmitted to the travelers all his modest advances in language interpretation, focused on an isolated small building with large signs and drawings outside. He had observed that people frequently entered and left. The front of the building faced a large space occupied by four-wheel vehicles which humans seemed to use for transportation.

Aruhu announced that he found Yttocs' hologram fit to go and the Manuh Yttocs' alter ego instantaneously materialized outside of the building designated by Aruhu. The expert in charge, watching from the ship, hesitated not knowing how the hologram could open the door that blocked the entrance to the strange building, until two human boys, which Yttocs found strange and surprising, came out revealing the mechanism. The door could be pushed or drawn open.

Yttocs's alter ego, who had found the door mechanism too primitive, walked inside. He noticed several tables with people seated at them and ingesting solid and fluid nourishment. He considered the situation and decided to take a place at a table, sit on a piece of furniture and see what happened.

A man at a neighboring table looked at him with curiosity. Yttocs recognized that their attires were dissimilar. This would require consideration for future missions. He studied the seated people and found them to be of two distinct kinds, men and women. This fact had already been observed and discussed by the group without reaching a conclusion. Why would there be two sorts of humans? Did they perform divergent functions or had different power faculties? What was the use? Were they allowed to freely choose or change being men or women? All couples were eating and drinking a dark fluid. This had been noted from the ship in some sites.

"Hi, you, the seated guy? Do you want to eat something? We have the best hamburgers in miles. Come to the front if you mean to order" loudly shot a young employee behind a counter in a white apron. Yttocs did not understand anything but interpreted the body language and signs of the server and decided to walk toward him.

"So, what is your pleasure, friend?" The boy was staring at the hologram with perplexity and some confusion. "Are you all right? How come you don't have ears? Does that run in your family or did you lose them? Ha, ha" He weakly laughed. Yttocs did not know what to answer. He was receiving comments from his crew and the skipper, but they were giving no advice. Kcops commented that the hologram should have had big ears. Yttocs decided to respond to the boy in his own language: "ZZZZ, rRrrrr, zzzzpf."

The boy opened the mouth. "Are you a recent immigrant?"

"rRzzzzzz, fjKkR", was the perplexing answer.

The employee, almost intimidated, took a decision: "Look man, I do not understand you, but I am sure that you are hungry and I happen to have a great hamburger here. Take it. It is five dollar."

"ZZZZ, rrrrrG" Scotty's hologram responded taking the hamburger in his hands. He turned around and started walking toward the exit.

The young man cried "What about the five bucks? In America you got to pay for food."

The hologram did not understand and was determined to bring the hamburger home for analysis. He walked toward the door. Furious, the employee followed him and reached him outside.

"Man, you cannot go without paying. If you got no money, find a charity that will feed you for free" He attempted to take away the food from the strange visitor. Surprised, the hologram opened wide the mouth. The interlocutor looked inside and shrieked terrified. "You have no tongue and no teeth" He turned around and ran back inside. A curious client came outside to also check the visitor. The creature had already disappeared *without a trace but keeping in his possession and teletransporting the precious hamburger that was his trophy.*

Back in the spacecraft, the community, clearly excited, was commenting on the outcome of the first encounter, which they had observed with great interest. The "tourist" placed the hamburger in the center of the group and everybody inspected it with displeasure. "Why is it warm?" "Are you sure that they ingest that as nourishment?" Everybody had a different opinion and nobody wanted to listen to the others. The Skipper intervened:

"If you continue talking on top of each other, I will disconnect myself." The electronic communication link obediently became silent. "We need to analyze the events of this visit and determine what will be our next step. "What is your opinion, Yttocs? You are first."

"Skipper, I found the creatures ugly. They were introducing strange materials in their mouth as you can see, probably some kind of sustenance, but I do not know why the man behind the counter wanted to take away from me something he had freely given to me by himself before. The person referred to my hologram as not having ears. I was not aware that this would cause a problem, because I regarded them as optional ornaments. Now I will put ears on all future holograms. And I did not expect anyone looking inside the mouth. I should not have opened it, because the inside was not ready. I will figure out what is the meaning of teeth and tongue."

Aruhu explained that they had all been unable to know human anatomy but that he would identify the nature of tongue and teeth and put them inside all expeditionary holograms.

Yoccam intervened: "Do you remember the planet FG56? The intelligent inhabitants used to buy and sell items and the recipient had to pay."

"To pay with what?"

"In FG56 they had metal pieces or paper thought to represent value and they called it money."

"Why would anyone value paper over metal or trade his property for them?" asked somebody. He was ignored.

"It is an important observation. Every time we go down and visit, the holograms should carry money. It must be what the boy demanded. How do we get it?" asked the Skipper.

The Vice-Skipper intervened: "I agree. The best course would be to have Aruhu check again the video pictures from the planet, identify transactions and try to see and copy the money used. Or maybe find a computer web that shows it." The community immediately agreed and Aruhu started working again. But Kcops was not finished. "The overwhelming problem we have is to communicate with the beings in their language. How can we decipher and learn it?"

Aruhu came back online. "I can also work on that. I have watched their public broadcasts of video scenes trying to correlate the images and action with the spoken sounds and I have made some connections. I found programs that show subtitles in some kind of lettering or alphabet that are helpful in allowing me to decipher their sounds. I need to make more progress before publicizing results and enabling teaching assistance to our community."

A voice asked: "Yttocs, why was the human scared when you opened the mouth? Is it important to have teeth and tongue?"

Aruhu again intervened "The beings, who call themselves humans, have a tongue and teeth inside the mouth. You also forgot to put ears on your hologram, as Kcops explained. They are used to perceive air vibrations representing sounds, possibly including human speech. They cannot connect with each other in different locations, as we do, without outside instruments that they carry in their pockets."

"And what is the nose?"

"I still do not know, but all of them have one. Maybe it helps with the vision because it is close to the eyes. The big ball on the top is called head. I suspect that it contains their central individual control and data processing."

Several astronauts objected "It cannot be, it is too exposed. Our controlling units are hidden in the safest part of our bodies, the center. It must be an evolutionary error because brains should be concealed and better protected."

The Skipper ended the discussion "We are here to explore new worlds and civilizations, not to criticize the creatures that live in them. Things, people, and worlds are the way they were born, as we are. Resume your work. We all depend on Aruhu for our next major step. Anyone who is idle must assist."

Aruhu was capable of doing arduous work for an extended period of time and was able to read or assess images much faster than humans, but this time he was almost overwhelmed. He detected numerous video sequences and radio stations but they appeared to speak different-sounding languages and he did not know how to decipher any of them. His companions shared his irritation: it was absurd and irrational that members of a single species used different languages. Even computers have a common machine language. How could they communicate with each other? The communications expert, however, was not ready to give up. His first real success was an internet web of a teaching program for children which included the alphabet, well-defined objects and their written names inserted in plain sentences. They even showed clearly how to pronounce the words. The second major breakthrough was achieved when he encountered spoken movies with subtitles: a computer analysis allowed the navigators to link written works with their probable pronunciation and associated action and suggest by comparison their possible meanings. One of the crew members had some useful training in linguistics and managed to discern some grammatical rules. He had been most helpful preparing the teaching material for the crew. They ascertained that their first learned language was in use in a number of territories over the Earth. Its name was something like Innisch or maybe English and they suspected that it was accepted in many places as a common language, what humans otherwise call a *lingua franca*. What perplexed them the most, however, was that people wrote or spoke multiple different tongues in broadcasts for the same areas, which they viewed as a trouble-making difficulty. The pronunciations and accents were also a serious challenge. It was difficult to find two actors or presenters with the same accent. They all welcomed the chance of viewing humans in various parts of the globe engaging in different activities but did not understand the reason for the different appearance, design, and color of their clothing. They had finally learned that the two human forms were men and women, but they still did not comprehend the purpose of that differentiation. Aruhu remembered having seen movie scenes revealing close interactions between unclothed representatives of both genres engaging in a physical activity. It could not be for reproductive purposes because it was practiced for life.

Skipper Krik attempted to summarize the work, which had been intently followed through the electronic link of the entire crew: "Finally we have identified and maybe understand at least one common language and soon we will learn more. Let's choose one of the territories that speak the common language and send down one or more of our enhanced holograms to see what happens."

Aruhu objected: "There is something else we need to resolve first. I have reexamined the scene between Yttocs and the restaurant employee, which I now understand. He complained and almost attacked Yttocs because he had evidently expected to receive money in payment for the food. If we go down, we need to have always money. All humans seem to have it and use it frequently for some exchanges or services, although we do not know the source. Strangers can get plenty in a robbery, but I do not know if you wish to engage in that."

"There seems to be no choice. We discussed this already. The holograms must carry money. How do we get money?"

"I need time but I know how to create it as an addition to the holograms. Money is either printed in paper with very elaborate details or coined on metal. I believe that the paper money is more valuable. It is printed in certain buildings and I can find images in the web."

"Do so, Aruhu, and I wish to congratulate you on your success. I want you to be the second to send a hologram under your command to the surface. If everything goes well, I would like that after your hologram's return everybody, including myself and the Vice-Skipper, sends down separate images in the entire crew's presence and attempts to learn something. For the time being, I do not authorize anyone to travel to the surface in person because it seems to be too uncertain and dangerous. We need to inhale hydrogen, do not handle water well and are not invulnerable. After each return, we can discuss and summarize our observations."

Aruhu's holographic replica with human features was walking the streets in Manhattan. It was still early in the morning and many stores were empty. He had chosen to appear of black color in a female shape in the feminine clothes he had observed in an earthly video, although he did not understand why it had no sleeves. He had reproduced the two awkward but symmetrical thoracic bulky areas without comprehending their meaning and required size. He announced to his community that he was going to enter a store and try to acquire something with the $10 *notes he had fabricated. He would pretend to be taking them out of a hand purse that he, like many women, would be carrying.*

He stopped at the display window of a store on Madison Avenue. What were they selling? Inspection of the display windows revealed some pretty ornaments in the shape of rings with attached shining hard crystals and some long metallic yellow and white chains with non-understandable symbols. He decided that the best way to study what these ornaments meant or what its use was, would be to purchase some of them. The hologram entered the store.

The salesclerk was surprised and mistrustful after seeing Aruhu, but she forced a smile and approached the supposed client offering her assistance. The astronaut-controlled figure took the opportunity to analyze in detail the figure of the human employee. Her arms were partly covered by much too short sleeves and the bilateral thoracic bulks were less prominent than her own. Arahu also attempted to smile, without understanding the exact meaning of this action.

"Me have seen the articles inside the bright display and liked to buy" said he/she.

The clerk did not respond at all. Was the supposed client a visitor from a foreign country? Many of them dress differently and do not mind spending thousands of dollars without performing the antics, hesitation and conversations that would precede a substantial purchase by a local resident. She had heard of similar cases involving oil barons and billionaires and decided to take the visitor seriously.

"Are you interested in one of the diamond necklaces and bracelets you were watching? I can show you the best ones." She discreetly nodded to a security employee to come closer and watch while she was retrieving items. She came back from the display window carrying a bracelet Aruhu had been admiring.

"It is a magnificent piece" A human would have examined a long time to reach a conclusion but not Aruhu.

"What does one do wiz it?"

Flabbergasted, the clerk answered that many women would be proud to wear it in their arms. That most be the reason for the short sleeves, though Arahu. After a while the saleswoman added "I will bring for your consideration similar bracelets at a more modest price" She retrieved two non-displayed items from the back of the store.

"How come you not possess duplicates? I and you own two arms. That is, I need two relatively similar."

"Well, if you can afford it, why not? Do you need the price for comparison? The first one costs 3,600 dollars and the other two respectively 2,000 and 1,800."

Aruhu wanted to investigate the bracelets further. That's why he decided to purchase them.

"All right, then. Me the three take away."

"Madam? A great acquisition. You mean to say that you would like to purchase all three bracelets? Do you realize what is the total purchase price?" The woman looked at the security guard with perplexity, while the astronaut answered:

"Of course, seven thousand four hundred dollars."

"Yes, plus tax, but how would you wish to pay?"

"See no problema. I have here cash. Look. I got $10 bills. Here are the moneys. Exactly 740 bills, all new."

Aruhu started taking out an inexhaustible supply of 740 ten dollar notes out of her purse. The employee opened her mouth as widely as medically possible while watching the growing pile of money, which had not been visible as a bulk in the purse. She was sure that it was all crooked, a stupid con. She had an idea.

"Madam, would you have some identification with you? We will make a copy to keep you in our list of preferred customers."

Aruhu stopped. "Identification? What be that?"

The woman exploited. "Enough of that! You are either a fool or think that we are all stupid!" The security man moved forward to secure the bracelets.

Arahu was astonished. "What war wrong? You like not my dollars?"

"We are going to call the police."

Police? Aruhu had seen police, judges, and prisons in his videos. Policemen occasionally shot people. He turned around and left the store. The security man and the salesclerk attempted to follow but Aruhu had mysteriously disappeared outside. The woman remembered that Aruhu had left in a hurry without taking back the money which, she was sure, had to be falsified. But all bills were also gone. They tried to view the visitor in the house security system but it had not captured the figure of the astronaut. Had the whole incident been a dream? Or a magic trick? They did not understand the real problem: video cameras were unable to register this type of holograms. The clerk was noticed talking to herself for a while.

The holographic traveler, always in touch with all the crew, which were following with attention but had volunteered no comments, moved across a wide river to a different territory and noticed a large crowd of people with more children than usual moving around. There were barracks with offerings, food, and drinks. Aruhu saw an enormous vertical wheel with people seated inside attached suspended cabins. What was it? Some kind of test or punishment? He walked around and noticed some very strange constructed instrumental assemblies that seemed specially made to torture people, but most visitors were laughing and were forming lines to enter outside. He asked the listening crew in the ship whether some colleague could identify the nature and purpose of the site but nobody answered. She decided to try something different and moved back across the river to Broadway, in Downtown Manhattan, an area he had explored from the ship. The number of pedestrians, their clothing and the density of the traffic fascinated the aliens in the ship who were now talking again.

"Ask them why they are wearing different clothes. This is unneeded and irrational" said one voice. "The number of vehicles is completely out of line, it is dangerous and must be poisoning the air" added another one. "Besides, the dense traffic cannot move which defeats the purpose."

Aruhu's alter ego stopped, surprised, in front of a store. Over the entrance, she read BOOKS. He did not recognize the word from his studies, but he had seen books and noticed several of them in the display window. He needed to know what this item contained and what was the purpose of fabricating it.

The hologram entered and asked an employee behind a desk: "Which ones be books?"

"You mean where are the books? Everywhere. Just look around" was the response of the perplexed man. He still asked: "What language do you speak?"

Aruhu hesitated: "What language speak? How many be there? Which one you speak?"

The employee laughed: "Me speak English! Go to the back of the store on the left. There are books in different languages and dictionaries. You may find what you are looking for."

The alien entity moved inside the store. He grabbed a book and was astonished "So, they print their words or thoughts in some white materials and they distribute them. The electronic and hertzian waves I found are not all, and the books' contents seem variable" He could barely read the titles and he guessed about the book's purpose. At last, he identified something that he really liked: an English-German and German-English Dictionary. He knew nothing about German but the book contained only words with short explanations of their meaning and even pronunciation. He decided to buy it and feed all its contents to his co-travelers. Dictionaries would be helpful in facilitating future visits. He took the volume and walked toward the employee, who clearly also functioned as cashier.

"Aha, you found a book. I am surprised. Sind sie Deutsch?"

Aruhu was perplexed. "What said you? Want buy that book."

"Okay, lady. I just wondered why you would want to purchase an English-German dictionary. Your accent is unusual, not German at all. It will be thirty-five dollars" And he smiled.

Aruhu was again surprised. "Why you laughing? Is book no good?"

"It is excellent! Thirty-five dollars, please" He wrote the figure on a paper and held it in front of the hologram, pointing at the number with a finger.

"Me understand. You expect currency. I have" He still carried the same bag she had used in the jewelry store. He extracted four shiny $10 bills from it and put it on the desk in front of the man. How could he pay only 35 with $10 bills? What was the protocol?

"Give me four of your bills and I will give you change."

The cashier took the money in his hands and looked at it carefully. The notes were completely new but they did not smell nor feel properly. The print was careful and correct, the numbering progressive. Yet, the man felt uneasy. Something was wrong, but what? He called an older individual, probably the owner, who also became suspicious and asked the employee for a measuring tape.

Upon completing his examinations, he exclaimed "Ah. You know, Madam, the American notes measure all exactly 6 1/3 by 2 1/2 inches, but your false currency measures only 6 by 2 inches. Whoever made them, must have been stupid. He could print it well but did not bother to check the dimensions! Compare them: Tom, put one of her bills over a real one. Don't you see the difference? You must be an accomplice! Return the book and leave this store or I will call the police!"

Was the size wrong? It had never occurred to Aruhu. Why did everybody want to call the police? He heard how the entire crew in the ship was making laughing-equivalent noise. He wanted the book but he really knew what the police was and did not care to face them. The hologram turned around *and started running away with the book. A man attempted to grab an arm of the fugitive but his hand closed empty through the arm and could grab nothing. Aruhu reached the door with the book and disappeared. Two men from the bookstore attempted to follow him but the hologram was nowhere to be seen. The book floated in the air several seconds but then also disappeared, being transported high to the heavens. The men in the store remained astonished, unable to understand.*

After closing the hologram, the real Aruhu in the ship said "We have learned something. I will prepare a better batch of money." The Skipper said that he agreed and noted that Aruhu had never been culpable of a mistake before and should not be ridiculed. The returned explorer announced that he would make the entire dictionary available for study and memorization immediately. All others paid attention. They would study the book, the first terrestrial object they had ever seen, after the hamburger. They had never seen a book before; in their culture everything they needed to know was in electronic files and screens. The visitors were learning a lot about humans. Vice-Skipper Kcops noted an additional problem. The holograms were speaking to real people downstairs, but what about the accent? Most crew members did not understand what an accent was. Aruhu reported that the dictionary followed each word with what might be a pronunciation guide. But did they know how to interpret the letter printed in the guide? Kcops closed the discussion noting that a long comparison of subtitled spoken videos with pronunciation was needed before proceeding any further and returning to the Earth. He was also worried that the terrestrial spoken languages might have structural rules and wanted to discuss that with the linguist. He pointed out that he had on his own noticed the considerable difference between a bookstore and a so-called library, both filled with books, but that libraries where free and contained very extensive information, especially a big one in New York City. This should be remembered and taken advantage of in the future.

An unexpected and shocking latest information unrelated to Earth agitated and concerned the crew. The star-gazing astronomy expert reported that the exit opening of the wormhole from which they had arisen had disappeared and could no longer be found or visualized anywhere in the galaxy. Did this mean that they could never return to their home planet?

"Not necessarily" answered the Skipper "but we all voluntarily enrolled in this exploration knowing the dangers. Wormholes have been observed frequently changing their location and it is possible that we find another opening."

"And where will it bring us? In what year? Should we not rather stay in this planet?"

The Vice-Skipper intervened "It would not be easy. They seem to have enough hydrogen in the atmosphere and water but not sufficiently concentrated for us. We would not know how to prepare our periodic sustenance. And water is dangerous for us."

"But, my friends," clarified the Skipper, "do not forget that we are performing the duty for which we volunteered and were chosen and we are sending detailed and surprising reports of previously unsuspected realities to the home planet. These will be received and our devotion to duty and success will be recognized."

"And remembered. But our report will be received in 90 years!"

"How do you know what year is it now there?" asked a curious crew member.

Another voice added "Can somebody figure out whether the humans would accept and tolerate us well?" Nobody answered. "We are most different. We are spherical and can morph in shape and appearance, from spheres to wheels, but humans are lengthy, tall, thin and cannot change their shape or size." Somebody else added "They look externally more complex than us, because we are only spheres," and Vokehc closed the argument: "Outside, humans may look more developed, but inside, I am sure, we are incomparably more complex, and we function at a much higher level. Besides our individual command center is well protected in the center of our bodies and theirs is very exposed in their heads."

"The main issue for me" said Kcops "is how tolerant these people are. Would they allow intelligent beings of alternative morphology and needs share their planet with them?"

* * *

Six terrestrial months had passed by since the spaceship's arrival. It had stayed continuously cloaked and was never discovered by the Earth's astronomers. The explorers had improved the proper appearance of their messenger holograms on the surface and they mastered soon multiple languages. Their probes had visited thousands of times the surface and the Namuhs might probably have found everything worth knowing, or so they thought. As the Skipper had demanded, each crew member had visited the planet's surface maneuvering his own holographic alter-ego as a puppeteer. The explorers were proud of their work. They had understood that there was no central power with authority on the entire Earth, and the dry territory was split in countries of variable size and shape with disparate governments, languages, religions, armies, and ideologies. The travelers found this divisions absurd and the countries had obviously been variably classified into friendly, adversarial, uncivilized, collaborative, violent, or threatening. Some of them partly dominated nuclear technology, which was dangerous and prohibited to others. The crew had been able to observe active wars with casualties. Like themselves, all humans should be united working toward collective progress and assistance, as the Namuhs had decided to do thousands of years ago. They found certain social relation-ships upsetting. Every newly born human had to fight to get a proper education, find a place to work and decent housing on his or her own. Even finding food to survive was an individual responsibility. In their home planet every newborn was assigned a comfortable appropriate position for life without fights or competition. Their communications method, what they called language, was based on air vibrations, but in their evolutionary stage they should have already found more rational, universal, and effortless ways of sharing their thoughts with others. Human speech was accompanied by gestures and changes in face expression. What information did these accompanying actions transmit? They seem to be the product of emotions. What were emotions? Brain circuits that could not be erased? They appeared to greatly influence human conduct and thinking, maybe ruling the Earth, and seemed to be based on preprogrammed circuits of their brains. Emotions informed resolutions rather than reason and blocked many forms of logical analysis. Humans seemed to be irrational.

The Skipper was close to declare the exploration of the Earth finished and resume the ship's travel, this time stressing an enhanced interest in finding another opening of the vanished wormhole. He told the crew that the displacement of the wormhole to an unknown address was not a severe problem, because the crew had a long survival time assured and many other planets may contain what they needed for hydrogen and for their sustenance. Unexpectedly Vice-Skipper Kcops changed the topic: "I have studied the human body and find it unreasonably built, because as noted by previous colleagues their main control organ, named brain, is located in an exposed area inside what they call head and has no backup in case of destruc-tion. Yet, the rest of the body is built to accommodate its needs and execute its orders. Their belly is filled with structures needed for the digestion of the brain's sustenance and they require replenishment at least three times per day; they have large legs for the sole purpose of displacing the individual as ordered by the brain; all internal organs serve the brain's leading purposes and preservation; only the arms appear reasonably developed to achieve ends similar to what we can accomplish when we display our own hidden mobile appendages. They die when their brain dies. These findings point to an evolutionary error. A human is a brain supported by massive and excessive differentiations."

"Include these observations in our report to the home planet" advised his superior.

Skipper Krik was unable to understand and interpret an important finding that worried him. How were wars and violence possible on Earth? What rational explanation did it have? Vice-Skipper Kcops, in a talking mood, remembered the audience that the last intergalactic war had occurred only two thousand years ago and that even in their own species archeologists had formulated suspicions about possible early episodes of physical and instrument-mediated violence among early Namuhs in the home planet. Irrationality had existed among Namuhs, although it was now overcome. Krik was not appeased by these comparisons. The parties involved in the last Galactic War had been unions of consenting planets, something impossible on Earth, and humans, unlike current Namuhs, did not think of themselves as being in an early stage of evolution, as their former ancestors had been. In his view, it did not make sense and defied rational analysis that intelligent beings were willing to kill each other at great personal risk of self-annihilation. The stronger always wins, why would the weaker expose himself? The rational resolution would be to have a group of experts examine the resources of the parties in conflict and assign the victory without causing death or destruction."

Hours later, still worried by the issue, the Skipper made an unexpected announcement. "I have chosen Uluz and Vokehc as my companions and security guards to do something else more adventurous and riskier, which I have not allowed anyone else to do before. We three are going to descend in our real bodies to the Earth's surface. To make our sight acceptable to humans, Aruhu will generate covering holograms that will disguise and conceal our real appearance by covering it with a human hologram image, and we will also be equipped with a small, flat, and well-hidden individual hydrogen tank to cover our necessities. We will descend inside one of our cloaked and covered space dinghies that will stay down cloaked, will follow us above our new heads in the air and will always remain in our immediate vicinity within reach. This will allow an emergency return if we were to feel in jeopardy. I never forget that we are also mortal. During my absence, the Vice-Skipper will be in charge of everything. My purpose is to try to identify and try to understand the reason for the existing massive wars and violence, which appear both to be officially banned and despised but are practiced in many corners of the Earth. Most of it is conducted by entities named armies. North of the city of New York, which we have studied so well, across the wide river I have identified a large place named West Point, where young people are trained to join the army and prepare for wars. I would like to inspect the institution and talk to the students to try to understand"

The hydrogen tanks and the special holograms made to hide the real bodies were readied, and a hologram was projected to completely cover the Manuhs' appearance.

The landing in an empty field was, as always, perfect. Their disguise mimicking humans was credible, except that the bellies concealing the hydrogen tanks were a little more prominent than usually. The three visitors determined that randomly encountered people accepted without comments or worried reactions their physical appearance and decided to enter a large commercial mall. The Skipper saluted and praised Aruhu in the ship for his excellent work. The hydrogen tank in particular was discreetly and easily accessible. He immediately responded, thanking.

Once inside the mall, the three aliens were astonished by the presence of so many large, well-lit stores on both sides and by a huge shopping crowd. Such sites had been previously missed. They stood in front of a counter offering frozen ice cream. "They seem to eat cold items", noted Uluz. "What about the small humans? Do you believe that they grow and differentiate?" "With the passage of time, yes." All three resumed their walk, reaching an area named Food Court. The Skipper immediately requested from the crew back in the ship information about the possible meaning of the label. He could not link the usual interpretation of the word "Court" with his observations. "We, neither. I suggest that you observe what humans do inside" was Kcops' answer. A moment later, the astronauts had figured it out: people were seated at tables and eating. They walked past the different counters reading the unintelligible list of sustenance offerings and noted that they were always linked to a currency figure. Did people have to pay for food although they needed it to stay alive? Did their employers not care? Should eating not be simply an employment benefit or a right? "No" answered Kcops in the ship. "They need to work for a fixed amount of currency to survive and must set aside funds to nurture the entire family, no matter of what size and secure their future. Everybody needs to find a suitable, well-paid job or alternatively they may survive with help of the government or of charitable organizations" Krik concluded: "They must be very concerned about the family to accept such responsibility for other people, but by what mechanism are they attached to certain individuals but not to others?" "Emotions" was the dry response from the ship "They seem to like or dislike other people" The Vice Skipper continued to be intrigued by the topic. "Emotions rather than reason run the humanity. Even when they argue, their appeals to reason are unreasonable and absurd, often contradictory."

The three aliens easily found West Point. It had been far away from their original landing point but they had no problems moving fast on the Earth's surface and had studied the territory from the air. They arrived in the late afternoon. Leading to the entrance of the institution on a public highway, establishments, a visitor center, and a big hotel were visible. A road past the entrance gate led to a series of buildings on both sides. Unseen, the three aliens easily bypassed the security at the gate and moved inside. A view to the magnificent and wide Hudson River at the bottom of a downslope appeared to the right. The main feature, a large building facing a green esplanade, was adorned by bronze statues of two old generals next to the entrance. Playgrounds for several sports surrounded by bleachers were present, and a coastal road lead north traveling through an art of small town with a well-identified home for the boss. A large unoccupied and empty area was of no interest to the visitors, as they were looking for people. The three Namuhs were unable to appreciate the rules of human beauty but studied everything with great interest. The community of astronauts on the ship was watching and recording the exploration but had so far offered no comments.

After a while, while waiting in a little garden adorned with a large old cannon placed above the Hudson River, they noticed three cadets, two young men and a young woman, all uniformed, coming their way. The Skipper decided to attempt a conversation with them outside without entering any buildings. The young cadet's names were Jon, Terrell, and Dawn.

"Hi, people, good evening."

"Good day, Gentlemen" answered Jon. "Can we be of help?"

"We do not require help, but we saw that you are in good mood and appear to be friendly."

The three cadets looked at each other and laughed. Terrell, who was black, answered "Yes, Sir, we are in good mood. We went outside to a Restaurant and had some food and drinks."

Hesitantly, Vokehc, asked "Do you carry weapons?"

"No, Sir" yelled almost simultaneously the three humans. "It is strictly prohibited."

This time, the three visitors looked surprised to each other. "But if you are learning how to make war, you must master the use of weapons."

"We don't know if we will ever be in a war. I hope not. We are trained to protect the Constitution of our Country and the liberty of all citizens and their self-government and we do not look forward to wars, although we are ready and willing to engage in one if our Country or our Constitution were ever threatened."

Now Uluz was interested: "I see. You do not declare the wars yourself."

"No, Sir" cried again unanimously the three cadets. "Only the President and Congress can do that, and their orders are transmitted to us through the chain of command and executed as indicated by our superiors."

"The chain of command? Could we meet it" asked Krik, while the other extraterrestrials companions watching the scene were equally perplexed.

The three cadets paused with a gaping mouth without answering.

"Can you imagine an enlightened, intelligible, rational world without violence or wars?" inquired the Skipper.

"We all would like it, but it is unrealistic and unimaginable. It has been shown many times."

"Where is your chain of command located?" Krik wanted to know. Uluz, however was more precise:

"Is it like a branching tree inserted inside the earth level but which finally branches and can reach everybody?"

Now the three cadets were irritated. "Excuse us, but we are busy. Goodbye, gentlemen. Have a nice evening."

The three visitors did not want lo lose the opportunity. "Oh, please, wait a moment. We just need some information. This chain of command must start somewhere. Who has the authority to declare war, and why do you do it if you don't like it?"

"The President of the United States. Go to the White House and they may explain it to you."

Actually, the visitors had twice attempted to explore not only the White House but also other government houses in several countries and found it impossible to understand anything about their dealings, resolutions, political situations, and problems. Besides, security guards had limited the mobility of their previous holograms and the group could not hear anything without holograms being in proximity of the action.

The Skipper had a last question: "Are you also being trained in the use of nuclear warfare?"

Terrell, incensed, turned around and faced Krik. "You are a fool. Or are you a spy? Where did you get your accent? Do you believe that we are also stupid? Who allowed you to enter this facility without escort?"

Unable to contain himself, Terrell attempted to push away the Skipper by placing a hand over his chest. The cadet's hand penetrated without resistance through the chest wall of the Skipper reaching his hydrogen tank. The three visitors, unable to express more horror, cried simultaneously "Noooo!, ZZRRRT, RWX!" as Krik lost his hologram-based balance and human appearance and bent backwards. He completely lost his hologram, which disappeared from human eyes, exposing the hydrogen, located in the area where the hologram had hidden his belly, and the rest of Krik's spherical body. He fell over the banister located at the end of the park, landing on a slope of considerable incline between the garden and the river, with a grade higher than 100 feet. The Skipper, while dangerously accelerating during his fall as a round sphere, managed to morph and flatten into the cylindrical shape that could be better controlled and continued his free descent on the slope toward the river. The entire crew in the spaceship shriek, as Uluz and Vokehc also cancelled their holograms and jumped behind their leader in their spherical shape to assist him. Krik had fully become a wheel before falling to the water. It had flattened out after entering the water leaving him helpless and causing a considerable splash. This was dangerous as the Namuhs were unused to water in their home planet and could neither manage these situations nor swim. The two associates had recognized the grave danger of their boss' situation. They thought it best to also morph into wheel-like cylinders and to accelerate their controlled downslide to the water edge. Both were able to stop close to the water on dry ground and rescue their boss. They had extruded their extremities extending them toward the Skipper, who grabbed them and was able to safely reach dry land. He was saved. Celebratory, relieved voices from the ship could be heard: "ZZZZZSFGD! ZZZXCZZ!" During the incident the hitherto invisible flying dinghy had approached the visitors and became discernible. Uluz and Vokehc took possession of the vehicle, carried Krik aboard and pulled the cover closing the passenger space. The craft was immediately cloaked and after becoming invisible, it left Earth returning to the spaceship. The crew decided that they never again would attempt to explore the Earth's surface in person. They were not used to sloping grounds or running water.

The three cadets, Terrell, Jon, and Dawn had silently witnessed the entire scene. When the space dinghy disappeared, all three opened their mouths at the same time without saying anything. It took almost one minute before Dawn asked "Boys, have you seen the same as I have? I am under the impression that the three people had become first a sphere, then a wheel and that a little spaceship picked them up. Maybe I had too much to drink."

"I don't know. Who were these creatures? What was the vehicle that disappeared? Would it represent a danger for the Academy?"

"It was your fault, Terrell. Why did you attack the man?"

"Because hey were asking absurd and insolent questions."

They remained silent and immobile for a while, until Jon proposed that it would be a clever idea not to mention their experience to anyone.

The girl immediately agreed "Who has ever met men who can morph into a sphere and a wheel and disappear?"

"Or a dinghy that can fly, and also disappear? No, it is the first time. But we had taken the three people for humans."

"If it becomes known, this story could mightily hurt our academic record and maybe get us expelled on medical grounds. Not to mention the mocking. We would not graduate."

Dawn finally came up with an explanation: "I know what happened. In the bar the ugly waitress who was serving and did not like us, dropped some LSD into our beers and that is why we had a joint hallucination. LSD produces hallucinations."

The explanation made the three happy and they shook their heads. The encounter would not be mentioned to anyone.

* * *

The crew had witnessed the serious incident that nearly cost the life to the Skipper and all unanimously decided not to return in person to the Earth and to rely solely on interactive projected holograms for the completion of their tasks.

Two months later the Skipper and the crew agreed that their job was done and that they would send to the home planet a fair and balanced final report. Vice-Skipper Kcops pointed out that if a new wormhole appeared, the possibility existed that they might arrive to the home planet many years ahead of the report. Krik answered that in that case they would present a copy but their most urgent need was to find a favorable new opening of the wormhole. The crew made skeptical noises. "What if we find it, but it turns out that the exit opens in an unexpected very remote location?" Aruhu, however, had a serious objection: "If there were another opening nearby, the humans might be capable of entering it and reaching our home planet with their nuclear bombs."

Krik dismissed all concerns: "We all volunteered being fully aware of the dangers of our expedition and we have enough hydrogen and sustenance for at least 10 local years. We even may find a planet where hydrogen and food can be replenished. Tell me: don't you enjoy our astonishing observations? Our co-citizens have never seen or heard of a like place. The Earth represents no danger to our planet, which earthlings will never be capable of reaching. Even if they should find a wormhole, they would never survive the trip. Aren't you pleased?" This invitation to comment only triggered profound silence, which Kcops broke:

"Compared with other planets nearer to our home, the difference in physical nature, habits, personal contacts, life span and above all political and social functioning arrangements are truly astonishing, but I am not sure that the contrasting differences deserve praise. Look at the fragmentation of their world in countries with different laws, languages, religions, political systems, problems, beliefs, individual armies. Some things are mandatory in certain areas and illegal and punishable by law with jail or execution in others. So, right and wrong are relative concepts that depend on the area where you live. And look at the pollution and contamination. They are not capable of controlling it. The same is true of the climate change."

"Vice-Skipper" claimed Aruhu, "our kind will learn much from seeing unknown and different forms of life and convivence. Learning by studying what is still unknown is what we value above anything else. What we have seen will define better and teach to our citizens our real place in a universe that we barely know and we may be incapable of fully exploring."

Uluz had a particular concern. "Should they not at least speak one single language, and guarantee to every human the same access to food and health care? Are they really a caring single species?"

The Skipper weighted the issue. "Compared to us, a very short time has passed since they achieved self-consciousness and became intelligent, autonomous beings. They have achieved a lot of progress in only some 100,000 years, more than we achieved in a comparable time span. Give them time...if they manage to survive."

Here Kcops intervened again: "How much time do they have left? They have military alliances against each other, they have built barriers and walls to keep people from entering a country, there is migration in many places. How can they master all of this? Their peril of extinction is patent. It would help them a lot if we were allowed to teach them how to achieve and control nuclear fusion to produce clean energy or how to get rid of the uranium debris in their fission reactors. I give them credit in science for having been able to develop the foundations of quantum physics, but we have seen them using nuclear energy without mastering it and putting everybody in jeopardy. They are all in danger of succumbing to an explosion, accidental or intentional. What about their continuous wars? Some of them might use nuclear bombs again. Many believe that a righteous country will always prevail over their enemies and all are willing to impose suffering and death on the civilian population."

"Oh, Vice-Skipper," objected Vokehc "don't form such a harsh opinion. They enjoy their emotions, which help them to overcome adversity and setbacks and give meaning to the lives of individuals. They expect and believe in a better future with individual happiness. I have read so in many of the library books we have copied."

"Our people never had or needed any such thing to conduct a fruitful and useful existence based on history, logic and common experience."

The Skipper, fully recovered from his accident, decided that it was time to close the discussion. "Men are what they are, and so are we. In contact with alien civilizations our Prime Directive is not to interfere. Remember: no hurting, no helping, no assuaging, just watching and reporting. I congratulate and thank you all for a difficult but extremely well-done job. Our final report includes copies of human history and fiction, cards and pictures, books in several chosen languages sent to our home planet in a way that will allow to analyze multiple different facts and opinions while we fly away in search of new worlds and new civilizations. In the process we may find a way to return home, or we may identify a suitable uninhabited planet where we could settle. The more we see and investigate, the wiser we become, and there is no limit. Start the engines, friends, and let us aim forward to the next stellar system."

And he cried "ZZRRRYT, ZRW, ZRPW, ZRPPW!" and all answered.

As of now, it is unknown whether the Namuh ship has managed to return home or not, but their astonishing final report will survive.

CPSIA information can be obtained
at www.ICGtesting.com
Printed in the USA
LVHW012314270322
714551LV00001B/53